THE PEPPER GIRLS AT WAR

(Lexie and Nancy
win WW2 their way)

by

SANDRA SAVAGE

ISBN: 978-0-9931332-7-5

Acknowledgements

For Maggie Ashford, Gail Hadley, Jean Tomlinson
and Liz Young.

Thanks girls, for your friendship and support
in the Clevedon Years and beyond.

Also by Sandra Savage

Annie Pepper

Annie Melville

Annie MacPherson

The Pepper Girls

The Dark Heart of Roger Lomax

The Green Years

Chapter 1

Dundee was at war. Since 1939, the whole of Europe had taken up arms, fighting the mighty German Army, Navy and Air Force, under the command of Adolf Hitler. The jute mills in the city were working day and night, producing sacking and canvas to service the military and with so many men called to war, it was the women who were called on to work in the mills to fill the void.

Nancy Donnelly was one of them, a skilled weaver and with Billy, her husband, enlisted in the Scots Guards and somewhere in a camp in England, she had answered the call. Their son, wee Billy was eleven years old now and his big sister Mary Anne was twelve, well able to look after themselves and get to school, unaided, while their mum worked at the looms.

She didn't miss her husband, in fact, she'd been glad to see the back of him. Ten years ago, not long after their son had been born, Nancy found out that Billy had been visiting a local prostitute, Gladys Kelly, while keeping her starved of his love. Fear of getting her pregnant again, he'd said, but Nancy knew it was more than that. Billy liked the excitement and danger, knowing it was forbidden. For a long time now, well before the war began, she and Billy had grown apart, only keeping up the pretence of a happy family for the sake of the bairns.

But things were different now, Nancy had money in her pocket and the freedom to spend it and to make her own choices as to whether she stayed at home or joined the growing ranks of women who had taken to spending their evenings in the darkness of the cinemas or at the dancehalls that had sprung up to cater for the many servicemen in the camps around Dundee, looking for distractions from the deadly situation they found themselves in.

But for Lexie Melville, Nancy's cousin, life held little excitement. At 29 years of age, she was fast becoming an 'auld maid' as Nancy had called her one Saturday, when they'd met by chance in JL Wilson's Department Store. She'd done well in the business world, managing Baxter Brothers Head Office in King Street, since Amy Fyffe had passed away five years ago and had focused all her energy in continuing Amy's standards to the letter, but Nancy's comment had stayed with her long after it had been said.

She was leaning into the small mirror on the wall in her office, tracing her fingers over the fine lines that had begun to develop at the sides of her eyes when the sound of a discreet cough, made her jump back. Joanie Kelly, the Office Junior stood open-mouthed, as Lexie smoothed her hair and forced a smile, embarrassed at being caught by the girl, in the act of gazing at her reflection..

"Yes, Joanie," she clipped, "what is it?"

Joanie indicated a handful of envelopes. "It's gone five o'clock," she said, "did you want me to post them, afore I go hame?"

Lexie looked at her watch. Usually, the office was closed at five o'clock exactly, but here she was, so caught up in herself and her appearance, she'd forgotten the time. Joanie waited. She hadn't been Lexie's first choice for the job, but there hadn't been any other applicants who had the ability to type, so her dumpy figure and wild hair had to be overlooked.

"If you would, please Joanie," Lexie nodded, "and thank you for reminding me of the time."

Joanie backed out of the office. "Goodnight Miss Melville," she said nervously, "see you Monday."

Once Joanie had left her office, Lexie turned back to the mirror. The weekend loomed and she'd be spending it, as usual, in the company of her mother and stepfather. Nancy was right, she was turning into an 'auld maid' and if she didn't do something to change her life, she'd be on the shelf for good.

She slipped into her tweed jacket that matched her skirt and pulled on her white kid gloves. Amy Fyffe had gifted Lexie her first pair, when she'd learned to type and she'd replaced them herself every year since. She'd been sixteen then and the whole world had been her oyster, but a broken engagement to Charlie Mathieson followed by an emotional disaster with her first love, Robbie Robertson, had left Lexie feeling rejected and more damaged than she cared to admit.

She moved through the main office, tidying up loose paperwork and straightening blotting pads as she went, before taking a last look round and switching off the electric lights.

George, the doorman was waiting to lock the main door and saluted her as she approached. "Have a nice weekend Miss Melville," he said as she passed, "let's hope the 'Jerries' leave us alone again." Lexie nodded, Britain had been taking a battering of late, from the German Luftwafa, especially London and the news on the Radio and on Pathe News in the picture houses had been terrifying. "Let's hope so, George," she replied "let's hope so."

She crossed the road to the tram stop and looked at the sky. It was getting dark already and pretty soon, the city would be in total blackness with the Wardens patrolling the streets, to make sure that not a chink of light was showing at a window, which might indicate to the German bombers overhead that people were living below. Lexie shivered and checked her handbag for her torch as the tram clanked nearer to her stop.

Lexie's mum and Euan her stepdad were both home when she came through the front door. Euan was a police sergeant with the Dundee Constabulary and also an Air Raid Patrol Warden, while Annie did her bit for the war effort, along with the other middle-aged women in Dundee, by re-joining the Women's Institute, the WI as it was known, along with Isabella Anderson, her sister-in-law, to provide 'home comforts' for the soldiers, as they'd done in the first world war.

"Have a good day?" Annie asked, smiling at her daughter and patting the sofa, indicating she should sit a while. She loved her daughter dearly and wished for nothing more than for her to find the love and happiness she had found with Euan, but as time went on and now, with so many men away fighting, she felt that for Lexie, life would be forever spent alone.

Lexie discarded her jacket and gloves, tossing them over an armchair. Annie smiled, although she knew her daughter ran a 'tight ship' at the office, she'd never mastered the art of 'a place for everything and everything in its place,' at home.

"Not bad," she said with a sigh, still thinking about Nancy's comment.

Annie looked sideways at her, "you sound a bit fed up Lexie," she said, "not coming down with anything are you?"

Lexie shrugged, "don't think so, just a bit fed-up with this war I suppose, with the streets blacked out and the shops short of everything." She picked up the newspaper from the little table beside the sofa, flicking through the pages and looking at nothing in particular. She was just

about to return the Courier to the table when she spotted it. There was a picture of a girl in uniform with the target emblem of the Air Force behind her and the words. JOIN THE WAAF TODAY. She folded the page over and looked at the wording closely. *The newly formed Women's Auxiliary Air Force is recruiting women, 18-43 years of age, to join the service in defence of their country.* It gave the address of the Recruiting Office in the City Square. Lexie stared at the picture of the girl and felt a rush of excitement fill her body.

"What's taken your eye," Euan asked, aware that Lexie was fixated on the page of print. Lexie looked up, her eyes gleaming, as she handed him the newspaper. "This," was all she said. Euan read the advert and felt a chill of apprehension. Lexie was safe here at home with him and her mother, she had a worthwhile job at Baxters and, with any luck, they would all ride out the war safely.

He handed the paper back to Lexie and said nothing. "What is it?" Annie asked, her curiosity aroused by Euan's silence.

"This," Lexie said again, pointing to the advert. "There's nothing to keep me here in Dundee," she said, hardly daring to believe what she was thinking, "and it's time I found another way to live my life."

Chapter 2

Lexie tore the advert out and folded it carefully. "I'll be back later," she said, "don't hold tea for me, I'll get something later."

Euan and Annie gazed in stunned silence at one another. It was Annie who voiced what they were both thinking.

"What's all this about?" Annie gasped, "what's wrong with the life she has here, with us?" A knot of fear had already formed in her gut. Euan rose from his chair and crossed the room to sit beside her on the sofa, recently vacated by his step-daughter. Although Lexie wasn't his by birth, it was he who had brought her up when he had married Annie and he'd grown to love her like his own. He took Annie's hand in his and pressed it to his heart. "Hush now," he whispered, searching for words to calm things down, "you know Lexie and her hair-brain schemes, she'll probably have forgotten all about it by tomorrow when she realises the daftness of it all."

"Do you really think so?" Annie said, barely able to speak.

But Euan had seen the gleam in Lexie's eyes, the excitement in her voice and knew that she had made up her mind and no amount of talking was going to dissuade her. Lexie would be going to war.

Sarah Dawson, Lexie's best friend from school days was marking some English homework when she arrived, unannounced at Sarah's door.

Sarah had followed in her mother's footsteps and was now an English teacher at Morgan Academy on Forfar Road. In their youth, Lexie had always been the one who drew men into her life like bees to honey, while Sarah had held back through fear of her mother Josie, whose ambition it had been that Sarah became a teacher, like herself. Josie had succeeded and apart from a brief encounter with a budding young doctor, John Adams, which her father, Billy Dawson, had abruptly put a stop to, there had been no other men in her life.

Lexie couldn't keep the sparkle from her eyes, as Josie invited her in. Josie had seen that look before on Lexie, but not for a long time now, not since that unfortunate business with Robbie Robertson, which had seemed to knock the stuffing out of her.

"Is Sarah in?" Lexie breathed, "I really need to speak to her."

Josie stepped back and inclined her head to the door behind her. "She's in the kitchen, at the table, doing some marking," Josie said, "just go in."

Lexie hurried through the door while Josie returned to the parlour and her husband Billy, who was reading his newspaper and shaking his head at the carnage that was unfolding on its pages.

Josie watched him for a minute. At 57, age was catching up with him now, his hair almost completely grey and his need for spectacles to read was permanent. He'd been working long hours at the mill, as General Manager at Baxters, the buck stopped with him and keeping his managers focused on production was getting more difficult as their lives became touched with grief. The arrival of a telegram from the War Office always bringing the worst of news of sons, killed in action and the need to carry on for the sake of those who were the survivors, becoming a daily struggle.

He became aware of Josie watching him and folded the paper. "Is everything alright?" he asked, reaching for a cigarette and his lighter.

"Sarah has a visitor," Josie began, "Lexie Melville," she added tightly, the usual edge to her voice when Lexie Melville, or her mother were mentioned, shining through.

Billy waited for her to continue. Despite thirty years having passed, Josie still hadn't managed to control the jealously she felt towards Lexie's mother, Annie MacPherson. She'd been Annie Pepper when Billy had fallen in love with her, and she with him, but the fates had conspired against the union time and again and Billy had married Josie after Annie had wed Alex Melville. After Alex's death, she married Euan MacPherson, but still it rankled with Josie and Billy knew it, but was powerless to reassure his wife he felt nothing for Annie, for what Josie feared in her heart, deep down Billy knew, was indeed true.

"So?" he said, inhaling the tobacco deeply and knowing that the evening ahead would now have to be endured in silence.

"So," Josie repeated, "what do you think she wants?"

Billy raised his eyebrows. "How should I know what she wants," he responded, quietly, "she's a grown woman, so maybe you should ask her, if you're that interested."

Josie tightened her lips into a narrow line. "She works in Baxters Office, doesn't she, thanks to you, so you must know what's going on with her."

Billy crushed out the cigarette in the ashtray. Here it was again, Josie working herself up into a fit of jealousy about Lexie or more accurately, about Annie. Would his wife never let go of this fixation, instead of continually inflaming it and reminding him that perhaps he should have married Annie and not her after all.

"I need some fresh air," he said, quickly planning his escape "and I've a meeting at the Lodge to arrange, so don't wait up." With that, Billy left the room and Josie, sitting silently in it. There was a war on for God's sake, he fumed inwardly, didn't she understand that. Men were dying and all she could think of was her bitterness towards Annie Pepper. He took a deep breath as he turned into the darkness of the blackout and without even wanting to, his heart filled with thoughts of Annie, all those years ago in Ireland, when he'd made love to her down by the river and then, unknown to him, Annie had bore him a son, John, who he'd only found out about when John came to Dundee on an exchange visit during his training to be a doctor, eighteen years later.

He turned down Albert Street, heading towards the Masonic Lodge in Princess Street, his torch pointing downwards to guide his steps. Annie had chosen Euan then and not him, but she had finally given him John's address in Belfast and letters had been exchanged. Josie had never found out about John's existence and never would, but one day, Billy was determined to meet his son, face to face and tell him how much he loved him... and his mother.

Chapter 3

"You looked pleased with yourself," Sarah smiled, "found 'the one' at last?" Both she and Lexie had decided long ago that 'the one' the man who would love them madly and change their lives forever, would one day ride by on his white horse and claim them for his own. This hadn't happened for either of them and now, with this damn war on, the only men available were either too old or too young.

Not that either woman was looking any more, Sarah had her job as an English teacher which she loved and Lexie had all but given up on men since Robbie Robertson had rejected her so cruelly and disappeared into the arms of the Merchant Navy and a life of travel and adventure.

Or so Lexie had believed, but the reality was that now, with the war on, Robbie Robertson was captain of a supply vessel that was running the gauntlet of German submarines in the Atlantic, as it brought much needed supplies from the United States of America.

"Have a look at this," Lexie said, excitedly, unfolding the advert and handing it to Sarah."

Sarah pursed her lips in disinterest. "Women's Auxiliary Air Force" she said aloud, handing the advert back to Lexie with a shrug. "Do you know someone who's going to be daft enough to volunteer to go to war then?" she asked.

Lexie folded the piece of paper again and returned it to her pocket. Daft, she thought, wondering now whether to tell Sarah that the daft person who was going to volunteer, was in fact her!

"I don't think it's daft, as you put it," Lexie said defensively, "I think its brave really..." her voice trailing off as she tried to justify her decision to her friend.

Lexie now had Sarah's full attention as she realised where the conversation was going. "Tell me you don't mean YOU?"

Lexie pulled back her shoulders and raised her eyes to meet Sarah's.

"That's exactly who I do mean," Lexie countered, stoutly, "and I thought you'd be pleased for me, doing something with my life instead of wasting it on filing Invoices and typing letters."

Sarah was now getting worried. "But Lexie," she began, "you're the Office Manageress at Baxters, not a filing clerk or a typist and everyone thinks you're doing a wonderful job there. Only yesterday dad said how well you ran the office and kept everything in order."

Lexie clenched her fists in her lap. "I'll soon be thirty years old," she said quietly "and if I don't do something to change my life now, I'm going to end up like..." she almost said, like YOU, an old maid, as that was the fate of women like Sarah who went into teaching, they weren't allowed to marry, but instead she added, "everyone else."

Sarah sat back in the basket chair in her bedroom. She knew what Lexie had been going to say. But going into teaching hadn't meant never marrying, she reminded herself, it was just that if she did meet 'the one' she'd have to stop working at the Academy and become a wife instead and right now, with the war on, this was becoming increasingly unlikely.

"Does your mum and Euan know?" Sarah asked.

Lexie shook her head. "Not yet."

"Isn't your brother a Corporal in the Army already?

Lexie sighed. Ian had enlisted almost immediately the war had started and over the two years since, he'd been promoted to Corporal and was based at an army training camp in the Southeast of England.

She knew what Sarah was getting at. Her mum and Euan had their only son risking his life for King and country and they wouldn't take kindly to Lexie also putting her life at risk.

"I don't need reminding of Ian's life," Lexie huffed, unhappy at Sarah's response and realising that leaving home and joining the WAAF was going to require all her powers of

14

persuasion to get her parents blessing.

"I'm sorry, Lexie," Sarah said, softening and realising the enormity of what her friend was contemplating. "It's just such a dangerous thing to do but if it's what you really want then...come here."

Sarah stood up and hugged Lexie close to her, willing her to change her mind but knowing Lexie of old, she also knew that once she'd made her mind up about something, nothing was going to change it.

There were tears in both their eyes as Lexie said goodbye and headed back home to face Euan and her mum.

She crept quietly into the house, not wishing to start the confrontation which she now knew would ensue and hoping it would keep till morning, but the grim expression on her mother's face, as she announced her intention to go straight to bed, said otherwise.

"I'm worried about you," Annie stated, trying to keep the tremor from her voice, "Euan says it's nonsense, but I need to know..." Two pairs of female eyes locked, "you're not thinking of volunteering to join this women's air force thing are you?"

Euan broke into the silence. "Maybe Lexie would like a cup of tea, Annie," he began, manoeuvring Annie towards the kitchen and Lexie towards the sofa, "and maybe one of your scones."

Lexie lowered herself onto the sofa, crossing her hands in her lap and keeping her eyes downcast. Euan sat beside her.

"Your mum's just worried for you, that's all," he said gently, "what with Ian away at the war and not knowing if...". his voice trailed off.

Lexie began to waver. Ian was Euan and Annie's son as well as being her half-brother, but they'd been proud of him when he'd enlisted, so what was the difference?

Annie hurried into the parlour with a tray of tea things and scones and looked anxiously at Euan. He'd make things alright with Lexie, just like always, she prayed to herself.

All eyes were on Lexie as the silence built. It was now or never.

She raised her eyes to meet those of her mother and with a voice stronger than she felt, announced her intentions.

"I want to do more with my life," she continued, "not just work in an office till I die an auld maid..." There it was again, the real reason she wanted to leave Dundee and go somewhere else, anywhere, just away from everything and everyone and especially away from the memories of Robbie Robertson, that lived deep in her soul.

Annie felt panic forming in the pit of her stomach. "What are you talking about?" she asked incredulously, "you're a lovely young woman and once this stupid war is over and all the men are back, you'll meet someone..." Euan held up a warning hand. He knew how much Lexie had been hurt by men and one man in particular and no amount of reassurance from either Annie or himself would heal her broken heart. If this was the only way she saw of leaving the past behind, perhaps it would be for the best. "Let's all sleep on it," he said, "things will be different in the morning."

Two white faces nodded and the scones and tea lay untouched as Lexie rose from the sofa. "Tomorrow," she whispered, leaving the room and wondering how things could be better then, as her decision would still be the same. She was going to join the WAAF the next day before anyone, especially her mum, could change her mind.

Annie and Euan sat late into the night, trying to accept that Lexie meant what she said. "She won't be in any real danger," Euan tried to assure her, "women don't get sent to the front lines to fight and if joining the WAAF is what she really wants to do, then I don't think we should try to stop her."

Exhaustion finally overtook them both but by the time they awoke the next morning, Lexie had already left the house.

Euan picked up the note he found on the sideboard in the kitchen.

"Sorry mum," it said, *"I know I'm doing the right thing, so be happy for me, please."* He filled the kettle. He'd take a cup of tea to Annie in bed. Looking around the kitchen, its familiarity comforted him, it didn't seem that long ago that Lexie and Ian

were children, safe and happy, but now, the war had changed all that, forever.

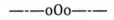

Chapter 4

It was Friday at last and the weavers were 'knocking off'. Tomorrow was Saturday and for Nancy, this meant only one thing, DANCING.

She pulled off her turban and ran her fingers through her dark hair, shaking her head as she walked from the weaving flat.

"Hey, watch it," a deep voice said, catching her arm and stopping her in her tracks. "What's the big hurry?"

Nancy blinked and looked into the eyes of her Gaffer. Jim Murphy was grinning ear to ear as he brushed his hand over her hair removing strands of jute from her curls and dropping them to the floor.

"Sorry Mr Murphy," she said, "cleaning tonight or no dancing tomorrow."

Jim Murphy raised his eyebrows. "When the cat's away the mouse goes out to play," he said, "is that it?"

Nancy lowered her eyes before returning her gaze to his. "What's it to you Jim Murphy?" she teased, "are you thinking of saving the last dance for me?"

Jim felt himself heat up. Nancy Donnelly was a beauty and he knew her husband was away with the Scots Guards somewhere down South.

"Maybe," he said, "if I felt like it." Now it was Nancy's turn to feel the rush of heat to her face. "Why Mr Murphy," she said coyly, "are you asking me to meet up with you at the Palais on Saturday?"

Jim smiled to himself. "Just make sure you get that cleaning done tonight," he murmured and with a squeeze of her hand, he was gone.

Nancy was giggling to herself when her friend, Di Auchterlonie caught up with her. "Hey, wait up," she called running to catch up with Nancy. "What was all that about?" she asked, breathlessly, pointing over her shoulder to the disappearing back of Jim Murphy. "He looked like the cat who'd got the cream when I passed him, didn't even seem to see me."

Nancy linked her arm into Di's. "I think it's me who's got the cream," she said, "he's only asked to meet me at the Palais tomorrow."

Diane's mouth dropped open. "But he's married isn't he?"

"So what," Nancy retorted, "so am I."

Di frowned. Nancy was getting more and more daring with men, the more freedom she got, but a married man was going too far.

She pulled Nancy to a stop. "What if Jean Murphy finds out?"

"What if she does," Nancy shrugged. "There's a war on, isn't there, so who knows if we'll live to see tomorrow." She freed herself from Di's grasp, "and I don't intend to waste a single day of the rest of my life worrying about Jean Murphy."

Wee Billy and Mary Anne were playing at Snakes and Ladders when Nancy came into the small kitchen. Mary Anne had the fire going and the table set for their tea and Nancy had brought home fish and chips for them all from Capitelli's chip shop in King Street.

They ate with their fingers and licked the greaseproof paper of its salt and vinegar before screwing it up and throwing it on the fire.

The bairns knew that Friday night was for cleaning both the house and themselves and by nine o'clock they were scrubbed and damp and in their pyjamas drinking some hot milk before going off to bed.

"Remember and behave yourselves tomorrow," Nancy said, "mum's going to be out for a little while, but Mrs Jeffries next door will be keeping an ear open, so if there's any nonsense, I'll know. So best behaviour!"

Mary Anne and wee Billy nodded solemnly. They were used to the Saturday night routine by now and always knew there would be a bag of sweeties for each of them when they woke up on Sunday morning provided, of course, they were good.

Once the bairns were bedded, Nancy sat beside the fire in the silence but for the ticking of the clock and thought of Billy. What would he be doing now, she wondered, but she knew the answer, probably in some pub somewhere, plying a whore with drink till she was drunk and biddable. Thoughts of Billy and Gladys Kelly hardened her heart again, bringing to life, once more, the hurt of what he had done and she could feel the softness of a tear making its way down her cheek.

She had loved Billy so much when they were wed and had never doubted his love for her...not until Gladys Kelly that is, from then on she had never trusted him again. With an effort she shook off the thought and reached for a cigarette. Tomorrow, she'd have her own fun, she told herself, when Jim Murphy takes her in his arms and makes love to her. Gladys Kelly straddling her husband would once again be forgotten.Next day, with Mary Anne off to the shops to buy her mum's messages and wee Billy out playing, Nancy hung last night's washing out on the pulley before making a pot of Stovies for their tea. Mrs Jeffries knocked on Nancy's door around mid-day. "Alright for the nicht?" she asked grinning a toothless grin, knowing that Nancy would be coughing up two shillings and a packet of Woodbines for her child-minding services later on.

"Fine, Mrs Jeffries," she said, "and are you alright for the night as well?"

Mrs Jeffries nodded enthusiastically. "Jist wish I waz young again, like you," she said, "I'd show them 'sodgers' a thing or twa."

"I'm sure you would," Nancy responded, rummaging in her apron pocket for the money and fags she'd dropped into it. She handed them over to her neighbour. "The bairns'll be fine," she said, "just keep an ear open for any nonsense and I'll be back around eleven."

The crone help up the coin, "you can count on me," she said, "and enjoy yirsel' lassie, cause one day, you'll be like me and no' be able." Cackling to herself Mrs Jeffries returned to her own door, leaving Nancy with the terrible thought in her head of ending up like Mrs Jeffries.

She chased the image from her mind and set about getting everything ready for the evening ahead. She was meeting Di at the Wellgate Steps and together they'd make their way to the dancehall. With a bit of luck, she'd be escorted home by Jim Murphy, confident that Di would find herself a soldier to make sure she got home alright too.

She washed and set her hair with Wavers and brought out her black skirt and beaded blouse from the wardrobe. Her Auntie Annie had gifted it to her on her last birthday and it was one of her favourites, glittering and sparkling as she moved around the dance floor to the music.

Mary Anne returned with the messages and her eyes lit up at the sight of the beaded blouse. "Can I try it on," she said, "just for a little while?"

Nancy smiled. "Not this time, young lady, maybe next year I'll let you have it for keeps." Mary Anne looked crestfallen. "But that's forever away," she wailed. Nancy ruffled her hair and guided her back into the kitchen, "now did you get all the messages," she asked, surveying the brown paper bags nestling in the shopping basket.

Mary Anne nodded, handing her mother the note and the change.

Nancy thanked her daughter and gave her a thrupenny bit. "There," she said, "that's for being a good girl, so out to play with you now till teatime."

Mary Anne skipped from the house and headed for Mr McInroy's sweetie shop. The thruppence would buy a nice bag of Dolly Mixtures, her favourite.

By seven o'clock, Nancy was ready to go dancing. Mary Anne gazed at her in awe. Her mummy was like a beautiful angel and one day, she told herself, she'd be just like her.

Nancy kissed both their heads, "now behave for Mrs Jeffries," she said, "and read your books till bedtime. Mrs Jeffries will be in to say goodnight at 8 o'clock." Both children nodded. Wee Billy didn't like when his mummy went out and left them to be looked after by Mrs Jeffries, but he'd been told by Nancy, that once daddy came back from fighting in the war, mummy wouldn't be having to go out again, so he had to be brave, like daddy, till the war was over.

Nancy closed the door of her little house and took a deep breath. She was free again, at last.

Chapter 5

Lexie's shoes clipped along the pavement as she made her way down Albert Street towards the City Square. She usually took the tram, but today she needed the walk to calm her thoughts. Today, she would join the Womens Auxiliary Air Force and nothing now was going to stop her.

As she passed Baxters Offices, she glanced at the glass entrance doors, the next time she'd go through them would be on Monday to tell Sarah's dad, Mr Dawson, that she would be leaving her job as soon as possible as she had joined the WAAF.

She could feel her skin tingle with excitement at the prospect of her new life. She hadn't felt so alive for a long time and quickened her step towards the recruitment office in the City Square. Early morning shoppers and last night's drinkers peppered the streets but Lexie was oblivious to them all. Then suddenly she was there, looking at the same poster she'd seen in the advert in the Courier. She took a deep breath and opened the door.

A man in his RAF uniform smiled at her and beckoned her to sit down, but said nothing. For the first time, Lexie felt unsure of herself.

"I've come about the advert," she said, "In the Courier."

The man nodded but still said nothing. Then a door behind her opened and a tall, middle-aged woman, also in uniform, entered the room. "I thought I heard the door," she said, "this way," she added briskly.

Lexie followed. "I take it you've come about joining the WAAF?"

Lexie took a seat in front of the desk and nodded. "Speak up!"

"Yes," Lexie stuttered, "I saw the advert and..."

"And you thought you'd join the WAAF and save the world eh?"

Lexie felt confused. What did this woman mean, save the world, I don't want to save the world, she thought, I want to change my world. Intelligent blue eyes watched her.

"Well?"

Lexie felt herself panic. What did this woman want her to say?

"I want to join up," she repeated lamely, "I think I'd be useful," she ended.

The blue eyes smiled. "Useful at what?" she asked.

Lexie tried to gather her wits, she hadn't known what to expect, but she had at least expected to be welcomed.

"I can type, touch type that is and do all sorts of office jobs."

"Good," came the response, "then the WAAF will be able to put you to good use." The female officer handed Lexie a form.

"Fill this in," she said, "and providing you can pass a couple of tests and a physical examination, I'll recommend you be accepted."

Lexie took the form and for the first time realised that what she was joining wasn't some cosy girls club that would fill the void left in her heart by Robbie Robertson, but a real armed force.

The Officer stood to leave. "When you've done," she said, "give your form to the sergeant at the front desk."

She turned to Lexie as she reached the door. "We need women in the WAAF to be strong and stay the course," she said, firmly, "there's a war on and time-wasters are no use to us." The door closed behind her.

Lexie gazed at the form. If the Officer had intended to make Lexie think about her decision, it had worked. Why *did* she want to join the WAAF?

Sure, she didn't want to be an old maid and she didn't want to live the rest of her life at home with her mum and Euan and she certainly didn't want to get involved with another Robbie Robertson, so WHY?

Her thoughts turned inwards and Lexie pictured her life as it was, yes she was safe and comfortable, but why wasn't that enough? The reason then struck her as so obvious. She wanted to feel alive again, break out of the confines of her narrow existence and find out what she was really made of and she wasn't going to find that out in Dundee. She started to fill out the form, she was going to join the WAAF and face whatever life threw at her. It was now or never.

With racing heart she completed it and handed it to the sergeant, who smiled as he placed her 'future' in a wire tray on the desk.

"We'll be in touch," he said, genuinely smiling this time, "soon."

Lexie almost skipped home, she'd done it, actually taken control of her life again, all thoughts of past hurts and fears dissipating with every step. She smiled at everyone she passed, wanting to shout out about her decision and already planning her exit from Baxters and her mundane life in Dundee and she couldn't wait to tell Nancy about joining up. She wouldn't be able to call her an 'auld maid' now.

Her enthusiasm abated slightly when she entered her home to find mum and Euan drinking tea at the kitchen table, their expressions saying everything about how they felt.

Lexie brought a cup and saucer to the table and poured herself a cup.

"Well," her mother said, unable to keep the anxiety out of her voice, "have you joined?"

"I have."

Annie winced. "Then we're happy for you Lexie," Euan interjected before Annie could say anymore.

"We'll worry, of course," he added, "but if it's done, then we're very proud of you."

In the silence that followed, Lexie knew that her mother was unhappy with what she was doing, but she'd expected that and sought to reassure her.

"I'll be fine," she said softly, "it's something that I have to do for me," she added, "please understand?"

Annie blinked back the tears of fear for Lexie's future. "I know," she said, "you're just so precious to me..." Euan folded Annie into his arms and nodded to Lexie to go, indicating that everything would be fine.

Lexie ran to her room and threw herself onto her bed, tears running unchecked down her cheeks. She loved her mother so much but knew she couldn't live her life through her mother's fears and that to join the WAAF and leave Dundee was truly the right decision for her. Euan understood and, one day she prayed, so would her mother.

Billy Dawson was surprised to find Lexie waiting outside his office on Monday morning. He unlocked the door and ushered her in, keeping his manner calm but knowing that something was amiss.

Lexie took a seat uninvited and placed her gloved hands neatly on her lap. "I'm sorry to bother you so early," she said, before Billy could ask her anything, "but I'll be leaving Baxters soon, so if you want me to help the new person get used to our system..." Billy held up a stopping hand. "Whoa! Lexie," he said, more sharply than he intended, "slow down."

Lexie took a deep breath. She knew her resignation would cause problems for Sarah' dad, but it was just another hurdle she had to get over before she could start her new life. "Leaving Baxters," Billy said incredulously, "but why, what's wrong?"

"I've joined the WAAF" she said, "so I'll be leaving my job and going to war." Lexie could feel a surge of pride rising in her at the statement.

Billy's eyebrows drew together in confusion.

"You've done what?"

"It's the Womens Auxiliary Air Force," Lexie said, clearly, "I've joined up."

Of all the things Annie Pepper's daughter could have told him, he hadn't expected this.

"Does your mum and Euan know?"

"Yes."

"And they're happy about it?"

Lexie tightened her interlaced fingers and shook her head.

"They're getting used to the idea," she said, "and I hope by the time I leave, they'll understand it's something I have to do."

Billy's mind raced back to his own experience of war. He'd come back from the Great War shell shocked and almost broken and it was only his love for Annie Pepper that had finally brought him back to life. He knew what Annie would be thinking and how much she would be fearing for Lexie going into another war situation.

Billy lit his third cigarette of the day. "You don't have to do this," he said, quietly, "war is for men, Lexie, not women. It's dangerous and bloody and people get killed. Is that what you want?"

Lexie felt her chin quiver. Billy Dawson had no right to try to frighten her, she wasn't his daughter.

She tilted her chin up and met his eyes.

"I've made up my mind," she said firmly, "and I'll be leaving as soon as I get word I've been accepted." Lexie stood up and extended her hand to Billy. "Thanks for everything," she said, "but I think it's time to move on." With these words and without his handshake, Lexie left Billy Dawson's office clearing another hurdle to her new life as she went. Nothing and no one was going to stop her now.

Chapter 6

Nancy met up with Di as planned at the Wellgate Steps and together they made their way to the Palais in Tay Street. Uniformed men jostled with civilians and excited women, all heading in the same direction.

"Do you think he'll turn up?" Di asked as Nancy flashed a smile to a passing sailor.

"Do I think *who* will turn up?" she asked, innocently.

Di nudged her in the ribs, grinning. "You know who," she said, "Jim Murphy."

Nancy shrugged, enjoying the game. "Maybe he will, maybe he won't," she replied, "we'll just have to wait and see, won't we."

They paid their money at the door and entered another world. Music, lights, laughter and flirting was going on all around Nancy and she loved it. Her husband and children were moved to the back of her mind as she became young and single again. She'd married far too young, she told herself and this was her chance to make up for the last twelve years of unholy matrimony. What was wrong with that? Nothing, she told herself, nothing at all.

A strong arm circled her waist attached to a khaki uniform.

"D'you fancy a dance beautiful lady?" the male voice asked.

"Anything for you soldiers," she said, giggling as she was swept onto the floor.

"Do you come 'ere often," the squaddie asked, grinning at his own cheek and Nancy's 'knowing eyes'.

"Every Saturday," she said, sweetly, "it's my reward for all the hard work I do during the week."

The soldier pulled her closer. "And what might that be then," he whispered in her ear, "looking after your hubby maybe?"

Nancy leant away from him. She'd heard the line many times before and knew how to answer.

"Hubby's away at war," she said, smiling, "and probably doing the same thing you're trying to do to me."

The soldier grinned and shrugged. "Can't blame a bloke for trying," he said, releasing his grip on Nancy. "Just a dance then?" Nancy nodded.

The evening sped by with Nancy and Di both basking in the attention of the army, navy and air force, breaking only to meet in the Ladies to discuss their successes and reapply their lipstick.

"No sign then?" Di asked, fluffing the waves in her hair and wiping the back of her neck with a wet hankie.

"If you mean, Jim Murphy, then no, not that I was waiting for him to make an appearance," Nancy added, carefully pressing some face powder to her flushed cheeks, "Jean probably has him shackled to the bed."

But when the girls returned to the dance floor, Jim Murphy had indeed turned up and wasted no time in making his presence known to Nancy.

"Fancy meeting you here," Nancy said, coyly. "Yeah," came the reply, "small world isn't it."

Nancy felt his arm sweep round her waist, "care to dance with another admirer?"

Di signalled her concern, shaking her head at Nancy as Jim led her onto the floor, but it was ignored.

He pulled her closer to him and for Nancy the world was suddenly very still. All around her was noise and movement and music, but in the circle of Jim Murphy's arms, there was only sweet passion. Neither spoke as the lights dimmed and the music moved into a slow foxtrot. Husbands, wives, children and even the war were forgotten as they moved as one around the swaying bodies. They were the last to leave the floor at the end of the dance with Jim's arm never releasing its grip on Nancy's waist.

Di was waiting, her arms crossed and her lips drawn into a tight line.

"I think your friend's waiting for you," Jim whispered, finally releasing his hold on Nancy "and that," he added, "was the most wonderful moment of my life."

Nancy knew what he meant. She'd felt it too and the knowledge that she could feel that way about another man, both frightened and thrilled her.

"Till the next time," Jim said, kissing her lightly on the forehead, "if you want there to be a next time, that is?"

Nancy nodded, "till the next time," she breathed.

"What do you think you're playing at," Di hissed in her ear, as Jim Murphy headed to the exit and home to his wife. If Jean was asleep, he'd slip in unnoticed, but if she was awake, he had his excuses ready.

He'd played this game many times before, Nancy wasn't the first and she wouldn't be the last.

Nancy shook Di's hand free. "It was just a friendly dance," she insisted, "nothing wrong with that."

Di wasn't convinced. "He's MARRIED Nancy," she reminded her, "and Jean Murphy isn't going to take too kindly to you and her man getting close."

Nancy shrugged her sequined shoulders. "C'mon," she said, flatly, "party's over."

The walk home was as dark as the mood that had settled on Nancy's shoulders. Why shouldn't she be loved, really loved by a real man, she asked herself, there was nothing left in her marriage to Billy except the bairns and they'd be grown up soon enough, then what would her life be like, just her and Billy, living out the rest of their lives hating one another.

By the time the friends had parted, Nancy had convinced herself that despite both of them being married to others, they were meant to be together and when Jim Murphy called again, she would answer and the answer would be YES.

Jean Murphy was awake when her husband's key turned in the lock.

She'd been awake for hours, her mind looking for reasons for his lateness, but deep down knowing that he was up to no good...again.

Jim feigned surprise at his wife still awake. "I thought you'd be in bed by now," he said, lightly, "its dark as tar out there." He filled the kettle and lit the gas. "There was a bit of a scare in Eliza Street earlier," he prattled on, "but we all pitched in to help and I'm sorry I'm late, but I couldn't walk away from people in distress."

Jean's eyebrows grew together. "What sort of a scare?"

"Unexploded bomb," Jim lied, warming to his deceit. "The ARP's had to cordon off the whole street and commandeered all us passers-by to help calm things down till the Army boys arrived."

He handed Jean her tea. "And, how have you been sweetheart," he smoothed, "anything exciting happen while I've been out?"

"Nothing," she said, wearily, placing the untouched tea on the tiled grate, knowing that there had been no unexploded bomb and that her husband was probably 'at it again' with yet another 'floozie.' "And now you're home, I'll be off to bed," she added, bleakly, "and next time there's an unexploded bomb, let the ARP do their own calming down."

Jim watched her go. How easy it was to fool her and how easy it was going to be to bed the sexy Nancy Donnelly.

He sipped his tea and closed his eyes, awakening again the image of Nancy in his arms and feeling her wanting him as badly as he wanted her.

Nancy tiptoed into the back room where Mary Anne and wee Billy were asleep and placed the two little pokes of sweeties on the chair between their beds. Watching them in the silence of the dark room, Nancy felt a pang of conscience. Could she really jeopardise their future lives by letting Jim Murphy into hers? Her mood darkened further, why did Billy Donnelly have to be unfaithful to her and make her even consider another man. It was all his fault if their children had to suffer. He was the one who'd ruined her trust in him, what was she supposed to do, join a convent!

She lit a cigarette and tried to recapture the feelings that Jim Murphy had stirred in her, but it was no use, the moment was gone for now, but there was always next Saturday.

—·—oOo—·—

Chapter 7

The sound of the post rattling through the letter box a week later brought Lexie running from her bed. With shaking hands, she read her name on the official looking envelope and tiptoed back to her bedroom to read the contents.

Lexie had to report for enlistment into the WAAF at an RAF Training Camp in Wilmslow in Cheshire, England in seven days time. More travel details and instructions were added, but for Lexie, the important thing was that she had done it. She was going to be a WAAF. She clutched the letter to her chest and allowed the surge of excitement to course through her body.

"ENGLAND", she said softly to herself, wondering what this foreign land would be like. She'd never been further than Perth before and that had been on a bus with Euan and her mum.

The thought of her mum stopped her in her tracks. There would be no turning back now and she hoped and prayed that she would be able to accept her going without any more tears.

Lexie waited till breakfast was over before producing the letter.

"This came this morning," she said calmly, "it's about my enlistment into the WAAF."

Euan took the letter and read it while Annie sat watching him.

"Cheshire, eh?" he said, "and in England," he added, nodding sagely at Annie.

"The RAF Training Camp's in a place called Wilmslow," Lexie said quickly, before her mother could say anything, "it's where you go to get your uniform and everything..."

Her voice tailed off as Annie's expression became fixed in a grim look of acceptance. Euan had talked to her at length over the past few days and convinced her that it was better to send Lexie off with a smile and a hug, as she was going no matter what either of them said, but now that the moment of acceptance was here, Annie felt only fear for Lexie's future.

"Well," said Lexie, wanting to run to her mother and tell her she loved her, but she knew this would only make matters worse, "I'd better go round and let Sarah know what's happening. I promised I would, so..." Lexie stood up, putting the letter back in its envelope and forcing a smile.

"This silly war won't last much longer," she said desperately, with more confidence than she felt, and anyway, once they see me, the Jerries will head for the hills..." No one laughed and Lexie hated herself for her nervous flippancy as she closed the kitchen door behind her.

"It's definite then," Annie said, casting a long glance at Euan hoping he would contradict her. "She's really going."

Euan took her hand. "She is Annie love," he said gently, "but I'm still here," he told her, "you'll always have me."

Annie tightened her grip on his hand and blinked back a tear.

How glad she was that she'd chosen Euan over her long ago love for Billy Dawson. Although still living close by with Josie and their daughters, Billy felt a million miles away from her, even with him knowing that she had given birth to his son in the poorhouse all those years ago, hadn't changed her mind about choosing Euan.

"Will you never leave me Euan," she begged, "no matter what?"

"I'll never leave you," Euan echoed, earnestly, "no matter what. Now let's get on with the business of the day and I'll make us another pot of tea, I think we need it."

Lexie hurried through her morning routine and quietly slipped out of the house, heading for Sarah's with her news. Dealing with her mother's distress was getting a bit easier and the confidence that she'd made the right decision was slowly growing but by the time she reached Sarah's house, her eyes were still bleak. Sarah was supportive, as usual and suggested they forget about things for a while. "Let's make up some sandwiches and a flask of tea and take the tram to the Ferry," she suggested, "get some Scottish wind in your sails, before the sun goes in again."

The activity helped and Lexie was regaining her optimism as they stepped off the tram into the bustle of the little town. The river was sparkling with life and so now was Lexie. She breathed in the salty air as they wandered along the sand looking for a sheltered spot amongst the grassy dunes to eat their sandwiches. It had been a long time since she'd felt so much part of life. There were shortages everywhere and no one wasted anything anymore and their picnic was going to be a meagre affair, but for Lexie it was to be the most wonderful food she'd ever tasted.

"So, you leave next Sunday," Sarah said, briskly, once they'd eaten their sandwiches and downed the last dregs of their tea.

Lexie nodded enthusiastically. "Will you come and see me off?" she asked, "I don't really want mum and Euan to be there, but I would like you to wave me off."

Sarah raised her eyebrows in surprise. "But, surely, they'll want to say goodbye?"

Lexie's lips tightened, "better to say our goodbyes at home," she said, "I think mum's going to be a bit upset."

Sarah wasn't so sure. Lexie's mum and Euan had always been there for Lexie and she didn't think they'd let her down now. "I'll be there," she said, "and maybe by next week things will be easier and they'll want to say goodbye at the station."

The week flew by with getting Baxters Office ready for the new incumbent and packing her belongings for the train journey South.

"We'll miss you," Billy Dawson said solemnly, as he took back the office keys and thanked her for her good work. He'd had doubts about Lexie's ability to make anything of herself, but under Mrs Fyffe's capable wing, she had flourished. She was also Annie Pepper's daughter, he told himself, so how could she not turn out well.

"You'll take good care of yourself, Lexie," he added, gruffly, opening the door of his office for her to exit, "you'll be in our thoughts till all this damn fighting is over."

Lexie cast her eyes to the floor to hide the flush of embarrassment she felt at Billy Dawson's words, he was after all Sarah's dad and she had enough people worrying about her without him adding himself into the mix.

"I will," she said quietly without shaking his extended hand and quickly left his office. She looked around her as she neared the glass door at the entrance of Baxters Jute Mill where George stood, as usual, guarding his domain. He saluted Lexie as she passed. "Well done, Miss," he said, "I'll feel safer now that you're going to war for us." Lexie blinked. Was he serious? But the glint in George's eye told her that he too would worry about her till the war was over and she was back home.

Wordlessly, she nodded, touched that so many people cared about her.

Only one more day, then she would be off, leaving behind her everything she knew and loved and setting out on a path unknown. Where it would all lead, she didn't know, but staying in Dundee was no longer an option and with a deep breath she boarded the tram for home and the future.

As Sarah had predicted, Euan and her mum would be taking her to the railway station. Much as she wanted to 'just go,' she agreed and the three of them set off to the Station to say their goodbyes.

Sarah was there before them and was thankful to see the small party arrive, Euan carrying her suitcase and Annie walking purposefully alongside Lexie. There was an awkward silence as the train pulled into the platform. Euan lifted Lexie's suitcase aboard then stood back while Lexie joined it. She loosened the strap that held the window and it dropped open. Annie couldn't contain herself any longer and large tears began to make their way down her cheeks. She reached up and grasped her daughter's hand. Words weren't necessary, her expression said it all. DON'T GO.

It was Sarah who saved the day, shouting 'good luck Lexie' and waving her hand to catch her friend's eye. It broke the tension and Euan stepped forward and extricated Annie from Lexie's hand.

The Station Master blew his whistle and waved his flag to the driver to start the engine. The little trio moved further back from the train and Lexie waved goodbye to her world. No war was going to be as bad as this moment, she told herself, but Lexie was wrong. Her life as a WAAF was just beginning, but the war would be continuing for many months and years to come and test Lexie to the limit.

——-—oOo——-—

Chapter 8

When Nancy got home from work on Monday, Mary Anne rushed to meet her at the door.

"There's a letter came," she said excitedly, waving a crumpled brown envelope in her hand. "It's for you."

"Let me get in the door first," she chided her daughter, taking the envelope from her. The postmark was blurred and she couldn't read it, but the only person who would be writing to her would be Billy.

The single sheet of grubby lined paper was extracted and unfolded.

Been put on embarkation leave it said. *See you on 14th June for a few days. Say hello to the bairns and tell them daddy loves them.*

Your husband, Billy.

"What does it say?" wee Billy wanted to know, "is it from daddy?"

Nancy gazed at his expectant face and nodded. "It is," she smiled at him and he'll be home...TOMORROW." The children jumped up and down with glee and starting dancing round the kitchen, but Nancy felt only a creeping sense of foreboding.

Embarkation leave meant Billy was being sent overseas, she knew that much, but where overseas, only the powers that be knew that. She folded the letter and pushed it back into its envelope. She had to pretend she loved her husband for the sake of their children and it would only be for a few days, she told herself, then he'd be gone again and she would have her new life of dancing and being lusted after by men, especially Jim Murphy, back again.

"Calm down," she ordered, laughing, "let's get our tea down us first, then it'll be early bed for you two, while I get the place tidied up for daddy coming home."

Mary Anne and wee Billy didn't need telling twice. This was better than anything they could think of and the quicker they got off to sleep, the quicker tomorrow would be here.

By nine o'clock the bairns were asleep and the house spick and span. She couldn't have Billy accusing her of neglecting things, it would be hard enough to pretend she still cared about him without giving him an excuse to get drunk, or worse, reacquaint himself with the prossie Gladys Kelly. Even the thought of Billy with the woman filled Nancy with disgust and reinforced her rejection of all Billy's attempts to build a bridge back to the time when they'd loved one another so much.

Tomorrow would be work as usual for Nancy and, hopefully, the chance to see Jim Murphy and tell him the bad news. Next Saturday was out.

Nancy didn't sleep well that night and by morning her stomach was in knots of guilt and desire. Jim Murphy was nowhere to be seen and by the end of her shift, Nancy knew that her pretence that she and Billy were happily married would begin.

Mary Anne met her as she climbed the stairs to their dwelling.

"Daddy's home," she squealed, "and he's brought me and Billy this.

She held up an orange, shiny and bright. "This one's mine," she prattled on and wee Billy has one as well..."

"Hush now Mary Anne," Nancy said, her finger pressing against her lips, "don't tell everyone," she said, "someone might come along and pinch it from you." With that, Nancy grabbed the orange and ran up the stairs ahead of her daughter.

They both burst through the door at the same time as Billy was polishing his son's orange on his khaki tunic.

He nodded to Nancy, as Mary Anne snatched back her orange and ran to her father's side.

For a moment, Nancy too wanted to run to Billy's arms, but the memory of Gladys Kelly was too strong and she stayed where she was, the smell of jute clinging to her hair pervading the small kitchen, along with the tension of the unknown.

It was Nancy who broke the silence. "Out to play you two," she said, "go and show your pals what daddy brought you." The bairns didn't need a second telling, and jostled with one another to be first out of the door.

"Mine's bigger than yours," yelled Mary Anne, waving her orange over her head and yelping as wee Billy kicked her leg. "No its not, no its not!"

"They're getting worse," Nancy said, turning her attention to the stove and filling the kettle. She sensed more than heard Billy's approach as she lit the gas. His arm encircled her waist and he turned her towards him. "No welcome," he said hoarsely, "for the conquering hero?"

Nancy struggled, but he held on.

"We're still man and wife," he said, hotly, "whether you like it or not and

I have rights."

Nancy felt her blood run cold. "In name only," she hissed, "you made that clear when you went elsewhere for your 'rights' with a prossie."

But Billy held her tighter. "That was a long time ago Nancy," he said desperately, "and things change...people change...I've changed."

For a second she almost believed him, till she felt the urgency of his lips on hers and her skirt being raised. She pushed him back with all her strength, but it wasn't enough. Billy was determined to have his home-coming 'welcome' whether Nancy liked it or not. Her body rigid with resistance couldn't stop Billy in his drive to claim his place in Nancy's life but as soon as his lust was satisfied, Nancy rolled away from him and ran from the room.

By the time she'd calmed down and changed her clothes in the back room, Billy had gone. "And good riddance," she muttered to herself as she came back into the kitchen, shaken by Billy's forcing himself on her and her dread of what the next few days would bring.

Billy headed for the place he knew best, the Thrums Bar. It was thick with tobacco smoke and the smell of beer as his fellow warriors drowned their fears with whisky.

Billy Dawson saw him at once, being the only sober man in the pub.

He knew the history of Nancy and Billy's marriage and debated whether to make himself known. He was Nancy's father and he felt it was his duty to find out what his son-in-law was doing drinking, instead of being at home with his wife.

"On leave then, Billy?" he asked indicating the barman to replenish Billy's glass.

Billy's eyes were black as coal and he turned to face his father-in-law. There was no love lost by either of them, their only mutual interest being Nancy and the bairns.

"Embarkation Leave," he said stonily, "if it's anything to you."

"France, is it?" asked Billy trying to stem the rush of anger that rose every time he encountered the man.

Billy shrugged and returned to his beer.

"Nancy and the bairns alright?" Billy persisted. He could see his son-in-law's jaw muscles tighten into granite.

"Why don't you go and ask her," Billy retorted bitterly, "you don't believe anything I tell you."

It was Billy's turn to bristle. "I'll be sure to," he said, letting the young man know that his past was still alive in the present. He drained his glass, "just make sure you keep your nose clean," he said "and the rest of you, as well" he added pointedly.

"I've been trained to kill people, Mr Dawson," Billy said quietly, "I don't have to do anything I don't want to, so keep your advice to yourself."

The barman was polishing a tumbler and stopped abruptly.

"We don't want any trouble now, do we lads," he said nervously, trying to
avert what could turn into a punch-up. "Enough fighting going on in the world as it is."

"No trouble," said Billy, "Mr Dawson's just going."

"No, no trouble," Billy echoed, "I'll see you later, Albert."

The barman nodded his relief. "Right you are, Billy, right you are."

"What waz that ah' aboot?" a voice said next to Billy. "Has he got a problem wi' fighting men then?"

Billy tossed back his drink. "He's my father-in-law," he said coldly, "and can't keep his neb out of my business."

His new companion nudged Billy. "Whut you need is somethin' to cheer you up," he said, "know whut I mean?"

Billy knew exactly what he meant and visions of Gladys Kelly filled his head and his loins.

"I'll find my own fun," Billy said, "but thanks for the reminder."

The pavements leading to Dens Brae and Gladys Kelly were all too familiar to Billy. Despite all his protestations of innocence to Billy Dawson, he'd never stopped visiting the prostitute. In the beginning, he had believed it was to keep Nancy safe, but very soon it became obvious that he kept going to Glady's door because he loved the excitement and danger of being with her. Everything about her intoxicated him and the mere thought of her straddling him, naked and uninhibited, kept him coming back for more.

"Well, well," said the husky voice of Gladys Kelly, "look what the wind's blown in."

Billy's eyes never left her face. "I'm off to France in a few days," he said, hungrily, "and I need something to remind me what I'm fighting for." Gladys stepped back, indicating he was free to enter. Since their first encounter, when Billy had came to work at Baxters and lodge at her mother's boarding house, there had been forces at work in his heart that Gladys barely understood, then as their meetings kept happening, despite grim warnings from Billy Dawson and Nancy finding out about her, he'd keep visiting her every chance he got.

She didn't delude herself it was love that Billy felt for her, but whatever it was she knew that he would always want her more than anyone else, especially Nancy.

Sex with Gladys always left him satiated, unlike with his wife which always left him feeling empty.

"When do you go?" Gladys asked, once the heat had ebbed from their bodies and Billy lay with her, her hand stroking the hair that whispered over his chest.

"End of the week," he said, his eyes closed and his breathing steady. He'd heard word back from others about the power of the Nazi's and their weapons, but there was no fear in Billy. When you've got nothing to lose, he reasoned, fear doesn't hold you in its grip. He turned slowly towards Gladys.

"If I don't come back," he said, suddenly bleak, "will you always remember me?"

Gladys pulled back, the better to see his eyes. "What kind of talk is that?" she asked, trying to hide the fear inside that he might, indeed, never come back, "you know I'll never forget you, Billy Donnelly, and when you're canoodling with all these French tarts," she added, trying to lighten the mood, "remember I'll be right here, waiting for you to come home again."

Abruptly, Billy sat up and began to pull on his clothes. "Well, at least someone will miss me," he said almost to himself, "so keep the bed warm for me Gladys Kelly, because my wife won't be caring if I live or die."

Gladys flinched. Word in the Thrums was that Nancy Donnelly wasn't exactly living the life of abstinence while Billy was at war with the Hun.

Men and drink are easy bedfellows and Glady's customers were no exception. With tongues loosened by whisky and inhibitions gone west, she'd been able to find out just how far Nancy Donnelly was going to ease her 'loneliness.'

"I'm sure she cares, Billy," Gladys said, choosing her words carefully, "it's just that sometimes temptation gets in the way of Godliness."

Billy froze. "Meaning?"

Gladys fussed around the bed, smoothing the coverlet and plumping the pillows. "Meaning," she said, cautiously, "while the cat's away..!"

Billy could feel temper rising from the soles of his boots through to the top of his head. His hands pulled Gladys round to face him.

"And who is this mouse playing with?"

Gladys knew she'd said too much. If she ever thought Billy wanted her more than he wanted his wife, she knew now that she was wrong.

She blinked back a fearful tear. "Jim Murphy."

The slamming of the door told Gladys all she needed to know.

Billy Donnelly would never be back.

Chapter 9

Lexie found a carriage and slid the door open. A young girl with huge blue eyes gazed at her.

"Mind if I join you," Lexie asked, stowing her case on the overhead luggage rack and sitting herself in the seat opposite without waiting for an answer.

The girl nodded. "If you like," she said, "I don't think there's anyone else getting on at Dundee," she added, as the whistle sounded the departure of the train.

"Was that your mum and dad at the station," she asked, "waving to you?"

"It was," Lexie answered relief that she was now on her way, relaxing her. "I'm off to join the Womens Auxiliary Air Force," she said proudly, "how about you?"

The blue eyes widened further, "me too," she said, excitedly, leaning forward in her seat, "I've to report to a place called Wilmslow in Cheshire."

"Me too!" Lexie exclaimed. Already it felt like everything was going to be alright, as the last of her nerves vanished. The girls giggled and Lexie introduced herself. "Lexie Melville," she said, "Dundee born and bred."

"Winifred Adams," the girl replied, "but everyone calls me Winnie and I'm Montrose born and bred," she added.

The train pulled out of the station and the girls watched from the carriage window as it turned onto the bridge over the river and Dundee, with its mills and smoking chimney stacks, began to recede into the past. Lexie felt a wave of emotion hit her, what would her future hold in the WAAF, she wondered, now that everything she had ever known was being left behind.

"I felt like that too when the train pulled out of Montrose," interrupted her companion, as a small tear escaped Lexie's eye.

Lexie sniffed. "Sorry," she murmured, brushing the tear away, "not usually this wobbly."

"So, what made you join up?" Winnie asked, moving the subject away from the unknown.

Lexie gazed at her clasped hands, searching for reasons that made sense. "I think I just wanted to find a better life for myself," she began, "you know, do something different." The fear of becoming an old maid, the hurt from Robbie Robertson's rejection, getting older and older and still working at Baxters, were the real reasons, but Lexie wasn't ready to go into them yet. "How about you?" she asked Winnie, switching the limelight onto her fellow-traveller.

"Same as you really," she said, "both my brothers are in the Army and dad was a soldier in the last war, so it seemed sort of natural, I suppose. And there's an Airbase just outside Montrose," she continued, "and the town is always full of RAF blokes in air force uniforms, so when I saw the recruitment poster for the WAAF, that was it."

"You saw it too?" Lexie exclaimed, "how strange is that?"

Winnie smiled, "not strange really, these posters were everywhere, just waiting to be noticed by girls like us."

"Girls like us?" Lexie asked.

Winnie's smile widened, "I know there's a war on and all, but it would be nice to meet some handsome pilot, don't you think..." Lexie dissolved into embarrassment. "You're blushing," Winnie said, surprised at Lexie's reaction. "Don't tell me it hasn't crossed your mind?" she said, surprised, adding quietly, "you must have led a very sheltered life."

"Sometimes you can't see the obvious," Lexie said, "I guess being hurt in the past sort of puts you off men a bit..." there, it was out, Lexie was running away from her past and Robbie Robertson.

Winnie felt sorry for Lexie. There had been men in her own life, plenty of them, but none of them had ever hurt her the way Lexie seemed to be hurting.

"Hey," she said, gently, "there's plenty more fish in the sea and someone as pretty as you isn't going to need much of a net to catch one."

"Lexie nodded. Winnie was right, she needed to shake off the past and enjoy the future whatever that held and this war, with all its evil, might prove to be her way back to living again.

The train chugged on throughout the day and the light was going by the time Wilmslow Station came into view.

The two girls stretched and pulled down their luggage from the overhead storage nets, as the train squealed to a halt.

"This is it then, Lexie," Winnie said, "the first day of our new lives."

Lexie nodded. "I'm ready," she said firmly, amid the noise of slamming carriage doors and chattering passengers.   She followed Winnie onto the platform, realising for the first time, that she was no longer in Scotland, but England and the thought of being in another country, albeit in the same island, filled her with excitement.

A uniformed woman was there to meet them and beckoned them over to the waiting truck.

"In you go girls," she said, briskly, indicating the step up to the canvas- covered back of the truck. There were four other girls already seated on the wooden benches either side as Lexie and Winnie took the last two places.

The woman joined the driver and they were off. "RAF Wilmslow, here we come," Winnie whispered to Lexie, nudging her gently in the ribs.

The drive to the camp was long and rutted and by the time they arrived, everything was in blackout darkness.

"Keep close together," their guide said as they alighted from the truck, "and follow me."

The six new recruits were ushered into a wooden billet and once the door was closed a weak electric light was switched on. The walls were lined with eight beds, each with a small wardrobe and locker, with a huge black pot-bellied stove, unlit, in the centre of the room.

"Right," shouted the woman, "find a bed, dump your bags and

follow me to the Mess Hall. There's tea and sandwiches for you all and then it's back here for some kip." Her eyes roved around the pale faces and Lexie swore she saw her smile.

"Any questions?"

"It's a bit cold in here," said Jean Bailey, the biggest girl in the group, "is someone going to get that 'thing' going by the time we get back?" She nodded towards the black monstrosity. Everyone was wondering the same thing but no one had the courage to ask.

"THING," came the short reply, as Corporal Beryl Samson crossed the room to where the iron stove sat. "And here's me thinking you Scottish lassies never minded the cold," she said, icily, before turning her attention to Jean.

"Name."

The atmosphere became colder than the stove, as Jean gave her name.

"Well, JEAN BAILEY," began the Corporal, "why don't you fetch some wood and coal from the coalhouse and get a nice fire going, while the rest of us go the Mess Hall for our sandwiches, or maybe you'll decide to put up with the cold instead."

"Riiigggghhhhttt," Jean replied, warily, knowing when to accept who was in charge, before stepping back from the Corporal.

Lexie stood very still. If she had any thoughts that being a WAAF would be 'fun' she was now in no doubt that it was going to be hard going, very hard going.

Now sure that she had their undivided attention, the Corporal headed for the door, with the new recruits meekly following her without any further comments.

The sandwiches were awful. Winnie had described them as some kind of fish paste on cardboard bread and as for the tea, uuugghhhh! But everyone quickly ate them, before being hurried back to their billet by Corporal Samson.

"Wake-up bugle-call at 7 o'clock, then we'll get you checked and decked and signed up. You'll be pleased to know that I'll be looking after you during basic training and before you know where you are, you'll be ready to join the fight."

Everyone shuffled nervously. "ANY QUESTIONS?"

The silence was deafening. "Good," said the Corporal, "Sleep well ladies, the fun is just beginning."

"Fun?" Winnie whispered, after Corporal Samson had gone, "I can't wait."

The girls introduced themselves to one another, each calling out their names from their beds. Winnie, Lexie, Mary, Daisy, Jean and Pearl.

"Goodnight all," said Jean, pulling on her fleecy pyjamas as the others did the same. "Tomorrow will be better, I'm sure," she added, "at least I hope so."

Chapter 10

Annie and Euan walked slowly away from the Station. Waving Lexie goodbye had been heartbreaking for Annie. Since Alex's death, Lexie had been the focus of all her motherly love and not being able to see her every day was going to be painful.

Euan linked her arm into his. "She'll be back in a few weeks," he said encouragingly "and things will be better by then, you'll see."

But Annie wasn't so sure. There was so much danger in the world and her wonderful daughter would be in the midst of it all.

"She'll be safe, won't she?" she asked Euan for the umpteenth time.

Euan squeezed her hand. "She'll be fine," he said, "just fine."

They were nearly home when they met Billy Dawson. He could see at once that Annie was upset and he knew the reason why.

He nodded to Euan before turning his attention to Annie. "She's gone then?"

Annie nodded. The silence became uncomfortable as words seemed inadequate. Billy knew how much Lexie meant to her and how she had suffered at the hands of Alex Melville. He looked at Euan.

"Take care of her," he said, grimly. "This damn war will be over soon and Lexie will come back home fit and well before we know it." He took Euan's hand and shook it. "If there's anything I can do to help," he said, "just let me know."

He and Billy had joined forces to make Billy Donnelly see sense when he'd refused to marry Billy's pregnant daughter

Nancy and had a mutual respect for one another and their place in Annie's life.

Annie kept her eyes fixed on the pavement as the men talked. Although Euan knew about Annie's illegitimate son John and had even met him, he didn't know that Billy Dawson was the father and never would. Annie had made sure of that when she had given Billy the news that he had fathered her son.

As always, when Billy was around Annie, he wanted to take her in his arms and hold her to him, more than ever now, since knowing of their son. But Annie had chosen Euan and that was how it had to be.

"And how's our Mr Donnelly?" Euan asked Billy as Annie excused herself and disappeared into the close. Billy's lips formed into a thin line. "I just don't know Euan," he said, "we met in the Thrums Bar a couple of nights ago and I have to tell you, he's a troubled man."

"Didn't he join the Scots Guards?" Euan asked.

"He did and he's on embarkation leave this week, so who knows where he'll end up."

Both men considered the possibility of Nancy's husband surviving the war.

"And how's your Nancy dealing with things?"

"She's working at the mill and seems fine, but there's word about, that she's taken to going to the dance halls with some pal of hers. I just hope wind of it hasn't reached Billy and that he doesn't do anything foolish, like he did before."

"Gladys Kelly," Euan said, pointedly.

Billy shrugged his shoulders. He's a full grown man now Euan, fighting for King and country, his decisions are his own, but I just hope they both weather this storm for the sake of the bairns."

The men went their separate ways, Euan home to Annie and Billy to the Masonic Lodge.

It was gone midnight when Billy Donnelly finally returned home. He had walked the darkened streets, letting his anger abate. He knew Jim Murphy and what he was capable off and the thought of him sniffing round Nancy was driving him dangerously close to the edge. It didn't matter that he was satisfying his lust with Gladys Kelly, she was a prossie, Nancy was his wife and though there was no love left between them, no other man could even look at her in that way, never mind bed her.

He sat staring at her in the darkness, her dark hair spilling onto the pillow and her lips slightly parted, breathing softly. He switched on the light and shook her awake. "Having a nice dream?" he asked.

Nancy's eyes flew open in concern, as she tried to understand what was happening.

She pushed herself up on her elbows and squinted her eyes at her husband.

"Billy?"

"You looked so happy lying there," he told her, "I thought you must be dreaming about something nice...or someone."

Nancy felt a chill of anxiety. She picked up the clock sitting on the chair beside their bed. "It's nearly one in the morning," she said "and I've the mill to go to tomorrow morning."

Billy flexed his fingers and slowly picked at the dirt under his thumbnail.

"So you do," he muttered to himself, "but then tomorrow's Saturday and you'll be getting your wages and wanting to spend them on something nice or go somewhere nice, what do you think?"

Nancy began to feel uneasy. What was Billy on about?

"I'll be spending them, as usual, on the bairns and if I don't get back to sleep there'll be no job to go to."

"So, no dancing this Saturday then?" he asked.

So this was what Billy's questions were all about, Nancy quickly realised somebody had told him of her trips to the Palais with Diane.

"No, no dancing," she said, treading carefully and choosing her words.

"Di Auchterlonie asked me to keep her company at the Palais a few weeks ago, so I did, but it was too much bother, so we didn't go back.

51

Billy nodded silently. "Maybe you should go again," he said, "with me that is, rekindle our love before I go overseas and leave you alone again with no man to protect you."

Billy was choosing his words carefully too. He'd be at the Palais on Saturday with Nancy, if it was the last thing he did and God help Jim Murphy if he turned up.

Billy would be gone by Sunday night, so Nancy had only to keep on his right side till then. She knew there was something in the wind, but felt she'd played her cards right and decided to go along with Billy's game.

"Fine," she said feigning sleepiness, "now can you get into bed and let's get some sleep.

Billy undressed and turned off the light. Cold and hung-over, he climbed over Nancy to his side of the bed and turned his back on her as usual, but not before Nancy caught the familiar whiff of rotten fish. He'd been with Gladys Kelly again and her heart hardened further. There would be no 'rekindling' of anything, she told herself, war or no war, Billy and her were finished. Nancy closed her eyes and dreamt of Jim Murphy.

Nancy left for the mill early next morning, leaving Billy to sleep off the drink and Gladys Kelly. She must see Jim before the morning shift was over and make sure he didn't turn up at the Palais that night, expecting to be with her.

Luck was with her and she caught up with him as he was unlocking the Buckie door.

He turned towards her, his delight at seeing her evident in his smile.

"You're early," he said, smoothly, "couldn't wait till tonight to see me,

eh?"

"Billy's home," Nancy said bluntly, "and he's taking me to the Palais tonight, so..."

"Is he now," Jim interrupted, "and you're here to warn me not to turn up there?"

Nancy nodded.

"Someone's told him about me going to the dancing while he's been away and I don't want any trouble. If he thinks I'm there to meet you, I don't know what he'll do."

Jim Murphy was no fool, he fancied Nancy Donnelly, but not at any cost and although Jean wasn't a raving beauty, his wife kept a good house and fed him well and he wasn't about to trade that for an uncertain future with Nancy and her two bairns. Sex he could get anywhere, but home comforts were harder to come by.

"Now don't you worry your pretty little head about me," he murmured, running the fingers of his hand down her bare arm, "I'll be safely tucked up in bed by ten o'clock tonight with a cup of cocoa and a good book."

Nancy relaxed. "Maybe next week," she said hopefully, "Billy will be gone by then?"

Jim Murphy smiled. "Maybe," he said, "maybe."

Nancy felt a frisson of anxiety take hold. The more Jim Murphy tempted her the more she wanted him and evidence that Billy had been with Gladys Kelly again, only served to intensify her desire.

She watched as he entered the Buckie and began to enter up the yardage for the previous day. The other mill workers were beginning to arrive and a couple of them glanced her way, wondering why she was standing there and nudged one another.

Quickly, Nancy pushed a stray curl under her turban and straightened her apron before walking towards the Weaving Flat, nodding to the questioning eyes as she passed by.

Tonight she and Billy would go the Palais and now she knew that Jim wouldn't be there, she relaxed and got on with her work. Tomorrow, Billy would be gone, where, she didn't know and didn't care enough to even wonder.

—-—oOo—-—

Chapter 11

Despite the cold billet and the hard bed, Lexie was sleeping soundly when the trumpeting of a bugle blasted her awake. The journey and her first encounter with the camp at RAF Wilmslow and particularly Corporal Beryl Samson flooded back into her mind.

The door of the billet swung open and Corporal Samson breezed in.

"Everybody up," she shouted, "ablutions and bed making then breakfast in the Mess at 7.15." Without waiting for a response, the Corporal exited the way she'd come in. The girls, who had been sleeping were suddenly awake. "Ablutions?" said Daisy, "what's that?"

"Get washed and dressed," shouted Jean Bailey as she rummaged in her suitcase for her toothbrush. We've got 12 minutes to get to the Mess!"

Clothes were pulled on where they stood and blankets thrown over their beds, as the girls rushed to meet the deadline. Breathlessly, they filed out of the billet and headed for the Mess. Having arrived in darkness, Lexie hadn't taken in the size of the camp, nor the fact that they shared it with the MEN. She turned to Winnie, a look of amazement on her face.

"It's full of blokes!" she exclaimed. Winnie giggled, "Mmmmm," she said, "isn't it great?"

The noise in the Mess was deafening, pans and metal trays clanged and banged, as porridge and rows of shelled eggs were being served up by the cooks. "Move along luv," one of them urged Lexie, "what'll it be, eggs or eggs?" Lexie looked into the grinning face, sweat glistening on its brow.

"Eggs, please," she stammered. "Bread over there," he indicated "and tea at the end of the line."

Winnie pushed in alongside her. "Eggs for me too," she said, coyly. Even at this hour of the morning, Winnie was already into flirting mode and the cook responded, giving her an extra big smile but, to Winnie's disappointment, not an extra egg.

The men were raucous, even at the early hour of the day, but Lexie and the other girls just stared in silence at the sea of faces. Suddenly, one man peeled off and made for their table.

"Well, hello girls," he grinned, allowing his eyes to roam all over them, "up for the fight then?"

Lexie looked at Winnie, "fight?" she mouthed, "what fight?"

Jack Forsythe's grin widened even further. He leaned forward over the table, "why the fight you're going to have to put up to keep us boys in our place at the NAAFI dance on Saturday."

Everyone relaxed and giggled. Pearl White, or Pearly as she had quickly been nicknamed, rose to her full height of 5 ft 2 in. "You'd better watch out," she grinned, looking round at the rest of them, "there's six of us and only one of you, so good luck with that one."

The rest of the girls rose as one, taking their dishes with them to the plate-clearing station, leaving Jack nodding to himself, Saturday should be fun and the girl with the big blue eyes would be top of his list.

"What's all this about a dance?" Winnie queried, excitedly and where's this NAAFI place?

Lexie shrugged, you're as wise as I am," she said, "maybe Corporal Samson will know." Winnie flinched visibly.

At the mention of the Corporal, the girls quickened their step back to their billet. Beryl Samson was already there and waiting.

"Today we get down to business," she began, pacing up and down the billet. First of all you'll see the camp doctor for your medical, then you'll be issued with your kit, uniform, bed-pack and your ID Number. You'll wear your uniform at all times and salute all officers that you pass.

"Any questions?"

Winnie almost asked about the NAAFI, but immediately thought better of it. Jack Forsythe was a dish and, one way or another, she intended to be his 'afters' on Saturday night.

By the end of a frantic week of activities, the girls were ready to drop, but they had all survived their induction. Lexie admired herself in her uniform as best she could in the small hand mirror she'd brought with her from home.

"1482166 ACW Melville," she whispered, hardly able to believe she had done it. She now knew how to launder and press her uniform, make her bed perfectly, learned the history of the RAF and the WAAF, knew the ranks of the RAF Officers from Group Captain to Wing Commander and was getting to grips with the discipline of 'square bashing.'

"Penny for them," said Daisy Ramsey, or Petal as she was now known, as she and Pearly came into the billet, after taking their turn at cleaning the toilet block.

Lexie swung round and blushed at being caught admiring herself.

De ja vue, she thought, remembering the time that the Office Junior, Joannie Kelly had come into her office when she was checking her face for the beginnings of fine lines and wondering if she'd 'die an auld maid,' like Nancy Donnelly has predicted.

"I was just thinking," Lexie said, "that I'm the luckiest girl in the world."

Pearly and Petal exchanged glances. "Obviously hasn't just cleaned the loos!" Petal said sagely, wrinkling her nose, before the trio burst out laughing.

"What's all the giggling about then," asked Winnie, coming into the billet, tossing her cap onto her bed and unbuckling her belt.

"Lexie thinks she's the luckiest girl in the world," Pearly said, holding up her mop and bucket, meaningfully.

Winnie shook her head. "I think you'll find it's me who's the luckiest girl in the world," she said, warming to her topic. "I've just been invited to the NAAFI dance on Saturday by none *other than **Pilot Officer Jack Forsythe!***"

Lexie flopped down onto her bed. "You've spoken to him?"

she asked incredulously, as Pearly and Petal moved closer, clutching their mops tightly, mouths agape with surprise. This was news indeed and they

didn't want to miss a second of Winnie's encounter with a **Pilot Officer.**

"Well," began Winnie, trying to keep the excitement out of her voice, "you know we have to salute all Officers," the others nodded, "well, I was just passing the Training Control Offices when who should come out but...**Pilot Officer Forsythe**. Naturally, I saluted, but he stopped me in my tracks and asked my name."

"What did you say?" asked Petal, her eyes huge with curiosity, "I said what we've been told to say, name, rank and serial number, SIR."

"But how do you know..." Lexie began, trying to imagine how Winnie found out his name. "Then he said, *"Pilot Office Jack Forsythe* at your service. Report to me on Saturday at 8 o'clock in the NAAFI for the first dance! Then he saluted me back and walked off."

The girls held their breath in disbelief. "Honest, it's true," Winnie assured them, clasping her hands together and gazing into the future with a misty look in her eyes. "Saturday was going to be wonderful.

The NAAFI was a sea of air-force blue when the girls arrived and an ancient gramophone was blasting out American Big Band music. The women were outnumbered at least three to one and it wasn't long before they were all split up and whisked onto the floor. Lexie had been pounced on by the cook, Bert Wilmot, who'd served the boiled eggs on Lexie's first day at the camp.

"Enjoying camp life then?" he asked in his South London accent, as the music stopped and he guided Lexie back to the seats around the NAAFI wall. "Just fine," Lexie replied, not sure how much she understood his accent. "What's your tipple?" Bert shouted above the music which had started again, "Tipple?" Lexie asked. "Yeah," Bert said, leaning closer to her, "you know...drink?" He pointed to the bar and pints of beer being served by an Orderly. Lexie shook her head, "I don't drink," she said, "but maybe a lemonade would be nice though."

Bert saluted. "Back in a tick," he said, heading off to the bar, but before he could return, another blue-uniformed man pulled Lexie onto the floor.

"Glen Millar," shouted her new partner, "the music," he added, "not me."

Lexie blinked. From leading a very quiet and man-free life in Dundee, she now found herself surrounded by men and all of them seemingly wanting to dance with her.

"Clive Jones," the Welshman said, "from the Rhonda Valley in Welsh Wales," he added. "How about you?"

"Lexie Melville," Lexie shouted back, "from Dundee in Scotland."

"A SCOTTIE!" Clive exclaimed, "how bloody marvellous. Isn't this war just great!"

Lexie had to agree, as Clive danced her round the floor. Far from being a frightening thing, Lexie was beginning to feel that it was going to be the best thing she could have done to get over all the hurt and dreariness that had been her life for so long in Dundee.

It was gone ten o'clock before she met up with Winnie in the toilet block attached to the NAFFI hall.

Winnie was glowing and Lexie didn't have to ask how things had gone with Pilot Officer Jack Forsythe. "Well," she said, "did you report to him at 8 o'clock?"

Winnie's eyes were huge and glassy. "Mmmmhhh," she whispered, "and don't wait up," she added, heading for the door, "I may be back a little late."

"Don't get caught," Lexie hissed after her. But Winnie didn't hear a word, she was on her way to make love with Jack Forsythe.

—-—oOo—-—

Chapter 12

When Nancy's shift finished at 1 o'clock, she hurried home not knowing what to expect, but safe in the knowledge that Jim Murphy wouldn't be at the Palais that night. Mary Anne and wee Billy were playing on the sloping grass around the Air Raid Shelters, Billy and his pals pretending to be soldiers like their dads and Mary Anne and the girl next door, kneeling on the grass playing at being housewives like their mums.

Nancy watched history repeating itself. It wouldn't be long now before Mary Anne would be grown up and looking for the love and happiness that had eluded Nancy. A shiver of fear for the future ran through her heart.

She dropped her message bag and coat on the coal bunker inside the kitchen and made her way to Mrs Jeffries house to ask her to mind the bairns again tonight. A bemused Mrs Jeffries screwed up her eyes in confusion. "But, your man was here earlier and asked if I'd minded the wee ones in the past and when I said I did and was happy to do so, he said I wouldn't be needed in the future and that your Auntie Annie would be looking after Mary Anne and Billy the night."

Nancy's blood ran cold. So, Billy now knew she'd gone dancing more than once and would make sure she never did so again, especially after he'd gone back to his regiment. She was going to be watched.

Di Auchterlonie popped her head round the top of the stairwell.

"A'right for the night Nancy?" she asked breezily.

Nancy hurried her inside the house. "Billy knows," she stated bluntly, lighting a cigarette and inhaling the tobacco deeply to calm her nerves, "and he's taking me to the Palais tonight to see who knows me."

"You mean, he knows about Jim Murphy?" Di asked worried now for her pal.

"NO, NO, not Jim anyway I've warned him not to turn up tonight, but he spoke with Mrs Jeffries earlier and knows I went dancing more than once." Tears of fear and dejection filled her eyes. "If he stops me going back to the Palais then me and Jim will be over before we've begun."

"Do you want me to speak to him?" Di asked, trying to defuse the situation, "you know, tell him it was all my idea and..."

Nancy lit another cigarette from the first one and shook her head, "I think the less said the better, but thanks for the offer."

There was still no sign of Billy when Nancy called the bairns in for their tea. "Me and your dad are going out tonight, but your Auntie Annie is coming over to mind you." Mary Anne cheered, "I like Auntie Annie," she said, "she always brings sweeties."

"For me too!" exclaimed wee Billy, "I want some too."

"Eat your tea, or you'll be getting no sweeties from anyone," Nancy chided, peeping around the net curtain for signs of Billy's return.

The knock at the door made Nancy jump, until she realised that Billy wouldn't knock. She hurried to the door and opened it to Annie.

"Nancy," Annie smiled, "how are you... and Mary Anne and wee Billy...how are they?" Nancy took her coat and hung it on the hook at the back of the door.

"Just fine, Auntie Annie," she said, ushering her into the small kitchen. I'm sorry to have bothered you, but Billy insisted we go out tonight before he goes back to his regiment."

Annie reached into her bag and produced two paper bags of sweeties and handed them over to the bairns.

"There," she said, ruffling wee Billy's hair and patting Mary Anne on the shoulder. "Now are you going to be good while mummy and daddy go dancing?"

"We're always good when mummy goes dancing," Mary Anne said innocently. Annie turned sharply to Nancy. "I don't understand," she said, pulling up a chair and sitting down at the table. "You've not been out dancing while Billy's been away at war...have you?"

Nancy felt the colour drain from her face. She busied herself clearing the table while the children ran outside to eat their sweeties sitting on the stairs.

"Just the once," she mumbled, "Diane Auchterlonie needed some company, so...I went to the Palais with her...just the once."

"Does Billy know?"

Nancy nodded. Annie fixed her eyes on her niece. She'd always worried that Mary's temperament had come through in the blood and that Nancy would become flighty and promiscuous, like her mother before her.

The pregnancy and Nancy's hurried marriage to Billy Donnelly had done nothing to allay her fears and now, with the war on, women were becoming bolder in their dealings with men and it looked like Nancy had become one of them.

Annie stood up and faced her niece. "Is there someone else, Nancy?" she asked quietly.

"NO, NO," Nancy responded a bit too quickly for Annie's liking.

The silence deepened till Annie spoke again. "Then you'd better get yourself ready for your husband. Annie looked at the clock. Half past six. "He'll be here soon," she added, pushing her disquiet to the back of her mind.

Billy came in at seven o'clock. He was wearing his uniform and had grown even more handsome as he'd matured into manhood. He'd had a drink or two at the Thrums Bar but nothing like his usual capacity.

"Thanks for coming at such short notice," he said, shaking Annie's hand, "It's just that I'm off overseas tomorrow and this will be my last night with my wife till God knows when."

Annie noticed he didn't refer to Nancy by name, but only as his wife, but his eyes seemed to light up when she came through from the back room wearing the sequined top Annie had given her and a tight black skirt and high heels. Nancy kept her eyes downcast.

The usual blackout was already in place in the town, with no street lamps lit and windows covered with heavy curtains or blinds. "Mind how you go," she said to the pair "and Euan's going to come and get me at eleven o'clock, when his shift with the ARP finishes, so be home in good time," she stated "we'll both be ready for our beds by then."

The thought that Sergeant MacPherson would be here when they got back from the Palais, gave Billy caution for his behaviour, he'd felt the pain of a punch in the jaw from the policeman, when he'd been caught visiting Gladys Kelly...again and he'd no wish to repeat the experience.

"We won't be late," said Nancy, also glad that Euan MacPherson would be around when they got back.

The bright lights in the dancehall in Tay Street almost belied the fact that the country was a war and that at any minute bombs could be raining down on them from German bombers heading for the shipyards on the Clyde. The various uniforms of the men, however, ensured that no one was under any illusion that peace was anywhere at hand and the urge to make the most of this brief respite from the fighting was evident in their faces.

Billy scanned the dance floor for signs of Jim Murphy while Nancy checked her coat into the cloakroom. For a moment he wished with all his heart that he and Nancy were still in love and that the evening would end in a glorious sexual release for both of them, but cold reality soon brought him back down to earth as Nancy appeared next to him, her face a mask of indifference.

"Not enjoying yourself," he said, adding pointedly, "as usual."

Nancy sighed. "So, I came to the dancing a couple of times," she said, keeping her voice low and shrugging her shoulders, "so what."

Billy looked around him again. "No one here you know then?" he asked, "seeing as how you're a regular."

Nancy didn't answer. Surely, he didn't know about Jim Murphy.

"Are you here to dance or just to start an argument," Nancy

said, wishing the night was over and Billy was gone.

She felt his hand grip her elbow and push her into the crowd of dancers.

The band was playing a slow Foxtrot and Billy pulled her into him. "Like this," he whispered in her ear, "is this how you like to dance."

"You're hurting me," Nancy gasped, trying to push Billy away.

"Not as much as you're hurting me," Billy said through gritted teeth.

Nancy closed her eyes and let her muscles go limp. The dance would soon be over, she told herself, bitterly and so would her marriage.

Although Nancy recognised a few of the soldiers, she avoided eye contact with them and none of them approached her.

"Can we go home now?" she asked, as the clock crept towards ten thirty. Annie and Euan will be waiting for us.

"Get your coat," said Billy coldly, "I'll wait for you at the door." So, Jim Murphy hadn't turned up, but that didn't mean he wasn't after Nancy. Gladys Kelly knew about the dark side of life and wouldn't have mentioned his name for nothing.

The walk back to their home was cold, dark and silent and it wasn't till they came to the close leading to the stairwell, that Billy spoke.

"I go overseas tomorrow," he said, "but I'll be back. And when I am, I'll know if you and JIM MURPHY have been up to anything. UNDERSTAND ME."

Nancy flinched. So he did know about Jim, but how?

Nancy neither confirmed nor denied Jim Murphy.

"Do your worst," she said, "and make sure you say good night to Gladys Kelly from me." Nancy summoned all her courage, "that's where you're going isn't it?"

Billy placed his hands either side of her head and pulled her face towards his. He roughly kissed her before stepping back into the darkness. "Remember I love you," he said hoarsely, "and that you're my wife."

The darkness swallowed him up. Nancy wiped his saliva from her mouth and ascended the stair to home.

Euan and Annie were waiting. "Where's Billy?" Annie asked, concern for the couple mounting, "is he alright?"

"He's fine," Nancy said, "just gone to say goodbye to someone."

"Who,?" Annie queried.

Nancy sighed. "No one you know Auntie Annie."

"Anyone I know?" asked Euan, worried now. Surely Billy wasn't at Gladys Kelly's after all that had happened in the past.

Nancy didn't need to give him an answer, he knew by her face that there was no love left for her husband. Gladys Kelly had won.

———oOo———

Chapter 13

By the time a month had elapsed at RAF Wilmslow, all the new recruits had been duly sworn in and signed the Official Secrets Act. They'd be going home at the end of the week for a long weekend before returning to the camp 'to see if they were any good for anything useful to the war effort,' as Corporal Samson had put it, before being ordered to their first posting.

Lexie was writing to her mum about her homecoming and the time of her arrival when Winnie came into the Billet and sat down across from her.

"Have you told your folks about coming home?" Lexie asked, not looking up from her writing. The lack of response made her glance at Winnie and she saw the anxiety on her face.

She put down her pen. "Something wrong?" Lexie asked.

"Could be," replied Winnie, enigmatically.

She now had Lexie's full attention. "Meaning?"

"I'm late."

"Late," echoed Lexie, "as in...monthly late?"

Winnie nodded. "Jack Forsythe didn't take any precautions and I...well, neither did I."

"Oh Winnie!" Lexie put aside her letter writing and joined her friend on the bed. "Are you sure?"

Winnie nodded miserably. "Should have been three days ago."

"Does he know?"

Winnie shook her head. "No," she sighed "and he's been posted to another airfield somewhere in Wiltshire..."her voice tailed off as she felt the weight of her predicament pressing down on her shoulders.

Winnie turned tearful eyes on Lexie. "I know we don't know one another that well," she began, "but could I come home with you, please, I don't want to face my dad yet and I won't be any trouble, I promise."

Lexie felt a wave of compassion for her friend. The last time she had had to confront pregnancy out of wedlock was when Nancy had come to stay and Euan and Billy Dawson had to 'persuade' Billy Donnelly to marry her.

"Of course, you can," Lexie said, "I'll let mum know there'll be two of us to feed, she'll love to meet you."

She put a protective arm around Winnie's shoulders. "It'll be alright," she told her, "my mum will know what to do."

But Annie was already worried about Nancy. Both Euan and herself had felt something was far wrong between the couple and Annie decided she would visit her niece more often in future.

"I'm sure she'd like that," Euan had said, trying to sound reassuring, but silently he knew that a telephone call to Billy Dawson needed to be made. Billy had already hinted to Euan that there was talk about Nancy frequenting the local dancehalls and with his suspicions aroused about Billy and Gladys Kelly, he feared the worst.

"Are you certain about this?" Billy asked when Euan telephoned about his concerns that Gladys Kelly was 'still around.'

"I can't be certain," Euan replied, but Nancy seemed very unhappy when she came home alone on Saturday from the Palais. She said that Billy had gone to say goodbye to *someone*...and I think that someone was Gladys."

"I'll keep an eye on Nancy
at the mill," Billy said, decisively, his temper rising at his son-in-law's inability to control his urges "and maybe you can let me know if you hear anything being said about her around the bars. You know the way men talk, Euan, especially when they think there's a woman on the loose, they're like alley cats on the prowl."

"I'll do that Billy and Annie's going to look in on Nancy more often too, make sure the bairns are alright 'kind of thing.'"

66

At the mention of Annie's name, Billy tensed. Try as he might, his response was always the same and it had become stronger since she had told him he was the father of her son, John Adams.

"Keep me posted, Euan," he said, ending the conversation and replacing the receiver back on the office telephone.

He'd go and see Nancy the following Saturday, find out for himself if she was unhappy.

Gladys hadn't expected to see Billy Donnelly again, not after he'd stormed out in a jealous rage, so when she opened her door to loud knocking, her heart filled with fear that Billy had done something murderous.

Without any preamble, Billy pulled her through to the back room.

"I go back to the fight tomorrow," he said, his eyes black as coal. He handed Gladys a piece of notepaper with his name, rank and number on it along with the name and Box Number for his Regiment. "If you care anything for me," he said, "you'll let me know when Jim Murphy makes his move."

Gladys knew what he meant and slipped the notepaper down the front of her dress. "If that's what you want," she said, resignation softening her voice "you can rely on me."

Billy relaxed, Gladys Kelly may be a prossie, but he knew he could trust her and even wished at times he could love her, but no matter what Nancy felt about him, he couldn't stop loving her.

"Can I stay the night?" he asked, pointing to the double bed. "Just to sleep," he added, "before I head off tomorrow."

"Whatever you want Billy," Gladys said, sadly, "I'll sleep in the kitchen."

She closed the door quietly behind her. She had made the mistake of falling for a paying gent and now she must suffer the consequences. Once a prossie, always a prossie.

"It's a letter from Lexie," Annie called out excitedly, waving the envelope over Euan's sleeping head. "Wake up, quick," she said, already tearing open the envelope and unfolding the single page.

Euan struggled to open his eyes, rubbing his face and head to bring himself to wakefulness.

Annie read the words. "She's coming home this Friday and...she's bringing a friend with her. Isn't that wonderful?"

Euan was awake now. "Wonderful," he agreed, glad to see Annie coming to life again. Her daughter was coming home and she couldn't wait to see her.

"I'll need to make up the bed in Ian's room for Lexie's friend and find a way to make the rations stretch to another mouth and..."

"Slow down," Euan said, smiling, "It's only Tuesday, you've got plenty of time to get ready for Friday, so how about we have our breakfast before you do anything else."

Annie clasped the letter to her chest. "She's coming home, Euan," she said and that's all that matters."

Euan thought to remind her that they had two children and that their son Ian was in the Forces too, but he knew in his heart that she loved both of their children equally, it was just that Lexie had been so hurt by Robbie Robertson's rejection and he just prayed that her decision to join the WAAF had been the right one.

"There she is," whispered Annie, waving her hand to attract Lexie's attention, as the train disgorged its passengers. She'd promised she wouldn't cry, but the sight of Lexie in her uniform brought a lump to her throat and her grip on Euan's arm tightened.

Lexie rushed to her mother's arms with Winnie following on in the background and she was hugging Euan when she remembered Winnie.

She ushered her forward. "This is Winnie," Lexie announced, excitedly, "the one I wrote to you about."

Winnie extended her hand, "pleased to meet you Mrs MacPherson and thanks for letting me stay with you."

Annie barely shook her hand, before linking her arm into Lexie's and heading towards the station exit, leaving Euan and Winnie to follow on.

Euan smiled at Winnie, "she's not usually this distracted," he said, "but she's missed Lexie more than she cares to admit."

Winnie nodded. "I understand," she said wistfully, wishing

she had had the courage to go home to Montrose and her own family, but her shame was too great.

Euan picked up her suitcase. "C'mon," he said, his fatherly voice giving Winnie a feeling of safety, "there's a motor waiting to take us all home."

Annie had been cooking all morning and the smells of minced beef and apple tarts wafted through the whole house.

"Something smells good," Lexie said, glancing at Winnie, "the food at the Mess is pretty tasteless, so we have to fill up at the NAAFI."

Annie took a good look at her daughter. "You've lost weight," she said, a note of concern in her voice, before bustling about the kitchen making tea and lifting half a dozen scones from the cake tin.

It was while she was pouring their tea, that she finally acknowledged Winnie.

"So," she said, offering the plate of scones, "you're Winnie?"

The girl nodded and it was then that Annie noticed the paleness of her face, so unlike Lexie's, that was pink with happiness.

"Eat up then," Annie instructed everyone, "we'll be having a proper meal later on, so keep a bit of your appetites for then."

Lexie was bombarded with questions from Annie and Euan. What was the camp like, did they learn how to march like the men, were there lots of other girls there and were the beds comfy. No one, however, mentioned the War, nor asked if Lexie was happy with her new life. That would wait till Annie and her daughter were alone.

After their tea, Lexie showed Winnie her room. "It's my brother's really," she babbled, painfully aware that her friend may be there in body but her mind was elsewhere, "but he's in the Army, so it's yours for now."

Winnie sat down on the edge of the bed and burst into tears.

"Oh! Winnie," Lexie exclaimed, rushing to her side, "everything will be alright," she hushed, "just wait and see."

She held onto Winnie till the tears ebbed, conscious once more of the pain that came from loving a man who didn't love you back.

Despite herself, images of Robbie Robertson came uninvited into her head. Lexie shivered, if Robbie had wanted to make love to her, she knew she wouldn't have been able to resist him and, she too, could have been in the same predicament that Nancy had endured with Billy Donnelly and now Winnie with Jack Forsythe.

Her decision to join up and make a life for herself without a man was reinforced. Not for her, the pain of giving birth to an illegitimate child nor the shame of facing everyone alone and unwed.

"C'mon Winnie," she said, encouragingly, "why don't we both go to Montrose tomorrow...speak to your dad about all this. I'm sure he'll understand," she suggested, without much conviction in her voice.

Winnie's blue eyes widened as she shook her head.

"It's no use, Lexie," she said, "I can't go back to Wilmslow like this." She turned her attention to her tightly clasped hands. "I'll go to Montrose tomorrow alone, leave the WAAF and have the baby..." The tears began again, just as Annie knocked and came into the bedroom.

"Everything alright?" she breezed, before suddenly noticing the sobbing girl beside Lexie.

She looked quizzically at Lexie, but her daughter indicated she should leave well alone. She'd explain everything to her mother once Winnie had gone.

At their evening meal, Winnie looked even worse, her pale face now joined by red-rimmed eyes. If Euan noticed he said nothing, sensing that this was women's work and better left to Annie.

"Winnie's going home to Montrose tomorrow," Lexie informed everyone briskly, "her dad hasn't been well, so she didn't want to upset him...but he's better now..." Lexie's lies sounded surreal to her own ears so here's to what they sounded like to Euan and her mum and the silent Winnie.

"Why don't I give you a lift Winnie?" Euan suggested, filling the gap that the lie had opened up.

Winnie forced a wan smile. "That would be nice," she said, "my rail warrant to Montrose expired yesterday and I don't have much..."

Euan hushed her. "Now, don't you worry about anything," he told her, "I have to be in Montrose myself tomorrow, so it'll be no trouble."

Once again, Annie was conscious of Euan saving the day. She knew he wasn't going to Montrose the next day, but it was plain that Winnie was very unhappy and the quicker she was home with her family the better.

Winnie hardly touched the plate of food and as soon as she could, she pled exhaustion and went to bed.

Soon after, Euan took his newspaper and pipe through to the parlour leaving Annie and Lexie to clear the table and 'talk.'

"She's pregnant," Lexie told her mother bluntly, as she stacked the dirty dishes on the draining board beside the sink.

Annie stopped in her tracks. Here it was again, history repeating itself, her sister Mary almost dying at the hands of a back-street abortionist, her niece Nancy, pregnant and unwed and if Euan and Billy Dawson hadn't 'convinced' Billy Donnelly to marry her, God know what would have happened to her. Then there was Annie herself, giving birth in the Poorhouse in Belfast to her own illegitimate son, Billy Dawson's son, who'd been adopted at birth and had only found her years later when he turned eighteen.

Her fears for Lexie flooded her mind. If this could happen to Winnie, it could just as easily happen to Lexie.

Her experience with Robbie Robertson had stopped her from loving again, but the pain of rejection that Lexie had endured since then had damaged her in a way that didn't show on the surface and Annie felt it was the unspoken reason why her daughter had joined the WAAF.

Lexie swished some soap into the washing up water, her thoughts forming with the suds.

"Why is life so unfair," she said quietly, "for women that is?"

Annie joined her at the sink.

"You mean for Winnie?"

"For Winnie, yes, but for Nancy too and probably lots of others who made the mistake of..." her voice dropped to a whisper, "falling in love."

Annie felt the helplessness of all mothers, who knew the dangers for their daughters when it came to men and, like Annie, had experienced them for themselves and now, with this war on, the reasons men and women had for throwing caution to the wind had increased a hundred fold.

"I don't have any answers, Lexie," Annie said, mechanically drying the washed plates. "Just be careful, very careful, about who you give your heart to and if he loves you back, he'll understand your fears."

Lexie dried her hands on then end of Annie's tea towel.

"Bed, I think," she said, almost sadly, "goodnight mum."

Annie watched her go. Lexie was right, life was unfair and she knew only too well how lucky she'd been that Euan had found her.

—-—oOo—-—

Chapter 14

Nancy lay awake for hours that night, but Billy never came back.

Just like in the beginning, when he'd first went to work at Baxters Mill and took lodgings in Ma Kelly's rooming house, he'd left her alone and unloved again. As usual, she was torn between wishing things would go back to when wee Billy was born and their love was strong and the horror she'd felt on finding out, in the hot steam and gossip of the public washhouse, that her husband was bedding a prostitute.

She turned on her side and reached across the empty bed. Was this to be her life forever more, waiting for the right man to bring happiness back into her life? It was all so unfair.

Nancy only realised that she'd eventually fallen asleep when a rapid tapping on the kitchen window woke her. She squinted at the clock on the mantelpiece, NINE O'CLOCK!

She threw back the covers and ran to the window. The face of Di Auchterlonie greeted her. It was Sunday morning and Di had the look of someone who had something to 'tell.'

Nancy pulled on her dressing gown and let Di in.

"Sssshhh!" she cautioned, "the bairns are still asleep."

"Has Billy gone then?" Di asked.

Nancy filled the kettle and nodded. "What time did he leave this morning?"

Nancy lit the gas and turned to face her friend.

"What does it matter," Nancy said, wondering where the questioning was leading.

Di folded her arms and leaned back in her chair.

"He was seen leaving Ma Kelly's this morning at seven o'clock."

Nancy had been right. Billy had gone to say goodbye to Gladys Kelly after all.

"Seen by who?" she asked, setting two teacups on the table.

"Jock Garvie," Di told her, "he'd been on his way home from his night watchman job at the docks, when he saw Billy coming out of the close with his kitbag over his shoulder."

So much for love, Nancy thought, went to say goodbye to his prossie, but couldn't say goodbye to his wife. She suddenly felt very tired, tired of the deceit and tired of the drudgery of her life.

"Thanks for telling me Di," she said, "but make sure you don't tell anyone else."

Di shook her head vigorously, "of course not," she assured Nancy, but I think Jock Garvie may not be so careful the next time he's in the Thrums Bar, it's not just women who gossip."

Nancy felt defeated. She'd lost her husband to a prostitute and now that she'd be the talk of the pubs, she'd also lost any chance of being with Jim Murphy.

Di could see that there was no point in staying and, leaving her tea untouched, made for the door.

"Are we on for next Saturday?" she asked, a bit selfishly, "for the dancing I mean?" Nancy may have man troubles, but Di didn't.

"Sure," Nancy replied, despondently, "why not."

She was drinking her tea and staring at nothing in particular, when two sleepy bairns wandered into the kitchen from the back room. She held out her arms to them and Mary Anne and wee Billy snuggled into her.

They were her world now, she thought, till this damn war was over at least and if it meant living the life of an auld maid, then so be it.

A brief smile crossed her face as she remembered saying these words to Lexie not that long ago. She'd been so sure of herself then, waltzing round the Palais with soldiers and sailors at her beck and call, but what did it really mean...NOTHING. And look at Lexie now. Annie had told her about Lexie joining the WAAF, leaving Dundee and making a new life for herself.

Now who was going to die an auld maid?

"C'mon," she said to the bairns, forcing a smile, "let's get the porridge on and if it doesn't rain, we'll go for a walk to the Stannergate, maybe even pick some whelks."

Wee Billy cheered, but Mary Anne wasn't so sure. Her mum seemed different. "Has dad gone back to the fighting?" she asked, worried that something bad had happened to him.

"Yes, he has," Nancy told her, "but before he went he said to tell you and wee Billy that he'll be back soon and that you've to be good till then." Mary Anne brightened. In her child's head, everything was alright again and she'd be 'good as gold' for her daddy.

When Nancy went to work on Monday at the mill, Jim Murphy was waiting. He'd heard about Billy and Gladys Kelly, which meant that he had nothing to fear from the big Scots Guard. What's sauce for the goose, he decided, was sauce for the gander and Nancy was going to be a tasty treat.

On spotting her on her way to the Weaving Flat, he signalled her over to the Buckie. "How did the happy homecoming go then?" he asked, smiling, knowingly, at Nancy.

Still smarting from Di's news that Billy had spent the night before his departure with Gladys Kelly, she wasn't in the mood for flirting with Jim Murphy.

"What's it to you?"

"Whoa!" Jim said, as Nancy bristled before him, "I only asked 'cause I've been worried about you."

Nancy hesitated. "Worried" she queried, "about me?"

The other weavers were beginning to filter past the Buckie into the Flat, some of them glancing knowingly to one another. Jim's reputation as a 'womaniser' was well known, but the last thing he wanted was his attention to Nancy getting back to his wife, Jean.

"Look," he whispered, hurriedly, "this isn't the time or place for having this conversation, just make sure you're at the Palais next Saturday."

With that, Jim quickly returned to the Buckie and shut the

door behind him, leaving Nancy wondering what to make of the man.

She was trying to shake the confusion from her mind when Di came up behind her and linked her arm into Nancy's.

She'd seen her encounter with Jim Murphy and now, knowing what Billy was up to with Gladys Kelly, she knew she had to steer her pal back onto the straight and narrow before she got hurt again.

"Two wrongs don't make a right you know," she said, "and Jim Murphy's definitely a 'WRONG.'"

Nancy looked at Di, tight-lipped. "Thanks for the advice," she said, "but I know what Jim Murphy is like."

The noise of the looms whining into life brought any further talk of Jim Murphy to a halt as both women began their working day. Nancy knew Di was right about Jim, but somehow, she managed to convince herself that she could take him or leave him, just like Billy had done to her. No strings attached and no regrets and with or without Di's blessing, she'd be at the Palais next Saturday.

———oOo———

Chapter 15

After Euan had taken Winnie to the motor car, for their journey to Montrose, Annie and Lexie were left alone together for the first time since her return.

As usual, when Annie wanted to talk, she made a pot of tea.

Lexie took her steaming cup to the kitchen table and sat down. It seemed like only yesterday, when she'd announced her intention to join the WAAF and now, she was more confident than ever that she'd made the right decision.

Annie sat across from her. "Is it for you then," she asked, nervously, hoping that her daughter would say she hated the life and was coming home for good, "this women's air force thing?"

Lexie sipped her tea. "It's not a 'thing' mum," she replied, "it's the Women's Auxiliary Air Force and YES, it is for me."

"So, no going back on your decision?" Annie asked, the hope draining from her soul.

"How's Ian?" Lexie said in an endeavour to change the subject which would only end in tears.

Annie blinked and rose from the table, hiding her disappointment and opening the sideboard drawer. "We've been getting a letter now and then from him," she said, "and he sent this photograph."

She handed it to Lexie. This tall, handsome and well-built sepia figure stood before her. He'd grown a moustache and had a Captain's insignia on his tunic. Lexie remembered the gauche boy she'd grown up with and could hardly believe her eyes.

She handed the photograph back to Annie. "Do you know if he's still in the country?" she asked, aware that all letters home were checked by the Army for information on the writer's whereabouts.

Annie shook her head. "We only know he's well and Euan is very proud of him...as am I," she added quickly, "just like we're proud of you."

There it was, thought Lexie, her mother's first step of acceptance that she was right to join the WAAF.

"Would you mind if I went to visit Sarah?" Lexie asked, finishing her tea and pushing back her chair. "I go back tomorrow," she continued, "and it's the only chance I'll have to see her before I go."

"Of course," said Annie, reluctantly, "I'm sure she'll love to see you."

Lexie kissed her mother on the cheek. "I'll be back for tea," she said, with a sigh of relief, before leaving Annie alone with her thoughts.

Annie crossed to the window and watched her beautiful daughter hurry up the road away from her. She'd always love her and worry about her, but for now, she knew she had to let her go and find her own happiness, wherever that took her.

Sarah was delighted to see Lexie. It seemed to be that no matter how much time had passed between their 'get-togethers' it always felt like they'd met only yesterday.

"Tell me all about it then?" Sarah demanded "and don't miss a thing."

Lexie laughed, "there's not much to tell...YET..." she added enigmatically, "but it's the best thing I've ever done...EVER."

"Have you met a handsome pilot yet?" Sarah asked "and have you been up in his Spitfire."

"Don't be daft," Lexie said, grinning at Sarah's naivety "and the answer is NO and NO AGAIN."

"I've been learning how to clean EVERYTHING in the billet and how to wash, iron and press this uniform and to march in time till my feet were throbbing, but most of all to salute all officers and OBEY ORDERS WITHOUT QUESTION."

Sarah's eyes widened, "NO. Lexie Melville obeying orders, I

don't believe it."

"Believe it," said Lexie, "Corporal Beryl Samson's word is law."

No romance then?" Sarah asked disappointed.

Lexie considered whether to tell Sarah about Winnie, but decided against it. It was nobody's business but her own and would only colour Lexie's description of the WAAF.

"No romance," Lexie echoed, "but when I go back tomorrow, I'll be tested for skills that I could do to support the fighting men, then I'll be sent where I'll do the most good."

Both girls were quiet, their minds digesting each other's situation.

"I've missed you," Sarah said, wistfully, "it's not the same now you're not around. Don't get me wrong," she added quickly, "I guess I'm just thinking how boring my own life is."

Hearing Sarah's words made Lexie realise that changing her life had meant that other people had to change too, just like her life had changed when Robbie had left her standing at the park gates waiting for him.

And because of his decision back then, she was now in the WAAF and everything had changed for her again, but this time for the better.

"But your work is far more important than mine can ever be! And you love teaching, you said so yourself."

"Love," Sarah murmured, her dark eyes meeting the brightness of Lexie's, "I don't know the meaning of the word and, if this war goes on much longer, I never will."

So that was it, Sarah was still hurting over the loss of John Adams. Neither of them knew the real reason for Billy Dawson putting a stop to the budding romance, but stop it he did and once John had gone back to Ireland, he'd never been in touch again. Not because he hadn't tried, but Sarah had never answered his letters, so he'd finally given up.

Billy Dawson and Josie had breathed a sigh of relief when the letters stopped, Josie, because it meant her daughter would concentrate on her studies and Billy because he now knew, thanks to Annie's revelation, that John was his illegitimate son and, consequently, Sarah's half-brother.

Lexie felt again how unfair fate could be. None of the other women in her life seemed to be happy with their lot, except herself and her mum, of course. "The war will soon be over," she said, softly, "and I'm sure you'll meet someone special and live happily ever after, just like we dreamed when we were girls."

Sarah smiled and took a deep breath. "I'm sure you're right," she said, bringing the unsettling conversation to a halt. "I've got an idea," she added, brightening visibly, "it's Saturday," she said a note of mystery coming into her voice, "let's do what all the other girls are doing in Dundee, let's go the Palais de Dance tonight."

Lexie thought for a moment, but only for a moment. If this was what was needed to bring some sparkle back into Sarah's life, who was she to deny her. After all, she'd been at the NAAFI dance herself and it had been fun dancing with Bert Wilmot and Clive Jones and as long as it was just dancing where was the harm.

"Let's do it," Lexie giggled, "I'll come round at seven and we'll have some fun dancing the night away."

"Thanks Lexie," Sarah said gratefully, "for being you."

Lexie wasn't sure what Sarah meant, but knew it was heart-felt.

"And thanks for being you too," she said, turning to go. "See you tonight at seven."

Annie was a bit disappointed that Lexie was going to spend her last night at the Palais of all places, with Sarah.

"I think that place has got a bit of a reputation," she said, anxiously, "Euan tells me that it's full of men on leave and women with, well, low morals."

"It's alright," Lexie tried to assure you, "we're big girls now and quite capable of looking after ourselves, so don't worry...please."

But Annie wasn't convinced. She'd make sure Euan or his Constables would be around when the dance hall closed, to make sure Lexie and Sarah came out alone and got home safely.

"I won't be late," Lexie called, looping her handbag over her shoulder and straightening her cap as she passed the mirror in the hall, "but don't wait up specially."

There was no reply from the parlour, but she knew her mother would be knitting furiously and keeping a close eye on the time till she was back.

Sarah was looking great. She always had good taste in clothes and even with the restrictions on dressmaking material, she'd managed to make herself a pretty floral dress and matching bolero.

"Wow!" Lexie exclaimed, "look at you."

Sarah gave a twirl. "Will I do?"

"You'll turn every male head in the dance hall," Lexie said. She'd always seen Sarah as 'matronly' and plain even, but things had changed and so, it seemed, had Sarah.

The girls made their way to the dance hall, their torches pointing downwards to guide their feet in the blackout. Everything had been blacked-out for a long time now, no lights showing anywhere and people were getting used to moving around like rabbits down a warren and God help anyone who came to the attention of the Air Raid Patrol Wardens.

The nearer they got to the Palais the more the sound of clicking heels and marching boots increased. It seemed that the whole of Dundee was going dancing. Sarah had been right, everyone was doing it and by the time they'd paid their money at the door, the excitement all around them was tangible.

Lexie wished she had on a dress, like Sarah, but she'd been told to wear her uniform at all times, and that included at the Palais, but, once inside, she realised that she was actually in the majority.

The music was infectious and it wasn't long before both girls were being spun around the crowded floor, by partner after partner. It was just what both of the needed to remind them that they were still very attractive, in or out of uniform.

Lexie was taking a breather, when a scarlet-faced young man in khaki approached, smiling and determined. "Wid you like to be dancin'?" he asked, his Forfar accent as strong as his arms. Lexie smiled back. He must be boiling hot in his uniform, Lexie thought, but there's a war on, she reminded herself and it was her duty to keep the soldier's spirits up.

"I would," she said, before being pulled onto the dance floor. The music had slowed down and the overhead lights were dimmed, but Geordie Davison kept up his hectic pace as he steered Lexie through the crowd of dancers.

Bumping into yet another couple for the umpteenth time, Lexie turned to apologise for their clumsiness. "Sorry," she mouthed, but before she could say any more, the lovely face of Nancy Donnelly turned towards her. Lexie stopped dancing. "Nancy!" she gasped, "it's Lexie."

Nancy had been dancing closely with her partner and seemed to be either a little bit drunk, or 'in a world of her own.' Nancy put her finger to her lips and shushed Lexie. "You never saw me," she whispered, "understand?" before she was pulled back into the man's arms and waltzed away.

"Sorry, Geordie," Lexie said to the ploughman from Forfar, "I need to sit down for a bit."

Geordie shrugged and immediately left her to seek out another partner.

A roll of drums signalled that the last dance was about to begin and all the men knew it was their last chance to see a girl home and maybe be rewarded with a kiss for their trouble.

Sarah was waving from the pillar near the exit and Lexie moved quickly to join her.

"I've had a great time," she said, her face flushed and her eyes sparkling, "but I don't want anyone seeing me home, so...can we go?"

Lexie looked around to see if Nancy was alone and would like to walk home with them, but she was nowhere in sight.

"Let's get our coats then and leave before the crush."

The girls linked arms as they left the dance hall. The doorman nodded to them as they passed. "Well done," he said to Lexie, indicating her uniform, "with pretty girls like you in the war, we'll soon have Hitler on the run."

Lexie nodded her thanks and breathed in the cold night air

that was rushing toward them as the doors were opened to let them out.

Euan stepped back out of Lexie's line of vision. Annie had begged him to make sure she found her way home alright. "There they are," he indicated with a nod to his Constable, "keep your distance," he instructed, "but stick with them till they reach Albert Street, then call me from the Police Box at Mains Loan."

Constable Murchison saluted. "Right Sarge," he said, "leave it with me."

Euan was maintaining his presence at the dance hall to make sure no over-heated soldier was spoiling for a fight, when he saw her. Nancy Donnelly was being escorted from the hall by a man. His arm was round her waist and the smile on her face was for him alone. Euan watched as she stretched up and kissed the man's cheek. So Billy Dawson was right, Nancy was frequenting the dancing, but that wasn't all, the man holding onto her so possessively wasn't her husband.

Euan took the decision to follow the pair, hoping that they'd part company at some point further up the Nethergate, but it wasn't to be and it was with a mixture of anger and despair, he watched them disappear into the close leading to Nancy's house.

He'd telephone Billy Dawson in the morning and arrange a meeting.

—·—oOo—·—

Chapter 16

The next day, Lexie made her own way to the station for the early train back to the camp at RAF Wilmslow. Thankfully, the house had been silent when she'd returned from the Palais. She had told Euan and her mother not to set their alarm clock, as she'd be away long before their normal wake-up time on Sunday, which was true, but it also meant that she wouldn't have to go through another 'goodbye.'

She'd had fun with Sarah at the Palais and the sight of Nancy with another man had shocked her, but today it was back to the business of being a WAAF.

Her thoughts turned to Winnie as the train pulled into the deserted station and she was wondering how the news of her pregnancy had gone down, when the familiar huge blue eyes smiled at her as she entered the carriage.

"WINNIE," Lexie squealed, "YOU'RE HERE!" she exclaimed, bumping down into the seat opposite her friend as the train jerked into motion.

"But, HOW...?"

Winnie leaned forward in her seat. "False alarm," she said, the relief obvious in her voice. "They were a fortnight late," she explained, "it must have been all the excitement of enlisting and leaving home or something, but I was just about to confess all, when...ta ra."

Lexie was so pleased for Winnie, but knew it could all have worked out badly for her, if she had been pregnant.

No one mentioned Jack Forsythe's name and, as far as Lexie was concerned, 'least said soonest mended.'

The journey back to the camp was interminable and it was

late in the evening before the girls all met up again, but everyone was too tired for gossip, tomorrow would be soon enough.

None of the girls had changed their mind about remaining in the WAAF and Lexie was keener than ever to start her skills assessment.

Lexie beamed as the stop-watch was clicked off and she was told that her typing speed was 45 wpm and no errors.

"Well," said the Assessor, nodding in appreciation, "a touch-typist!"

"And I can do book-keeping and filing and invoicing..."

"Whoa," the Assessor said smiling, "I think we'll be able to make good use of your skills ACW Melville. "Have you ever used a Teleprinter?"

Lexie frowned and shook her head, "I haven't," she replied anxiously, "but I'm sure I could learn," she added quickly, fearing that she'd blotted her copybook already.

"Good." There was silence while the report was completed and signed.

"I'll recommend you for either Communications or Administration Services."

He indicated that Lexie should go now, "and send in the next person if you would," he called after her.

Pearly, Petal and Mary were also recommended for office work, but Jean Bailey and Winnie were classed as 'unskilled' and would be sent for further training, Jean to learn how to pack parachutes and Winnie to train as a driver.

At the Passing Out Parade, Lexie was almost bursting with pride. She'd never felt so good about herself nor her life and couldn't wait for her first Posting.

"I don't suppose we'll be altogether from here on," Jean said, her chin quivering slightly. She'd never been blessed with lots of friends and her new-found companions had filled a huge space in her life.

"But let's exchange addresses, so that we can all meet up once the war is over, or at lease write now and again."

So, it was agreed and just in time, as each one was issued

with their new Posting instructions the very next day.

"RAF Lossiemouth," Lexie repeated softly to herself. Although far from Dundee, it was still in Scotland and within striking distance of home if she got any leave time. The Airfield was under the command of Group Captain TC Monkton AFC CVO and Lexie was to report of Wing Commander Johnny Johnson on arrival.

The others were being deployed to various RAF Camps in Wiltshire, with Winnie being sent to Swindon itself to start her driving training and Jean to Woodall Spa in Lincolnshire for general duties and parachute packing.

"Let's go to the NAAFI tonight, celebrate our successes and drink a toast to the future," Winnie suggested, thankful now that she had a future.

The NAAFI was busy, as usual, the food being better than the slop served up in the Mess, albeit at a price. A group of airmen were raucously celebrating a successful raid over Germany by a Squadron of Vickers Wellingtons from Bomber Command at Middle Wallop in Hampshire when Jack Forsythe spotted Winnie and the rest of the girls.

"I need a couple of wingmen," he said, suggestively, to the rest of the squad. "Angels at 2 o'clock," he added. The men turned as one and fixed they eyes on the girls. "Bombs away!" said Nigel Allen, already lifting his pint from the bar and turning towards the target.

"Pick anyone you want," Jack told him, "but the blue-eyed beauty is mine."

Winnie felt a rush of colour to her face as Jack Forsythe pulled up a chair and pushed in beside her. "Can I buy a lady a drink?" he asked, never taking his eyes of her face.

She threw a glance at Lexie, which said 'rescue me' but Nigel Allen had already turned her head towards his and was regaling her with his exploits of 'daring do.'

Winnie felt Jack move closer, draping one arm around her shoulder and allowing his other hand to linger on her thigh.

"Have you missed me?" he whispered in her ear, "like I've missed you."

Winnie pushed her chair back and lifted his hand from her thigh. She was on dangerous ground and she knew it. There was no way she was going to risk her future again, no matter how much she wanted to throw herself into Jack's arms and let him make love to her again.

She abruptly stood up, knocking over a glass of beer as she did so, "we've things to do, Lexie," she said loudly, "REMEMBER!"

It only took one look for Lexie to realise that Winnie needed to make her escape.

"Ready when you are," she smiled, extricating herself from the attentions of Nigel, before joining Winnie and heading for the door.

"Night night all," she called over her shoulder, while marching Winnie quickly outside.

"What was all that about?" Lexie asked as soon as they were out of earshot.

"I just had to get away Lexie," Winnie said, still trembling, I couldn't risk another 'scare.' He's everything I've ever wanted in a man and I just know if he'd got close to me again I'd..." Winnie burst into tears.

"Oh! Winnie," Lexie said gently, wrapping her arm round her tearful friend, "you'll be out of here tomorrow and you'll soon forget Jack Forsythe."

Just like she'd forgotten Robbie Robertson, Lexie insisted to herself, knowing that forgetting someone you loved and yearned for, was far from an easy option.

The girls spent the rest of the evening back at the billet. Tomorrow they'd be going their separate ways, Winnie to Swindon and Lexie to RAF Lossiemouth and it would be up to the fates and the hostilities, if they ever met again.

"Keep in touch, if you can?" Lexie asked her friend and don't worry about Jack Forsythe, I'm sure you'll meet someone better than him in Swindon."

But Winnie wasn't so sure. Jack Forsythe had stolen her heart and she knew it was as much her fault as his that she'd had her 'close call.'

She sighed loudly. "What's done is done," she said, bringing the unhappy talk to an end "and I'll just have to get over it." But, Winnie knew, that wasn't going to happen, at least not for a long, long time.

Lexie had assumed that she would be going to Lossiemouth by train and wasn't looking forward to the many station changes that would involve, but the RAF had other ideas.

"Four Vickers Wellingtons are heading for RAF Lossiemouth today for servicing and maintenance," Corporal Samson told Lexie. "You're to fly with the rest of the crew at fourteen hundred hours today." She handed the paperwork to Lexie. "Report to Sergeant Hargreaves at Hanger 3, who'll explain everything to you."

"FLY!" Lexie blurted out, but I've never flown in an aeroplane before." Beryl Samson tried not to smile. "You do realise you've joined the AIR FORCE don't you?"

Lexie blushed with embarrassment. "Sorry Corporal," she said.

"You'll love it," the Corporal said, remembering the terror she had felt at her own inaugural flight. "The trip won't exactly be comfortable, but it'll get you to Lossiemouth quicker than any train and just make sure you wear something warm, these bomber fuselages are perishing."

Lexie pulled herself erect and saluted. "Yes Corporal," she said, getting back her composure and realising her nerves were excitement. She was going to actually fly, in the air, in a Vickers Wellington Bomber!

Thoughts of her mum and home suddenly invaded her mind, how far away it all seemed now, the office where she'd spent all her working life, the streets and people of Dundee going about their business as best they could and Nancy Donnelly, what was Nancy doing dancing in the arms of another man, while Billy was away fighting with the Scots Guards? She would ask her mother about Nancy and Billy the next time she was home.

Sergeant Hargreaves was waiting for her at the Hanger. He was in charge of Maintenance he told her and handed her a fleece-lined flying jacket. "You'll need this," he said, "and when you get to Lossie' hand it into Stores and they'll get it back to me."

Lexie draped the heavy jacket over her shoulders and waited, her excitement growing as the huge bomber was guided out of the hanger and onto the runway.

"Isn't she a beauty?" a voice behind her said.

Lexie turned to see the smiling face of Nigel Allen.

"Going my way?" he grinned, pointing to the metal steps that had been placed under an opening into the fuselage.

"Lossiemouth?" Lexie asked.

Nigel nodded and walked beside her to the aircraft, while the rest of the crew whistled and grinned as she struggled to board the Bomber swamped in the Flying Jacket.

"Ignore them," Nigel shouted over the roar of the propellers starting their work, "they're only jealous."

The fuselage was rigged with low seats and safety straps that Nigel showed Lexie how to fasten. "You'll need them if we hit any air pockets, especially over the Scottish mountains," he said, "but I'll be next to you, so if you feel sick, lean the other way," he joked, pointing away from himself.

Sick? Lexie thought, why would she be sick? The roar of the huge engines meant that no further conversation took place and as there were no windows to look out of, Lexie closed her eyes like the rest of the crew and tried to sleep. It was in this half-asleep state that the aircraft hit an air pocket and Lexie awoke abruptly, feeling as though she was falling through space. She reached out and grabbed Nigel's arm, as the engines roared on till the aeroplane stopped its descent and levelled out. Much to Lexie's horror, a wave of nausea swept over her and it was sheer willpower that prevented her from vomiting.

Nigel handed her a brown paper bag. "Just in case," he shouted, grinning at Lexie's discomfort.

The cold intensified as the Bomber flew further North and Lexie almost disappeared into the Flying Jacket trying to keep warm.

"Not long now," Nigel mouthed, pointing to his watch and indicating 20 minutes. "Lexie nodded, flying, she decided was not for her and after a terrifyingly bumpy landing at

Lossiemouth, she was very glad to be back on the ground.

Her whole body felt as if it would ache forever after the long flight as Nigel helped her from the belly of the Bomber.

There was hot tea and sandwiches on offer at the Mess and Lexie ate ravenously. "The first time's always the worst," Nigel said between mouthfuls of bread and tea, "you get used to it."

After an hour or so, Lexie became aware that the rest of the crew had left the Mess.

"I think your crew has gone," she said, looking around and wondering why Nigel Allen was still glued to her side.

"Who do you have to report to?" Nigel asked, ignoring Lexie's reference to the 'missing' crew.

"Group Captain Johnny Johnson, I think," she said, drinking the last of her third cup of tea, "and this jacket has to be returned to Stores"

"C'mon," he said, relieving her of the flight jacket, "I'll get this back to Stores and show you where the Ops Rooms are."

The base at Lossiemouth was huge. In the early evening light, Lexie could see the hangers and buildings stretching into the dimness, with Spitfires, Hampdens and Oxfords parked silently along the runways.

"What happened to your friend last night?" Nigel asked, lightly. "One minute Jack was talking to her and the next she was off, taking you with her."

"She had things to do," Lexie said, not about to mention Winnie's distress, "she's been posted to Swindon for driver training and I think she was a bit anxious about it, that's all."

"Mmmmm," Nigel murmured, not quite sure to believe Lexie or not.

"Jack was a bit upset about it," he told her, "he thought she was quite keen on him."

Lexie felt herself bristle, she was tired and didn't want to get into a discussion about Jack Forsythe.

"Are we near the Ops Rooms yet?" she asked, quickly changing the subject.

"We're just coming to them now," Nigel said, pointing to a low building to their left.

"Thanks Nigel," Lexie said, "I think I'll manage from here," just wanting to end the conversation and get settled in.

"Sure," Nigel said, "I'll probably see you around then," he added, hopefully, "I'm here for a week, so..."

Lexie was aware that Nigel was angling for a date but she remembered Winne's recent experience with airmen, or one airman in particular and was determined that she wouldn't be the next 'kill' on anyone's hit list.

"Probably," she said, taking the flight jacket back from Nigel "and I'll get this back to Stores myself," she added, completing the 'brush-off'.

She was ACW Melville 1482166 now and that was the most important thing in her world.

———oOo———

Chapter 17

Euan's phone call to Billy Dawson was not an easy one to make, but only her father could broach the subject of Nancy's behaviour at the Palais.

"Are you quite sure?" Billy asked quietly.

"I followed the pair myself, Billy," Euan replied, "all I can say is they both went into the close to Nancy's house together, but whether he stayed the night, well..." Euan hesitated to go further, the policeman in him unable to prove or disprove the possibility.

"Thanks, Euan," Billy said, "leave it with me to deal with, but if you find out anything else, I'd appreciate if you'd let me know."

It was with a heavy heart that Euan returned the receiver to its cradle.

Annie would be heart-broken if Nancy and Billy parted, especially if it meant that Nancy was to blame. It's the children who will suffer, she'd say, and Euan knew she was right. What would happen to them when the neighbours found out that Nancy was 'carrying on' with another man while her husband was away fighting in the war.

Euan shuddered. He'd tell no one, especially not Annie, till Billy Dawson had a chance to sort things out with his daughter.

Nancy's night of love with Jim Murphy was all she'd hoped it would be.

Jim was an expert lover and he had to cover her mouth with his hand to stop her calling out and waking up the bairns.

"It's been a while then?" he whispered, as Nancy lay limply in his arms, her whole being satiated. She nodded and snuggled into Jim's chest.

"But it was worth waiting for," she murmured, wishing that

the moment would go on forever.

The cold air in the kitchen swept over her as Jim pushed the bedcovers aside and swung his legs over the side of the bed, reaching for the trousers he had dropped on the floor, as he did so.

Nancy sat up abruptly. "You're not going already, are you?" she whispered, a begging tremor in her voice.

Jim turned back to face her and cupped her face in his hand. "I've been here long enough as it is, Nancy," he said, "Jean will be getting worried."

He pulled on his shirt and tightened the belt of his trousers.

"Jean!" Nancy said, almost as if she had never heard the name before.

"You know I'm married Nancy," he said, "as are you," he reminded her, "so...it's time for me to go home."

He tied his bootlaces and pulled on his jacket. "Don't get up," he said, blowing her a kiss, "see you later."

The door closed quietly and he was gone. Nancy flopped back onto the bed. She hadn't known how the night would end, but she had hoped that Jim would want her as much as she wanted him. She'd been willing to leave Billy and saw her future with Jim Murphy, but now, she wasn't so sure, not sure at all.

She was making soup for the bairns dinner on the Sunday morning when there was a knock at the door.

Nancy's heart leapt. Jim Murphy had come back to her, sure Jean would be upset, she reasoned, but she and Jim were meant to be together.

She flung the door open only to find her father standing on the landing, his face serious and his eyes locked onto hers.

She felt her face flush and her knees go weak. What was he doing here and on a Sunday too.

"Dad," she said, nervously, "this is a surprise."

Billy looked past her shoulder. "Where's my grandchildren then?" he said, forcing some lightness into his voice.

"Playing," Nancy replied, "but come in and I'll give them a shout." She stood back and allowed him to enter.

"No need," Billy said, "it's you I've come to see."

Nancy felt her blood run cold. Something was wrong and her guilt about Jim Murphy flooded her mind.

Nancy hurried to put the kettle on while Billy took a seat at the table and watched her.

"Did Billy get away alright then?" he asked, "I met him in the Thrums a few days back. He said he was on embarkation leave, so...has he gone?"

Nancy tried to control the tremble in her arm as she poured the hot water into the teapot.

"Left last week," she said, abruptly, bringing the teapot to the table.

"Bad business, this war," Billy continued, "puts a dreadful strain on everyone."

Nancy poured the tea, more sure than ever, that something was wrong.

"Are you...and the bairns...coping?" he asked, "with Billy being away, I mean."

Nancy's eyes levelled with her father's. "If you've something to say, dad," she countered, "then say it."

Billy put down his cup. "Alright then," he said, evenly, "there's word at the mill that you're spending your Saturday nights at the dancehalls instead of at home taking care of Mary Anne and wee Billy."

There, it was out and Billy waited for her answer.

She sipped her tea before replying. "That's right," she said, "in fact Billy and me were at the Palais last Saturday, before he went overseas. He's quite happy that I go dancing once in a while with Diane, you know Diane, one of the other Weavers at the mill."

Billy weighed her answer in his mind. "Just dancing?" he probed.

Nancy felt the colour drain from her face, surely her father didn't know about Jim Murphy.

Her eyes flitted around the small kitchen. Thankfully, she'd made the bed and had washed herself thoroughly. There was no evidence that Jim Murphy had been with her the night before.

"Just dancing," she replied, her confidence growing that her father knew nothing.

Billy finished his tea and stood up, replacing his bonnet and fastening his jacket. He fished in his pocket and produced a two shilling coin. "Get the bairns some sweeties from their Grandpa," he said, "and I'll see you at the Mill on Monday."

The visit was at an end and Nancy closed the door behind her father with a sigh of relief. She was going to have to be careful in future about meeting Jim Murphy. The Palais was too public and now that Jim Murphy had made love to her, there was no need to pretend they were just acquaintances. And, as for Jean Murphy, she was going to have to keep a close watch on her husband, she had competition.

Billy was turning into the close from the stairwell when he bumped into a woman. He caught her shoulders and was apologising before he recognised who she was.

"Annie!" he exclaimed, his eyes lighting up at the sight of her.

"I've just been to see Nancy," he added, still holding her shoulders, "I didn't expect to see you here."

Annie pushed herself away from his grasp.

"Nor I, you," she replied, quickly, unable to meet his gaze.

The silence grew between them till Billy's voice broke into it.

"I've written to our son," he said, gruffly, "John."

Annie's breathing quickened. Since telling Billy he was John's father, they'd not spoken about him again, till now.

"He's never mentioned you in his letters," she told him, wondering if Billy was telling the truth about contacting their son.

The sound of footsteps coming down the stairwell interrupted the conversation, as one of Nancy's neighbours walked between them, her eyes lingering on Billy as she went.

Billy cleared his throat. "I told him not to," he said, "not till we get to know one another a bit better."

So, Billy intended developing the father/son connection and Annie now wished she'd never given him John's address in Ireland. She was acutely aware that their relationship would always be a reminder to her of her coupling with Billy Dawson and the pain that had caused when he married her sister, Mary.

Annie felt her knees weaken and she leant against the close wall.

Billy instantly reached out to steady her, but again she pushed him away.

"I'm fine," she said, shakily, "just let me pass please, I need to see Nancy."

Billy felt his heart ache, as he stepped aside.

"Anything you say, Annie," he said, resigned to her leaving, "I'm sorry...for everything...but not" he added firmly, "for fathering our son."

Annie's chin began to tremble as she hurried up the stairs. Why did he always have to do this to her. She loved Euan and was happy in her life, but each time fate brought them together, Billy Dawson always seemed to stir up memories of the past, that she wanted to remain buried.

"Auntie Annie!" Nancy exclaimed as she opened the door to her second visitor that morning.

"You've just missed my dad," she said, "come on in."

Annie looked around the tiny kitchen as her heartbeat returned to normal. Are the bairns not about?" she asked, taking out two little pokes of sweeties from her message bag.

"Out playing somewhere," Nancy said, refilling the kettle, "but I'll be calling them in soon," she glanced at the clock on the mantelpiece, "get them ready for Sunday School."

Annie nodded, pleased that Nancy was looking after the children's spiritual needs as well as their physical ones. She sipped the hot tea and watched her niece as she gave the soup a stir before joining Annie at the table.

"Did Billy get home alright after we left?" Annie asked, casually. She and Euan had expected the pair to come home together from the Palais, but Nancy had come home alone.

She took a few seconds to get Annie's drift. "Oh, you mean after the dancing when he went to say goodbye to his pals?" she answered, remembering the awkward end to the night.

"Fine," she lied, "then he was off early for the train South on Sunday."

"Do you know where he's being sent?" Annie enquired, praying it wasn't to France.

Nancy shrugged her shoulders. "They don't tell them anything," she said, "or if they did, they're not allowed to tell anyone else. Something to do with 'keeping mum'", Nancy told her, putting her finger to her lips by way of explanation.

"But, enough of that," Nancy said, changing the subject. "This is a nice surprise, there's nothing wrong I hope?"

"No, no," Annie reassured her, "I just want to make sure you and the bairns are OK, with Billy being away and you having to cope with everything on your own."

"Oh! Don't you worry about us, Auntie Annie," Nancy told her, "the bairns are almost grown-up now, so they look after themselves while I'm at the Mill, especially Mary-Anne, she's turning into a proper little housewife, so we're managing very well."

Annie felt she was being reassured a bit too much and that Nancy really didn't need, or want, any more visits. She fleetingly wondered if Billy Dawson had felt the same way.

The sound of little footsteps hurrying past the window and into the kitchen stopped all further conversation.

Annie hugged the bairns and gave them their sweeties. "Now, that's for after you've been to the Sunday School and not before," she chided, knowing that the sweets would probably be gobbled before they got to the Sunday School in King Street.

Nancy ushered them into the back room to change their shoes and put on their coats, before turning to Annie again.

"Well," she said, "thanks for coming Auntie Annie, but as you can see, everything's fine here, so don't worry about us."

Annie had no option but to take her leave. "Now, if there is anything you need," she said, "or if you want the bairns minded, you'll let me know?"

Nancy nodded, guiding Annie out of the door. "And say hello to Lexie for me," she added, before suddenly remembering that Lexie had seen her at the Palais dancing closely with a man who wasn't her husband.

"She's a brave girl," she added, envious of Lexie's freedom, "enlisting like that."

"We pray nightly that she'll come home safely when this war is over."

Nancy felt a twinge of guilt. Here was Lexie risking her life to keep people like her safe and here she was, having an affair with Jim Murphy.

"I'll pray for her too, Auntie Annie," she said, closing the door quietly and leaning against it, her eyes filling up with regret at how her life had turned out.

Mary Anne and wee Billy clumped through to the kitchen in their Sunday shoes. "Can we eat our sweeties now," wee Billy asked, knowing that he would, no matter what his mother said.

Nancy ruffled his hair. "One only," she said, "Jesus will know if you eat them all."

His eyes widened in fright and he pushed the sweets back into his pocket.

When did lust overcome our fear of the Lord, she asked herself after the bairns had gone. Billy's excuse for going to Gladys Kelly was that he feared God more than he loved her and now, she was being bedded by Jim Murphy behind his back. The tears began to roll down her cheeks. She was as bad as Gladys Kelly, she realised, the only difference being that she didn't take money for her services.

—-—oOo—-—

Chapter 18

Wing Commander Johnny Johnson was as his desk when Lexie was shown in by another WAAF.

"ACW Melville 1482166, reporting for duty Sir," Lexie said, saluting smartly.

Johnny Johnson was red-haired and sported a 'handlebar' moustache, which covered his top lip and curled up at the ends. Lexie thought he looked quite comical till he spoke.

"Sit down," he instructed, before returning to finish the paperwork he was working on.

Lexie waited. "So," he began, "the training officer at Wilmslow tells me you're very capable with a typewriter."

"Yes Sir."

"Good. We need a Teleprinter Operator in the Communications Room. Do you think you could handle that?"

"If someone shows me how to work the machine, I'm sure I'll master it...Sir."

"Good," the Wing Commander said, "report to Sergeant Brady at eight hundred hours tomorrow in the Comms Room. He'll show you the ropes." For the first time since Lexie had come into the room, the Officer looked up and Lexie realised why he'd grown the moustache. Wounds to the left side of his face had been medically sewn together, pulling his mouth out of shape and puckering his chin and his neck was distorted with healed burn marks.

Lexie held her breath and shuddered at the thought of how the damage must have been inflicted and, in that moment, the reality of war was brought home to her. No wonder Euan and her mum had been anxious for her, they'd lived through the

First World War and knew what guns and fire could do to a body.

"That's all," Johnny Johnson said, "ACW McKenzie will take you to your Billet."

"Yes Sir," Lexie said, saluting and doing a quick turn before heading for the door.

"And, welcome to the war ACW Melville and to Lossiemouth."

Lexie nodded her head in acknowledgement without turning to look at Johnny Johnson's damaged face again.

Jenny McKenzie was waiting for Lexie at a filing cabinet where she had a good view of the Wing Commander's office door.

"ACW Melville?" she asked, approaching Lexie and noticing the paleness of her face, "I'm ACW McKenzie, assigned to show you the wonders of the Teleprinter," she added, smiling. Lexie met her eyes with questions of her own about the Wing Commander, but knew this wasn't the time nor place to ask them.

"But first of all, let's get you to your Billett." Lexie followed her out of the Comms Offices and over the tarred walkways to the familiar shapes of the billets, silhouetted against the yellow moon.

"Have you got your torch handy?"

Lexie fished into her kit bag pocket and produced one.

"Good," said her guide, "don't want to wake the others."

Once inside the Billett, Lexie switched on the torch at a bed just inside the door, indicated by ACW McKenzie. Silently, Lexie nodded and the ACW left her, quietly closing the door behind her.

Keeping the torch pointing downwards, Lexie managed to take her uniform off and pull on her pyjamas, switching the beam off once she'd slipped under the covers.

As her eyes adjusted to the darkness she could see that the other beds were all occupied, with the occasional sigh or snore drifting into the air. She closed her own eyes but kept seeing Johnny Johnson's face with its disfiguring scars and shuddered at the thought that 'real' war wasn't fun, as Winnie had told her and she became more determined than ever to do whatever she could to help win the fight against the Nazi war machine.

The morning call of the bugle brought Lexie to immediate alertness, followed by the need to get to the Comms Room and report to Sgt Brady at 08.00 hours.

There were smiles and nods from the other girls as they made themselves ready to meet the day, but conversation was at a minimum and it wasn't 'till they were in the Mess filling up on the day's offering of porridge and scrambled eggs that introductions were made.

"I'm Lucy Ashford," smiled the girl sitting opposite Lexie and this lot are May, Fran, Kath, Dot, Eddie and Pat," she said, indicating each one in turn. Lexie blinked, trying and failing to lodge all the names in her brain.

Lucy grinned, "don't worry, you'll soon get used to us."

"I'm Lexie Melville," Lexie said in return and I've been posted to the Comms Room, Sgt Brady."

A series of ooohhhhs and aaahhhhs from the rest of the girls met Lexie's ears.

"Well, you're in for a treat," one of them said, as the others nodded in agreement, "Sgt Brady is a 'DISH.'"

Lexie raised her eyebrows, was that all women thought about, she wondered, dishy men!

ACW McKenzie brought the daydreams about Sgt Brady to a halt as she came to their table to find Lexie.

"Ready?" she asked, looking at the Mess wall clock. Lexie nodded and quickly took her plates and mug to the dish racks for washing, before catching up with the ACW who was waiting for her at the Mess door.

The Comms Room was low and flat with camouflage draped over the roof and walls. "Don't want any bombs dropping on us," ACW McKenzie said, "if the comms go down, we're scuppered."

Lexie nodded, the importance of everyone doing their bit to win the war coming home to her.

"Sgt Brady's over there." She pointed to a man in his RAF

uniform, with its three Sergeant's stripes on the sleeve, sitting at a grey metal desk. "Let's get you registered then we'll start getting to grips with the Teleprinter."

Lexie had to conceal a gasp of surprise as Sgt Brady acknowledged her. The girls from the Billet hadn't been wrong, the Sergeant was, by far, the handsomest man Lexie had ever seen and that included Robbie Robertson. She'd never seen an Italian or any other Continental man in the flesh, but he reminded her of pictures she'd seen of Rudolph Valentino, the silent movie actor. The Sergeant stood up to fetch a docket from the filing cabinet and Lexie was almost speechless as she watched all 6 ft 2 ins of animal magnetism return to his desk.

It had been a long time since any man had rendered Lexie speechless, but Sgt Brady had done just that.

Jenny McKenzie nudged Lexie back to reality. "I'm sure ACW Melville will master the Teleprinter quite quickly," she said, "she's already an experienced typist."

"Good," said the deep voice of Sgt Brady, turning his liquid brown eyes to connect with Lexie's blue ones. "Dismiss." He turned back to his paperwork and after another nudge from ACW McKenzie, Lexie saluted and 'about turned', marching on slightly wobbly legs to the Radio Operators Room.

"Not you as well," said Jenny McKenzie, despairingly, when they were firmly out of ear shot, "what is it with you girls and men?"

Lexie tried to regain her calmness, but Sgt Brady had aroused something inside her that had been latent for a long time, not since Robbie Robertson had turned up in Harry Duncan's butcher shop in his dark blue Merchant Navy coat and seaman's cap, had she felt this captivated.

"Sorry," said Lexie, "I think I was just taken back a bit," she murmured, the girls from the Billet said he was a 'dish' but..." saying any more was pointless, she'd shown herself as a shallow girl in the eyes of her fellow WAAF, but was determined to make up for it by learning to use the teleprinter quicker than anyone had done before.

By the end of the day, Lexie was sending messages from the

Radio Operators via her teleprinter to the HQ in Edinburgh and before she knew it, her spell of duty was over for the day and ACW McKenzie was congratulating her on a job well done.

"I usually eat in the NAAFI," Jenny said, "you can join me, if you like...unless you're going to the Mess?"

Lexie didn't hesitate to answer positively, she wanted to make up for her embarrassing start to the day and maybe get to know her Trainer a bit better."

"See you at 18.00 hours then," Jenny McKenzie said, "and it's Jenny by the way, when we're off duty."

Lexie smiled as she followed Jenny to the door of the Comms Room. They had to pass Sgt Brady again on their way out, but Lexie didn't make the mistake of looking at him again, just saluted as she passed and hurried out of the door.

Sgt Brady shook his head and smiled to himself. Fortunately, for the girls at RAF Lossiemouth, Sgt Brady was a happily married man and had no intention of fulfilling the wishes of his army of admirers and that included Lexie.

The NAAFI was busy, as usual, when Lexie arrived and Jenny waved her over to her table. Lucy and two of the other girls were also at a table in the NAAFI and Lexie felt a bit uncomfortable about not sitting with them and, instead, joining Jenny McKenzie. However, she'd see them later at the Billet and bond with them in mutual admiration of Sgt Brady.

"Mince Pie or Fishcakes," Jenny announced as Lexie took her place at the table. "Oh! Fishcakes, I think," she said, also accepting the glass of beer already on the table and bought for her by Jenny.

"I'll go," Jenny said, getting up and trying to gauge the queue,"this one's on me."

"There's no need for you..." began Lexie, but she was silenced by a wave of Jenny's hand.

"I insist," she smiled, "be back in a tickety-boo."

Lexie sipped her beer and waved cheerily over to Lucy, Dot and Pat while she waited for Jenny's return.

Lucy gave a feeble wave back, while Dot and Pat offered only half-hearted smiles before all three turned their attention to their drinks.

Jenny plonked the plates down on the table. "Watch out," she said, "they're a bit hot."

"Thanks," said Lexie, "I'll be careful."

"How are you enjoying Lossiemouth then?" Jenny asked, brightly.

Lexie hesitated. "Well, I was enjoying it, but I waved to the girls while you were getting our food and...well...they seemed a bit...offhand."

Jenny's features tightened as she looked at Lucy Ashford. "Oh! Don't mind them," she said, "they're just jealous that you're nearer Sgt Brady than they are."

Lexie suddenly lost her appetite. How could they possibly be jealous, she wondered, she'd barely said a word to the man. He was handsome that was for sure, but Lexie was determined to become the best WAAF ever and that didn't include risking her goal for any man, no matter how tempting.

Jenny was watching Lexie carefully. She'd been attracted to her from the moment they'd met, but she had to tread with caution, she'd been burnt in the past by wearing her heart on her sleeve.

Lexie pushed the plate of half-eaten food away and stood up.

"Sorry, Jenny," she said, "I think I need an early night, it's been a long day and...well, sorry."

"Maybe tomorrow then," Jenny said hurriedly, before Lexie could turn away from her.

"Maybe," Lexie replied, lamely, gathering up her handbag and gasmask case. Something was wrong, but she didn't know what. Were the others really jealous?

She was about to say goodbye to the girls as she passed their table, but none of them could look her in the eye. More confused than ever, Lexie headed for the Billet. She had to find out what was wrong and soon.

It was two hours before Lucy and the rest of the girls returned, each one barely nodding in Lexie's direction before gathering at the other end of the room, giggling and nudging one another.

Lucy felt tension tightening her throat as she approached the group.

"Lucy," she said, "I know something's wrong...I just don't know what it is." Seven pairs of eyes turned in her direction, none of them welcoming.

Lucy looked at the others before turning her attention back to Lexie.

"I'll not mince my words," she said, coldly. "Are you one of them?"

"One of them?" Lexie echoed, not knowing what Lucy was talking about, "You know," continued Lucy, "fancy other women instead of men."

Lexie's confusion deepened. "I don't know what you mean," she said, waiting for further explanation and it wasn't long in coming.

"You do know what ACW McKenzie is, don't you?"

Lexie didn't know what the right answer was. "She's a WAAF, like us," she stammered, and she said you're all jealous because I work in the Comms Room, near Sgt Brady."

Lucy began to think Lexie was an innocent in all this, just like she had been when Jenny McKenzie had turned her attentions on her.

"She's a Lesbian, Lexie," Lucy said, bluntly.

Lexie shook her head. "What's a Lesbian?" she said, never having heard the word before in her life.

Lucy abruptly changed tack. "What did you think of Sgt Brady then?" she asked.

A picture of the dishy sergeant filled Lexie's mind and a smile flitted across her face. "He's lovely," she breathed, "but don't be jealous, please," she added quickly, "he'd never fancy me in a million years."

The atmosphere went from icy to warm in an instant, as all the girls had the same mental picture.

Lucy stood up and took Lexie's arm, walking her away from the rest of the group.

"We need to talk," she said, "about ACW McKenzie.

—-—oOo—-—

Chapter 19

When Annie returned from visiting Nancy, Euan was reading a letter from Ian. "Just saying he's well," Euan told Annie, his voice matter of face "and that the battalion are on the move soon."

Annie flinched. "Move to where?" she asked anxiously.

Euan shrugged. "He just says there's a move on the cards, but not where to. He folded the letter and returned it to its envelope.

He gave Annie's shoulders a squeeze. It didn't do to show he was worried about their son, as Annie hadn't been her usual self since Lexie had enlisted in the WAAF and there was no point in adding to her anxiety.

The bombing of the Scapa Flow Naval Base in March and the Nazis invasion of Denmark and Sweden had escalated the war to the point where Hitler and his armies were now seen by many as unstoppable. Churchill had to respond soon, everyone said, or the country was in danger of being Hitler's next target and Euan knew that Ian would be in the front line, leading his men to face the German guns.

"How was Nancy?" Euan asked, pushing his fears to the back of his mind and filling the kettle to make them some tea.

"She seems fine," Annie told him, warily, "but I'm sure there's something she's not telling me and Billy seems to be so far from her thoughts that she only speaks of him when she's asked. It's almost as if she doesn't love him anymore"

Euan filled Annie's cup and placed the Biscuit Barrel on the table.

He wondered whether to tell her about Billy's behaviour with Gladys Kelly and Billy Dawson's fears that Nancy was doing more than dancing the night away at the Palais, but thought better of it. There was enough to deal with just getting through the days without worrying about Nancy.

Ian's letter had brought back memories to Annie of when both Lexie and Ian were children and now, here they were fighting a war that Annie knew little about, except what Euan passed on to her from the newspapers.

"Are you alright, dear?" Euan asked, noticing Annie's far-away look.

Annie brought her attention back to her husband. How lucky she was to have this wonderful man in her life. He'd supported her through the many trials that had beset her and especially when she told him she had given birth to an illegitimate son. For a moment, she felt now would be the time to tell him that John's father was, in fact, Billy Dawson, but almost instantly dispelled the idea. She couldn't bear the hurt that the confession would surely inflict on Euan.

"I was just thinking how lucky I am to have you," she said instead,

"I don't know how I'd manage without you Euan," she added, a worried frown forming on her brow.

"Now, now," Euan said, reaching across the table and taking her hand in his. "Nothing's going to happen to me, so don't fret," he said, "it'll take more than Adolf Hitler to separate me from you."

Annie squeezed his hand and smiled. "I love you," she said simply, knowing every word was true. "And, I love you," Euan replied, his voice soft with sincerity, "till death do us part," he added, repeating the last line of their wedding vows. Annie felt a shiver run through her body at the mention of the word 'death.' "And beyond," she added, "for eternity."

It was two weeks since Nancy's coupling with Jim Murphy when Nancy realised that her regular monthly period hadn't started. Jim had kept his distance at the mill and Nancy hadn't gone to the dancehall the following Saturday, in the hope that Jim would miss her and knock on her door.

It was the anxiety of the last couple of weeks that had made her late, she told herself and anyway, Jim had been careful.

She busied herself around the house all weekend, polishing and scrubbing to ease the tension that was growing in her mind, but a few days later, Nancy fainted in Harry Duncan's butcher shop.

"I think it was the sight of all that Tripe that knocked me out," she said, weakly, trying to justify her blackout as she sipped the glass of water a concerned Harry had given her.

"Maybe you should see a doctor or something," Harry urged her, but Nancy brushed his suggestion aside. She knew the reason for the faint and it wasn't the dish of Tripe. She was pregnant and Billy Donnelly was the father.

Di Auchterlonie turned up at Nancy's house the following Saturday morning, as usual, to discuss their plans for the dancing.

"You can't miss another Saturday!" she exclaimed, as Nancy told her she 'wasn't in the mood.'

"Billy's away back to the Guards," she stated emphatically "and Jim Murphy will be beginning to wonder where you are," she added, winking a knowing eye, "so what's stopping you?"

Nancy turned her strained face toward Di. "I'm pregnant," she said despairingly.

Di's hands flew to her face. "JIM MURPHY?" she asked, horrified.

Nancy felt tears forming in her eyes. "No," she said, her voice quivering, knowing that her hopes for a life with Jim were now over, "it's Billy's."

"Does he know?" Di asked, before realising that, of course, he couldn't know.

Nancy shook her head, and reached for a cigarette, her hand shaking with fear for the future.

"What's to do, girl?" Di asked, gently, knowing that there was nothing her friend could do, but have the bairn and hope for the best.

"When I figure that out, I'll let you know," Nancy said, bleakly.

A part of Di was relieved that the bairn was Billy's doing and not down to Jim Murphy, but another part of her was concerned about Nancy's heart.

She knew how much she'd wanted Jim Murphy and how hurt she'd been by Billy's visits to Gladys Kelly.

"If there's anything I can do to help," Di ventured, "you know I'll do it."

Nancy shook her head and lit another cigarette.

"Thanks," she said, "but this is something I have to cope with myself."

Di nodded solemnly, "I'll leave you be then," she said, "I'll see you at the mill on Monday."

Di closed the door quietly leaving Nancy staring into nothingness, all her dreams of happiness lying broken at her feet.

"MUM, MUM," wee Billy shouted as he barged into the kitchen, "Mary Anne says I'm not big enough to go climbing on the Air Raid Shelters with her and Davie Innes. Tell her she's got to let me!"

Nancy burst into tears and her son turned white with fear. "Why are you crying?" he asked, rushing towards her and wrapping his spindly arms around her waist. "I won't go climbing with Mary Anne," he burbled, tears beginning to run down his cheeks, "don't be sad."

Nancy held her son closer. "Ssshhhh! It's alright," she said, "mum's not crying about you and Mary Anne," she sniffed, reaching for her handkerchief to blow her nose. "I'm just missing your daddy, that's all."

Her son turned his eyes towards her. "I'll look after you," he said, shakily, "I'm a big boy now, daddy said so."

Nancy felt a wave of guilt hit her. Here she was, crying self-pitying tears when her son needed his mum more than ever, now Billy was away fighting this damn war.

She wiped the tears from his face and forced her biggest smile.

"C'mon," she said, "let's find Mary Anne and we'll all go down to Woolies and you can spend a whole sixpence on anything you like."

Wee Billy whooped with glee, his tears forgotten. "Go find Mary Anne," Nancy said, "while I get tidied up." She turned her son to face her. "And, no more tears," she said, "not ever again."

Billy nodded solemnly, relieved that his mum was back to normal.

He skipped out of the kitchen to find his sister and Nancy splashed cold water on her face, running her wet fingers through her hair. Her destiny had been decided for her and from now on, she would push all thoughts of Jim Murphy from her mind and concentrate on her two children and prepare for the arrival of her next.

Jim Murphy was watching on Monday morning as the Weavers arrived for work. He'd had one wonderful evening with Nancy, but Jean had been suspicious when he'd finally got home and had started asking him awkward questions about his whereabouts, so he'd decided to cool things down, but now, the desire for Nancy was rising again.

She came hurrying through the loading bay heading for the Weaving Flat. She'd left her arrival as late as possible to avoid seeing Jim Murphy and falling under his spell again, but Nancy wasn't quick enough.

A pair of strong arms stopped her in her tracks.

"Hey, slow down," Jim Murphy said, "where's the fire?"

Nancy shook herself free. "No fire," she said averting his eyes, "just running a bit late."

"So late, you don't have a minute to speak to me?" he grinned trying to get her to focus on him.

Nancy took a deep breath and said the harshest words she could muster.

"Keep away from me," she hissed, "another minute with you would be a minute too long." Jim stepped back. "You'd better go then," he said, slowly, shocked at the venom in Nancy's voice, "don't want to waste your precious time."

Fighting back tears of hurt, Nancy ran to her looms, leaving Jim Murphy in her wake, confused and wanting her more than ever. He had to find out what was wrong and how he could fix it so that he was back in Nancy's good books and her bed.

110

It was the following Friday before he knocked at Nancy's door. Jean had been watching him like a hawk, but couldn't find a reason to stop him from going for his usual Friday night drink at the Thrums Bar with his pals and that's when he took his chance.

"Have you got a minute?" he asked when Nancy came to the door.

The sight of Jim at her door almost broke the resolve she had been building to keep away from him. She was on dangerous ground and she knew it.

"If you've anything to say," she replied, steadying her voice, "then say it and go." She crossed her arms in front of her and fixed her lips into a tight line.

Jim removed his bonnet and ran the fingers of one hand around the rim.

"Can I come in...please," he said in a begging voice, "the neighbours...you know..."

Annie looked along the paved landing, where at any minute a door could open and one of the neighbours would see Jim Murphy at her door and the gossip would start.

She stood back to let him in. "I suppose so," she said, "but just for a minute."

Jim didn't hesitate and quickly closed the door behind him, following Nancy into the kitchen.

"All alone?" he said. Nancy bristled and flashed a warning look at him.

"Why do you ask?" she retorted, "who were you expecting to see?"

"I just meant the bairns," he said quickly, "that's all."

Nancy's feathers were ruffled. Did Jim Murphy think she took other men into her bed!

"Billy's at the BB and Mary Anne's at her pal's house," she muttered, "and you can thank your lucky stars for that, or you wouldn't be standing here."

"What's wrong, Nancy?" he asked, his voice gentle and concerned, "I've missed you."

Nancy turned away, afraid to look at him as her head fought a losing battle with her heart.

"Nothing," she whispered to herself, "I've just had enough," she added, "that's all."

Jim was standing directly behind her now.

"Enough of me?"

Nancy felt her emotions weakening her resolve to hate him and her head dropped back onto his shoulder as his arms folded around her.

"There," he said hoarsely, "that's more like the Nancy I know."

"I'm pregnant," Nancy announced bluntly.

Jim's muscles tensed in unison and his arms dropped from Nancy's waist. He didn't know what he'd expected to hear, but it wasn't that she was pregnant.

She turned to face him, her eyes bleak. "Still want a minute of my time?"

"It can't be mine," Jim said, "I was too careful." He stepped further away,

panic beginning to overwhelm him.

"What's the matter Jim?" Nancy asked, seeing him for the first time for what he was. He'd never had any intention of leaving Jean to be with her, she realised, her heart breaking with the truth of it.

Nancy walked to the kitchen door and opened it wide.

"Thanks for nothing," she said as he hurried past her "and just for the record," Nancy added, before slamming the door, " you're not man enough to father a bairn."

Silence filled the room as Nancy filled the kettle and made herself some tea. She knew now for sure, that she'd had a lucky escape from Jim Murphy and the tears she'd expected to shed over him, never came.

Mary Anne came bustling into the silence. "We've been playing at Snakes and Ladders at Lena's and her mum gave us lemonade and a biscuit," she prattled on, as Nancy sipped her tea and listened to her daughter's news, "and she said I could come again next week, if I liked."

Oblivious to what had just happened, Mary Annne started to dust the furniture as part of her Friday chores to help her mum, before getting herself eady for bed.

Please let her life be better than mine, Nancy prayed silently, as she watched her daughter morphing into another wife and mother, just like she had done.

"Go read your book," Nancy said, taking the duster from her hands,

"I'll manage the dusting."

Mary Anne's eyes lit up. "Can I?"

Nancy opened her arms and her daughter ran into them. Despite war and Jim Murphy, she realised that her bairns were the most precious thing she had and she'd spend the rest of her life loving them and that included the next one. And Jim Murphy could go to Hell.

———oOo———

Chapter 20

Since Lucy's 'talk' about Jenny McKenzie, Lexie made sure she stayed as far away from her as possible during her shift in the Comms Room, but it didn't take long for Jenny to realise that she was getting nowhere in her pursuit of Lexie, especially when she saw her giggling with one of the Radio Operators and casting longing looks at Sgt Brady. And she knew who was to blame for putting a spoke in her wheels, Lucy Ashford.

RAF Lossiemouth was like a little village, Lexie realised, where everyone knew everyone else and gossip was rife. Her experience, by just being seen in the company of Jenny McKenzie, marking her down as 'one of them' had been dispelled, however, Lexie decided to keep herself to herself in future and not give the gossips any excuse to focus on her.

Fortunately, the work kept her busy during her shift and once she'd eaten in the NAAFI, she'd take herself off to the billet to read or write home, but the isolation that Lexie had imposed on herself was becoming depressing.

Alone in the billet, she gazed out of the window. Autumn was coming in, and before long the winter would begin, but Nature had produced a few days of an Indian Summer and Lexie decided to head down to Lossiemouth harbour to take in the sea air and watch the gulls swooping over the fishing boats tied up for the weekend.

The harbour, usually busy during the week, was peaceful and quiet and Lexie gave a jump as a gruff voice behind her wished her 'guid day.'

She turned to see the weather-beaten face of a civilian, with twinkling blue eyes and a mop of wind-swept brown hair, blowing around his head.

"Good day," Lexie replied, "lovely weather."

They both gazed at the scene before them. "It is that lassie," the man said, "makes you forget there's a war on."

Lexie agreed. It all seemed far away from this peaceful place, but she knew that was just an illusion. At the base, aeroplanes were being made ready to drop their bombs on Germany and men were pulling on all their reserves of strength to fly them.

"The name's Henry Stockwood," the man said with a slight bow of his head and an extended hand. "ACW Melville," Lexie said back, "but it's Lexie when I'm off duty. The roar of a Wellington Bomber reached their ears, stopping any further conversation, as it flew over the local golf course. A sudden noise, louder than a gunshot, made both of them flinch. "What was that?" Lexie asked as the bomber began to turn sharply and nosedive towards the water.

"I dinna ken, lassie, but that Wellington isn't going make it."

The huge aircraft hit the water, breaking on impact and spreading wreckage on the surface.

Without hesitation and fully clothed, Henry and Lexie leapt into the water and began wading and swimming towards the stricken aircraft. The crash had created a heavy swell and swathes of seaweed impeded their attempts but finally Lexie managed to reach the broken aeroplane. Two bodies bobbed up to the surface in front of her, both dead and Lexie identified them by their insignia as the pilot and co-pilot. She could do nothing for them.

Meanwhile, Henry Stockwood was struggling to maintain his head above water. Lexie spluttered as the water splashed onto her face and she was losing feeling in her right leg but she pushed herself off against the broken fuselage and headed towards Henry.

Voices were shouting from the Harbour Wall and the noise of a motorboat grew louder, as she grabbed Henry under his arms and managed to keep him afloat.

Strong hands of two fishermen pulled Lexie and Henry aboard their boat, gasping and spluttering and almost beyond the point of exhaustion.

"You're ah'right, lassie," Lexie heard one of them tell her from somewhere far off, before she collapsed into the boat.

It was in the dim light of the sick bay on the base that Lexie's eyes finally flickered back to life.

"She's awake," she heard a femail voice say, before a man's voice called her name. "Lexie," he said, gently, "everything's alright."

Lexie tried to force herself to sit up but almost instantly slumped back onto the pillow.

"Where am I?" she said weakly, "where's Henry?" she added anxiously, the memory of the ditched aircraft flooding into her consciousness.

"You're safe," the man said, "I'm Dr Carter and you're at the RAF base at Lossiemouth." Lexie turned worried eyes to the doctor. "Did anyone survive?" she asked. The doctor shook his head, "there were two crew members aboard the Wellington when the starboard wing snapped off and down she came into the sea."

"And Henry Stockwood?" Lexie said, "is he alright?"

Dr Carter shook his head. "We got him out alive," he said, "but the shock got to him and he passed away a few hours ago."

Lexie closed her eyes, to keep the tears in. One minute they were admiring the view and then out of a clear blue sky, the bomber came down in front of them.

And now, Henry Stockwood was dead. Lexie covered her face with her hands and wept.

Over the next week, Lucy and the girls visited her in her hospital bed and a Reporter from Inverness turned up and wrote up the story of Lexie's act of bravery for his newspaper.

"I'm fine," she told Dr Carter on one of his checks on Lexie's progress.

"I know you're fine physically," he said, "but I want to make sure you'll be able to cope with being back in the thick of things again."

Lexie knew what he meant, she'd been lucky to have gotten back to shore safely and the trauma of it all had given her nightmares for a few days, but she felt sure she could cope again. "I can cope," Lexie said simply.

Dr Carter smiled at his patient. "You'll do, ACW Melville," he said, signing off her discharge paperwork, "and well done, what you did was very brave."

Lexie coloured. She had only done what anyone would have done, she thought, but it was nice to hear the compliment.

On her first day back at her post, she was summoned by Wing Commander Johnny Johnson.

"Take a seat," he said to Lexie, his fingers laced in front of him and a glimmer of admiration in his blue eyes.

Lexie sat.

"I want to congratulate you on your bravery ACW Melville. To have risked your own life to save another is the highest act of bravery there is."

Lexie acknowledged the statement with a 'yes sir.'

"In order to recognise your courage, I have been instructed by HQ to advise you that the RAF is putting your name forward for consideration for an Empire Medal."

Lexie's mouth dropped open in disbelief. "Medal!" she exclaimed, "but I was only..." Johnny Johnson stopped her response with a wave of his hand. "I think 'yes sir' is all I need to hear," he said, warming to the modesty of the ACW.

He shuffled the paperwork on his desk before producing a single sheet part of which he read out to Lexie. "They've also recommended that you be promoted with immediate effect to the rank of Corporal."

Before Lexie could say anything, Johnny Johnson stood and saluted her. Lexie jumped to attention and saluted back.

"That'll be all, Corporal Melville," the Wing Commander said, "Report to Sgt Brady for further orders."

Johnny Johnson stroked his moustache, tracing the scars that ran from it down to his chin. He knew all about bravery, having flown numerous sorties in his Spitfire against the German Luftwaffe and had barely survived the last one, when his fighter plane had been shot down over the English Channel. And now, he was deskbound at RAF Lossiemouth and a little Scottish girl had shown him that bravery could be found in the most unlikely of places and people. With WAAF's like Lexie Melville around, he surmised, Hitler and his ilk had better watch out.

When Euan opened his newspaper, he couldn't believe his eyes. There was a picture of Lexie in her uniform and a story about how she and someone called Henry Stockwood had attempted to rescue the crew of a Wellington Bomber that had ditched in Lossiemouth Harbour.

"ANNIE!" he called through to their bedroom where she was brushing her hair and getting ready to meet the day. "Come and see this."

Annie hurried into the kitchen, the tone of Euan's voice brooking no hesitation. He handed Annie the Courier.

"You'd better sit down before you read this," he said, "I'll get you a cup of strong tea."

Annie read the story in awe, before bursting into tears.

"She could have been KILLED!" she wailed, "Lexie could have died."

Euan rushed to her side. "Hush now, Annie," he said wrapping his arm around her shoulder, "Lexie's fine and I'm sure we'll hear from her soon."

They both re-read the story again, with a mixture of disbelief and pride.

"Their little girl was a hero!

The letter from RAF Lossiemouth arrived two days later, explaining everything and advising Annie and Euan that an Empire Medal for Lexie was being considered and that she had been promoted to Corporal in recognition of her bravery and strong character.

Later that day, in a public house on Dock Street, Captain Robbie Robertson, was drinking his second tot of rum. Home on leave from sailing his freighter MV Northern Way across the Atlantic Ocean to safe harbour in Glasgow, he was back in Dundee, awaiting new orders from the Merchant Navy and hoping for an easier trip next time. The German U Boats had been waiting to torpedo the convoy of ships night and day, but the accompanying Destroyers had safely escorted them back home, with the loss of only two of the twenty cargo vessels.

So, Lexie was a WAAF, he mused, wondering what had happened to the meek spinster she'd become since he'd cruelly rejected her to satisfy his male pride. He looked closely at the newspaper photo. He still saw traces of the girl he'd fallen in love with and who he'd wanted to marry, until Sergeant MacPherson had made it plain that Lexie never wanted to see him again. That hurt had lasted till he'd gotten his revenge, but it wasn't long after that, that he began to hate himself for his stupidity and despite trying to write to her several times before the war started, he'd never had the courage to send the letters. Robbie winced with regret as he carefully tore out her picture, folded it and slipped it into his wallet.

He raised his glass and silently toasted the only girl he'd really loved, wishing, not for the first time, that things had turned out differently.

Chapter 21

Di had rushed over to her as Nancy took her lunch break in the canteen at Baxters. "Look at this," she squealed, waving a copy of the Courier at arm's length, "You're Auntie Annie's girl is famous!"

Nancy put down her bread roll. She didn't have much appetite at the moment with the morning sickness lasting longer than the morning.

She took the newspaper from her pal's hand and spread it out on the table.

"Do you mean, Lexie?" she asked scanning the headline,

'DUNDEE WAAF'S HEROIC RESCUE ATTEMPT'

Nancy read on and held the paper closer to make sure the photograph was indeed of Lexie.

"Well, well," she said, in admiration, "good old Lexie. Fancy that!"

Wasn't she the 'auld maid' of the family?" Di asked incredulously.

Nancy smiled, remembering how she'd called Lexie the name and how differently things had turned out. It was she, who was without a man and Lexie, well, she was surrounded by a whole air force of men.

"I'll take the bairns and visit Auntie Annie on Saturday," she told Di, "let her know how proud we all are of Lexie."

Wee Billy had been ecstatic when he heard the news. "Will Auntie Lexie get a medal?" he asked, his eyes gleaming. "Can I be a soldier like her too?" Mary Anne added, caught up in the excitement of it all.

"Your Auntie Lexie isn't a soldier," Nancy corrected her, smiling at her daughter's enthusiasm to be something other than a housewife and mother, albeit not knowing exactly what Lexie was.

"She's what's known as a WAAF and that means she's part of the Royal Air Force. That's the people who fly around in airplanes," she added by way of explanation at Mary Anne's confused face.

"Will Auntie Lexie be dropping bombs on people like us?"

Out of the mouths of babes and sucklings...thought Nancy. How was Germany dropping bombs on us, any different from what we were doing to them. Unwanted thoughts of Billy came into her head. He too had been catapulted into the war, asked to risk his life for 'King & Country' and be branded a coward if he refused.

"Of course she won't," Nancy reassured her, bringing her thoughts back to her daughter. "Auntie Lexie will probably be one of the girls who keep the airplanes clean and make tea for the men, just like I keep the house clean and make tea for you and wee Billy."

"Where's daddy?" Mary Anne asked, suddenly, now wondering about her father, "is he dropping bombs on people?"

Nancy blanched, how could she explain about war and killing to a young girl. She stood up and hurried Mary Anne over to the breakfast table. "No, he isn't," she said, "now let's get these dishes done and then we'll go and see Auntie Annie." She hugged her daughter "and don't be asking her if Lexie bombs people, alright?"

Mary Anne shrugged. She wasn't sure if she understood the words, but knew instinctively that it was her job to help her mum and not drop bombs on people.

Annie and Euan had just finished lunch when Nancy and the bairns turned up on their doorstep.

"What a lovely surprise!" she exclaimed, "look who's here," she called to Euan, who was reading his newspaper at the kitchen table. "Sit down," Annie said, taking the children's coats, "tea won't be a minute and I'm sure there's some Grannie Sookers in the sweetie jar," she nodded to Mary Anne, "I think they're one of your favourites."

"There mine too," jumped in wee Billy, afraid he'd miss out on the treat.

Nancy laughed, "I'm sure there'll be enough to go round," she said, ruffling her son's hair.

Annie looked at Euan, wondering if he too had noticed the change in her niece. The haunted look they'd seen before Billy went back to his regiment was gone and the calmness she now displayed was reassuring. Euan had been watching the dancehall at closing time as often as he could, but hadn't seen Nancy again, nor the mysterious man she'd been hanging on to.

Annie poured the tea. "I suppose you've heard the news?" she asked Nancy, unable to keep the pride out of her voice, "about Lexie I mean."

Nancy smiled, "she's the talk of Baxters," she said, "and probably the whole of Dundee." She leaned forward and squeezed Annie's arm, "I just wanted you to know how proud me and the bairns are of Lexie and hope she'll get some home leave as a reward. It would be great to see her again."

"Oh! I'm sure she'd love to come home for a spell, but we don't know how these things work, not during a war, that is. Do we Euan?"

"When we know," Euan said, "you'll be the first person we tell,"

he said, "but enough of us, how are things with you...and how's Billy?"

Nancy was conscious of Mary Anne's eyes fixed on her, awaiting her answer. She hadn't spoken to them much about their father, mainly because she wanted them to learn to get along without him, but it was plain that Mary Anne missed him.

"He's fine," Nancy said, "as far as we know," she added, included Mary Anne in the statement, but I'll be writing to him soon with news of my own."

Annie and Euan waited with bated breath, Annie fearing that something was wrong with the bairns and Euan fearing that Billy Dawson had found out about Nancy's secret dalliance and had confronted her...but she seemed too calm for that.

But none of them had expected the news that Nancy imparted.

"Mary Anne and wee Billy are going to be getting a new baby brother or sister," she said, smiling at the open mouths around the table, including Mary Anne and wee Billy.

Euan was the first to speak. "You're PREGNANT?"

Nancy nodded and waited.

"But HOW?" Annie added, "WHEN?"

Nancy smiled, "well, I think you know how," she said, coyly "and as for when, well, before Billy went back to his regiment, we..." she shrugged, indicating that she'd be saying no more in front of the bairns.

"Does Billy know?" Euan asked, when he'd recovered enough to think straight. He would have been delighted at the news that she and Billy were, once more, fully married, but there was a nagging doubt that Billy Donnelly might not be the father.

"Not yet," Nancy said, "I just hope he can get back before the baby's born," she added, keeping up the appearance that all was well in the Donnelly household. She'd be needing Annie and Euan's support when the pregnancy became more advanced and the more they thought everything was alright between her and Billy the better.

"Well!" Annie exclaimed, relieved that Nancy seemed happy with her pregnancy, "this has been a real 'red letter day' all round."

"Give our love to Billy when you write to tell him the news," Annie said, hugging her niece, before the little family left for home, "and if there's anything we can do to help, you just have to say."

"Thanks, Auntie Annie," Nancy said, relieved that her pregnancy was now out in the open, "you've always been there for me and I'll know where to come if I need anything."

She took the bairns hands, one at each side, and walked confidently down Albert Street. She'd deal with this pregnancy alone and the less Billy Donnelly knew about it the better. She wouldn't be writing to him, he may be the father but she knew where his heart really lay and that was in Gladys Kelly's bed and he was welcome to her and her to him. But the bairns were hers and hers alone, no matter what the future held and with Annie's help, Nancy would cope.

Once they were back home, Nancy sat her children down and explained about the new baby. "So you're both going to have to be very grown-up now," she said, "mum's going to need your help with shopping and cleaning, especially when it gets nearer the time for the baby to born. Will you do that for me?" She smiled as two intent faces nodded.

"Will daddy come home soon?" Mary Anne asked, the weight of her mother's news sitting heavily on her shoulders. She didn't know anything about bairns and wee Billy knew even less. Daddy needs to be here, she reasoned, mum needs him.

"You know he can't come home soon Mary Anne," Nancy said, trying to keep calm in the face of her daughter's needy question, "he's had to go and fight a war so we can all be safe," she said quietly but firmly, "but he'll be back as soon as he can, we've just got to be brave till then."

The answer seemed to satisfy Mary Anne, for the moment, but Nancy knew that Billy's absence, as the pregnancy progressed, would need to be spoken off again.

"C'mon you two," Nancy said too brightly, "out to play with you while I get our tea ready...and no climbing on the air raid shelters," she called after them as they disappeared out the door.

Later that evening, Annie and Euan were gradually getting used to the idea of Nancy being pregnant, when the telephone rang. Euan picked up the receiver.

"Sergeant Euan MacPherson speaking," he said formally. The Constabulary had installed the telephone in his home so Euan could be contacted in case of an emergency at the Bell Street Station or a call-out in his role in charge of the Air Raid Patrol Wardens.

"I'll be there at once," he said, "I'll meet the men at the gates."

"What is it?" Annie asked, anxiously.

"The Park Wardens have found an unexploded bomb in Baxters Park," Euan told her. The ARP lads are on their way and we'll make the area safe till the Army can get their experts there."

Annie jumped to her feet. "BOMB!" she exclaimed, but..."

Euan hushed her with the stopping hand he used to control traffic. "Now, now," he said, "don't take on. We're not in any danger and when the Bomb Disposal squad get there, our duty will be to keep people away, that's all."

Annie hugged him tighter than she'd ever hugged him before. Everything was so out of her control and now THIS. "You will be careful," she said, tension tightening her throat, "I'll wait up till you get back."

Annie listened as the sound of Euan's boots on the stairs faded. There was nothing she could do but wait. The minutes turned into hours and it was gone midnight when Annie was jolted from an uneasy sleep by a loud ringing sound.

She stared at the ringing telephone, she'd never answered it before but had seen Euan pick up the receiver and put it to his ear.

She lifted the black earpiece and immediately the ringing stopped. She put it to her ear. "Yes," she said tentatively. "Mrs MacPherson?" a male voice asked. "Yes," Annie responded. "This is Captain Millar, Bomb Disposal Unit calling." Annie felt her blood run cold. "Is there anyone with you?" the Captain asked. "No," Annie said, "no one."

"Then I will be over to see you shortly, so when I knock at the door, please don't be afraid, just let me in."

Annie nodded and replaced the receiver to its cradle.

Fear was now enveloping her, freezing all her senses into immobility.

The knock on the door when it came was loud and insistent and forced Annie's legs to move to go and answer it.

A tall man in Khaki uniform stood before her.

"Mrs MacPherson," he said, removing his hat, "may I come in?"

Annie stood aside to allow the Captain to enter. Her face was devoid of all colour as she listened to what he had to say, then blackness enveloped her as she fainted.

———oOo———

Chapter 22

The NAAFI was abuzz with excitement as Lexie took her place in the queue for the evening meal. Lucy Ashford was in front of her, ordering her food as Lexie tapped her on the shoulder.

"What's all the excitement?" she asked, looking around her again, "the war isn't over is it?"

Lucy gazed dreamily skyward. "It's better than that," she said, ignoring the signals from the cook to move on. Lexie nudged her forward, intrigued by Lucy's response. Surely, nothing could be better than the end of the war!

"There's a group of Canadian airmen due to arrive in the next few days for training to fly our bombers," Lucy whispered, "can you just imagine it?"

"Why is that better than the end of the war?"

"Oh! Lexie, my dear," Lucy chided gently as they made their way to a table, "Canadian Pilots! They'll be like film stars," she continued, her imagination taking over.

Lexie smiled, "I guess that's Sgt Brady out of the picture then?"

Lucy had pierced a sausage on her fork and was nibbling one end, her mind's eye conjuring up images impossible for any man to live up to. At the mention of Sgt Brady's name, Lucy came back down to earth.

"Oh! No," she said, "Sgt Brady is adorable, but as we have all found out, also happily married."

Lexie had to agree as she tucked into her bangers and mash, unable to get that excited about yet another batch of airmen, Canadian or otherwise.

Just as predicted by Lucy, a Canadian Air Force airplane landed at Lossiemouth on Sunday evening, disgorging a dozen travel-weary airmen.

"Well, guys," Group Captain McGhee said, looking around the expanse of flatness that was RAF Lossiemouth, "here we are at last." He stretched his arms and legs and buckled his flying jacket tighter against the North wind.

Wing Commander Johnny Johnson hurried across the tarmac to meet the new arrivals. They were going to be needed and soon, the North Sea and the Norwegian coast were being targeted by German U boats and battleships and the War Office wanted the Luftwaffe airbases in Norway targeted to stop giving their naval fleet air cover.

He shook hands with Captain McGhee. "Good to see you," Johnny Johnson said, "the Mess has food ready for your men and their Billet is at the end of the Southern runway, but I think I have something more edible in my Quarters, if you'd care to follow me."

Captain McGhee passed on the information to his men and followed the Wing Commander off the runway. Johnny Johnson's quarters were small but his hospitality to the Canadian Captain was generous. His Batman brought in hot food and once it was eaten, Johnny produced a bottle of Scotch Malt Whisky and poured each of them a stiff measure.

"Slange," said the Wing Commander, "Cheers," responded McGhee, holding the glass of golden liquid up to the light after his first sip.

"Well, I didn't expect anything other than beer," he said, "but this is going down nicely."

"There aren't many perks about being based this far North," Johnny Johnson said, swilling his drink, "but access to a whisky distillery is one of them."

The Wing Commander brought Captain McGee up to date on the need to get his men trained quickly to fly the Wellington Bombers. "We lost four of our bomber pilots over the North Sea," he said solemnly, "the Luftwaffe fighters were on us before we knew it on our last mission to the industrial heartlands of

Germany and intelligence has told us that 'Jerry' have set up an airfield at Stavanger."

"And it needs to be put out of action rapidly," Captain McGhee nodded.

"You got it," the Wing Commander said, standing up, "but enough of that for one night, you must be in need of a few hours rest." He pressed a button on the wall and the Batman returned. "Show Group Captain McGhee his quarters," he ordered," before saluting McGhee, "welcome to Lossiemouth Captain...and good flying."

McGhee saluted and followed the Batman to his new quarters. The room was adequate but he could have slept on the 'edge of a knife', he was so whacked with the journey. He tossed his flying jacket and uniform onto a small chair and fell into his bunk. Tomorrow was another day, tonight was for sleep.

Lexie was getting used to her new role as Corporal. She was now in a senior position to ACW Jenny McKenzie, who had to carry out Lexie's orders, and she made sure that the ACW was kept busy on the Comms Room Teleprinter where she could cause no further embarrassment to Lexie. She also now worked closer to Sgt Brady and was privy to the more confidential information that passed through the Comms Room.

"Here's the list of Canadian Pilot Officers who've just arrived," St Brady said, handing Lexie the details of the new men. Wing Commander Johnson wants you to see that they have everything they need and liaise with the Maintenance Sergeant at the South Hanger and the Training Control Officer to make sure all goes smoothly."

Lexie saluted the Sergeant and scrutinised the list.

Group Captain R McGhee seemed to be in charge, so once she'd been to the South Hanger and the Training Control Office to get a handle on the set up, she'd seek out Captain McGhee and his men.

Three Wellington Bombers were being made ready in the South Hanger by the Maintenance Crew, under the beady eye of Sergeant Ron Hammond and Flight Sergeant Dan Patterson had been given the task of training the pilots on the intricacies of the Wellingtons.

Lexie introduced herself to the Flight Sergeant and explained her role as go-between for Wing Commander Johnson. "So, if there are any problems with the training schedules, report them to me and I'll try to get things resolved."

"Will do, Corporal," he said, casually, "and maybe when you're not so busy, you and I could have a beer together."

Lexie was taken unawares. As an ACW she'd been approached by other men at the base, but her focus had remained on her job and, especially now, that she'd been promoted to Corporal, it was even more important to her that she wasn't seen to be fraternising with the male officers.

"Maybe," she stammered, saluting quickly and leaving the Training Room.

The Canadian pilots were sitting on old deck chairs around the outside of their Billet, drinking tea and awaiting their orders when Lexie marched up to them. She waved the list of names Sgt Brady had given her and saluted the pilots. "Can I have a roll-call," she said, her pen at the ready to tick off their names. But instead of a roll-call, Lexie was on the receiving end of a series of 'wolf-whistles'. "Well," said one of the group, "what have we here?"

Lexie flushed scarlet and saluted again. "Corporal Melville," she said, "Womens Auxiliary Air Force."

"Hey," the ring-leader said again, "brains as well as beauty." The comment was met with another round of whistles and Lexie was just wishing that the ground to open up and swallow her, when another voice made itself heard above the noise.

"That's enough guys," the owner of the voice said, stepping out of the Billet and crossing to where Lexie stood. "You'll have to forgive them Miss," he said in a deep Canadian drawl, "they've been too long away from the company of fine young women like yourself."

Lexie stood transfixed, for the second time in her life, lost for words.

The Canadian gave her a half-hearted salute. "Group Captain

Rainbow McGhee," he said.

"Corporal Melville," Lexie murmured... "roll-call," she was able to say indicating her list.

Rainbow McGhee grinned at her as he took the list from her hand and skimmed through it. "All here," he said, handing it back to Lexie.

Lexie took the list back and forced her legs to move, while the now silent group watched the interaction between their Group Captain and the Corporal.

With as much confidence as she could muster, Lexie saluted and walked away. The last time she had felt such an impact as the one she had just experienced on meeting Rainbow McGhee, was when Robbie Robertson had come into Harry Duncan's butcher shop, dark handsome and dangerous and rendered her speechless with desire.'

"Hey", said one of the men, "I think I'm going to like Scotland, if that's an example of the women here."

Captain McGhee silenced him with a look. "We're here to bomb the Germans," he said, his authority sitting easy on his shoulders, "not flirt with the natives." He looked at his watch. "Training begins at 09.00 hours," he said, "so get your asses over to the South Hanger and the only woman I want you making eyes at is called Miss Wellington."

"Yes sir," a chorus of male voices responded, as they shrugged into their flying jackets and folded up the deck chairs. They knew from past experience, that when Group Captain McGhee gave an order, the only answer was 'Yes Sir.'

The walk back to the Comms Room in the cold air, gave Lexie time to cool down before she reported to Sgt Brady, but despite her head telling her time and again not to be so foolish, her heart was saying something quite different. "Rainbow McGhee," she muttered to herself, who calls a child 'Rainbow' Lexie wondered, especially a boy!

"Everything alright Corporal?" the voice of Sgt Brady broke into her thoughts, bringing her back to the business in hand.

"Everything's ready for the Canadian pilots," she said, forcing sternness into her voice. "Sgt Hammond has three Wellingtons ready to go and Sgt Patterson is on his way to the South Hanger to start their training at 09.00 hours." She handed over the list of pilots' names, now duly ticked. "All present and correct," she said, taking a step back and saluting.

"Well done," Sgt Brady said, saluting back, "and Wing Commander Johnson also wants you to join him and the Canadians for dinner at the Officers Mess this evening at 19.00 hours."

"But..." Lexie began, "I can't..." Sgt Brady held up his hand. "That's an order," he said, "the Wing Commander wants you to be his liaison officer, making sure that the training goes ahead without any hitches, these pilots need to be ready to fly the bombers within two weeks."

Lexie saluted and turned towards the Comms Room Teleprinters, forcing her attention on the job at hand and determining that, in future, she would give Rainbow McGhee a 'wide berth.'

The Canadians and Wing Commander Johnson were having a pre-dinner drink in the Officers Mess when Lexie arrived. She'd pressed her uniform and polished her shoes to within an 'inch of their lives.'

Johnny Johnson waved her over. "Corporal Melville," he said, "I believe you've met Group Captain McGhee and his fellow pilots," he said nodding towards the Canadians.

"Yes sir," Lexie said smartly, saluting the Wing Commander and keeping eye contact with him. "I've been telling the Group Captain that you are our liaison officer and the one to go to if there are any problems."

"Yes sir," Lexie said again.

"So," Johnny Johnson said, bringing the introduction to a close, "let's eat."

The meal was served and Lexie managed to swallow most of it, never daring to look at Rainbow McGhee and speaking only when spoken to by Johnny Johnson. At the end of the meal, the men went to the bar and Lexie was dismissed with a nod of thanks from Johnny Johnson and a salute.

With a huge sigh of relief, Lexie picked up her things and

hurried from the Mess. She only had to be around Rainbow McGhee for a couple of weeks and then her liaison duty would be over. She was half-way back to her quarters when a voice called out behind her. "Corporal Melville, wait up."

Lexie stopped and turned. Rainbow McGhee emerged from the darkness.

"I never got the chance to thank you," he said, "the first day of training went well, thanks in part to you."

Lexie's eyes adjusted to the shape of Rainbow McGhee, her voice still deserting her. "Just doing my job," she managed to say, "but thank you."

She turned to go but he gripped her elbow and turned her back to face him.

"May I walk you back to your Quarters?" he asked, removing his Captain's hat and releasing her elbow.

Lexie nodded silently as Rainbow walked beside her on the short walk to her hut.

They stopped at the wooden door. "Do you have a first name?" he asked, trying to break through the resistance that surrounded her. For the first time Lexie looked into the black eyes of Rainbow McGhee and felt as if she could dive right through them into his soul.

"It's Alexandra," she said, "but everyone calls me Lexie."

"Lexie," he said softly, nice name.

"Rainbow McGhee," he stated offering his hand, "dad was an Irish fur trapper and mom was a Cherokee Indian," he told her, "hence the name 'Rainbow,'" he added, but my friends call me Bo."

"Bo," whispered Lexie. "Can I call you Bo?" she asked, wanting to know him better.

"I insist," he said, shaking her hand gently. "Now we've been introduced," Bo said, "how about you show me around Lossiemouth?" he suggested" as my liaison officer, of course."

"As your Liaison Officer," Lexie said, forgetting all about her decision to avoid him and focus on her job, "how can I refuse?"

"How about Saturday then?" Bo asked, "if you're free, that is."

"I'm free," Lexie replied.

"Great," he said, "It's a date. 13.00 hours at the NAAFI." Bo released her hand and replaced his hat back on his head.

He stepped back, saluted and was gone.

Lexie stood staring into the darkness till the shadow of Bo McGhee disappeared.

What was happening to her? She'd thought she was immune to male attention since Robbie Robertson had broken her heart, but now...once again, she was flooded with desire for the irresistible Bo McGhee.

—-—oOo—-—

Chapter 23

Annie became aware of voices around her, that got louder as she came out of the blackness. Her sister-in-law Isobella Anderson was calling her name and her husband, John, was speaking quietly to Captain Millar.

One of the ARP men had known of the Anderson's relationship to Annie and had been despatched to bring them, at once, to Annie's house by Captain Millar, as soon as she had told him on the telephone that she was alone.

The news he had to give was not good and Annie was going to need someone with her.

"She's coming round," Isobella said, patting Annie's hand.

"Fetch her some water, John," she said, raising Annie's shoulders and helping her to sit up.

Annie's eyes gradually focused on the faces around her, before widening with fear as she remembered Captain Millar's news.

Euan was dead. The unexploded bomb that had been found in Baxters Park had been fitted with a timer and exploded before the bomb disposal unit could even begin to defuse it. Euan and two of the ARP men had been killed instantly.

Annie felt herself crumble again under the weight of her husband's death.

"Isobella," she whispered, her eyes begging, "tell me it's not true?"

Isobella held Annie closer. "Hush now," she said, softly, "John and me will look after you, just hold on Annie, hold on."

"Can you come to Maryfield Hospital?" the Captain asked John Anderson, "identification and all that," he said, quietly, "though the damage to his body is quite extensive, so it won't be easy, but his wife must be kept away from him till the Undertakers have done their work."

John nodded. "I'll follow you up to the hospital as soon as I can," he said, "let's take care of the living first," he added, compassion filling his soul at the sight of Annie lying stunned in Isobella's arms.

Euan, who'd been so strong and steadfast by Annie's side all these years now lay dead in Maryfield Morgue. John Anderson pulled on his Salvation Army great-coat and knelt down beside the two women.

"Annie," he said softly, wanting her to focus on what he was saying, "Isobella will look after you till I get back," he said, "I have to go to the hospital with Captain Millar...sort things out...and..." He watched as Annie nodded imperceptibly. He realised that she understood Euan was never coming back and for her, the future was now as bleak as the Scottish winter.

Isobella guided Annie to the sofa and wrapped a woollen blanket over her knees. "I'll get us some tea, Annie" she said, poking some life back into the coal fire, "I won't be a moment."

Isobella headed for the kitchen and Annie gazed at the flicker of flames that were beginning to reignite. The shock of loss had settled into her bones and muscles rendering them numb and useless, while her mind kept repeating Euan's name over and over, as if calling him to come home to her. But somewhere, in her heart, she knew he was gone and nothing would ever be the same again.

The wailing sound that came from Annie's mouth stopped Isobella in her tracks. She hurried through to the parlour. The dam of Annie's emotions had burst and she shook with sobs that wracked her body. Isobella wrapped her arms around her distraught sister-in-law, holding her in their safety till the weeping ebbed and Annie fell into an exhausted sleep.

Isobella eased Annie down onto the sofa and covered her with the blanket. Sleep was the best thing, she reasoned, letting Annie's body calm down to face tomorrow and all the rest of her days as a widow.

She put more coal on the fire and sat in the chair opposite. It was going to be a long night, but Isobella knew that she would be there for Annie no matter what, just as she had been by her side when John had deserted her with Mary and her brother had hanged himself, unable to handle the guilt of his cruelty to Annie.

There was a quiet knock on the door, rousing Isobella from her catnap. She looked at the clock, it had gone six and the first signs of dawn were creeping into the sky.

Billy Dawson stood, ashen faced in the dim light of the gas lamp in the stairwell. "I had to come," he said, lines of worry etched deep into his forehead. Isobella was never sure about Billy Dawson and his motives regarding Annie, but he'd always been a gentleman and Euan himself spoke highly of him.

"Annie's asleep in the parlour," she whispered, "you'd better come into the kitchen." Billy closed the door quietly and followed Isobella into the coldness of the kitchen.

"How is she?" he asked simply.

"Not good," Isobella said, "the shock of Euan's death has hit her hard."

Billy hung his head. "Me too," he said hoarsely, "he was a good man who loved his family very much...does Lexie and Ian know yet?" he asked suddenly, realising that Euan and Annie's son and step-daughter would have to be told.

Isobella shook her head. "John's at the hospital with Captain Millar of the bomb disposal unit, identifying Euan's body and dealing with the Undertakers, maybe he'll know more when he comes back, but Annie's in no fit state to tell them their dad is dead."

It would be up to Isobella and John to get in touch with Ian and Lexie, but it would be up to Billy to get in touch with his and Annie's son in Ireland, John Adams.

Billy stood to go. "If there's anything she needs, that I can help with, please let me know," he said, "anything at all."

"There's nothing," Annie said, tonelessly, appearing in the kitchen doorway, her eyes red with weeping and her face tight with sorrow. "He's gone," she said, looking at Billy directly, "why is it that the good end up dying while the cowards live on."

Was Annie referring to him, he wondered, remembering how he'd been branded a coward when he'd come back from the First World War, shell-shocked and broken and unable to fight anymore.

"I'm sorry, Annie," he said, pulling his bonnet down over one eye, "I'll leave you be now, but if there's anything..."

Annie stood aside as he left the kitchen.   She didn't want his sympathy, she didn't want anybody's sympathy, she just wanted the one thing she couldn't have, her husband.

Isobella re-boiled the kettle and sliced some bread for toast, all the time watching Annie from the corner of her eye.

"John will be back soon," she said, placing the cup of hot sweet tea in front of her sister-in-law, "then we can get some of your things together and you can come home with us."

"Home?" Annie said, looking around her, "this is home and this is where I'll stay."

Isobella knew this wasn't a time to insist she come with her and John.

"If that's what you wish Annie," she said, "then I'll stay too, just for a day or two."

She knew Lexie and Ian would have to be told of Euan's death today and hopefully, one or both of them would get compassionate leave and come home to be with their mother, at least till the funeral.

Isobella raised her eyes heavenward.   "Please God," she murmured, "help us all."

Chapter 24

Bo McGhee was waiting, impatiently, outside the NAAFI. He couldn't wait to see Lexie again and had thought of nothing else since his encounter with her after Johnny Johnson's dinner, when he'd followed her back to her Quarters.

She wasn't his usual type, he told himself, but there was something about her that seemed to draw him in, despite the war, despite her being Scottish and him Canadian, despite everything, Bo McGhee knew this slip of a girl in her WAAF uniform had stolen his heart.

As soon as he saw her in the distance, he almost ran towards her, taking her arm in his and steering her towards the camp gate. They both handed over their passes to the sentry and couldn't stop grinning at each other as they hurried down the road to Lossiemouth Harbour.

Lexie grew quiet as they neared the harbour wall, remembering the crashed Wellington Bomber and Henry Stockwood. It seemed wrong, somehow, that she should be the one being considered for a medal when Henry and the airmen were all dead and she was alive.

She gazed at the sunshine sparkling on the water and breathed in the peace of it all, once again, grateful that there was still peace to be found in the midst of so much suffering.

Bo McGhee's voice interrupted her thoughts. "Hey," he said turning her to face him, "what's wrong?"

Lexie couldn't just say there was nothing wrong and for the first time, she poured out all her feelings about the accident. Bo waited till she'd finished before taking her hand and leading her away from the harbour.

This girl was not only beautiful, she was also brave, Bo realised, a quality seldom found anywhere, but here it was in the shape of Lexie Melville and he loved her all the more.

Bo told her of his life in Moose Jaw and Lexie giggled at the name of his home town. "Moose Jaw!" she exclaimed, "what kind of a name is that for a town?" Bo joined in the banter. "What about Lossiemouth?" he asked, "what's a Lossie and why does its mouth get a mention?"

They both dissolved in fits of laughter, clinging to one another for support. "May I kiss you?" Bo suddenly asked, tipping Lexie's chin upwards with the tip of his finger. Lexie closed her eyes, she wanted nothing more than for Bo to kiss her, but instead of allowing herself to melt into the moment, she drew back, the old fear of trusting a man again, rearing up into her mind.

"I don't think that's the role of a Liaison Officer," she stammered, stepping away from the closeness of the man. Bo's eyebrows pulled together in a frown. "I'm sorry," he said, "I just thought...I'm sorry."

Lexie felt the chill of the North wind plucking at her hair. She wanted to say so much, to explain about Robbie Robertson, but the words wouldn't come.

"I guess we should be getting back," Bo said, struggling with the change in Lexie's mood. The walk back to the camp was taken in silence, each lost in their own thoughts and Lexie hating herself for letting the memory of Robbie Robertson's rejection still reverberate through her emotions.

"Are you alright?" Bo asked, as they stopped outside Lexie's Quarters.

"No, not really," Lexie replied, "but it's a long story and...I did want to kiss you Bo...I was just...scared, that's all."

Bo felt himself relax. So, there was something, but it wasn't him that was the problem, he was sure of that now.

"A heroine like you," he chided gently, "scared!"

Lexie blushed. "I'm not that brave," she said, "especially when it comes to kissing."

Without saying anything more, Bo pulled her towards him

and kissed her softly and tenderly on the lips. "There," he whispered, as she relaxed into him, "that's wasn't so bad was it?"

Lexie shook her head, "no," she said, trembling slightly "not bad at all."

"Does that mean you'll see me again?" Bo asked.

"Only if you want to see me again?" Lexie replied.

"Tomorrow then," Bo said, "same time same place?"

"I'll be here," Lexie smiled, everything was going to be alright, she told herself, Bo's kiss had broken through her defences and she couldn't wait to see him again.

It was early on Sunday morning that Lexie was summoned to Johnny Johnson's office. A surge of panic washed over her, surely no one had reported seeing her with Bo, she thought worriedly, they'd just gone for a walk after all and...the panic was followed by guilt at allowing Bo McGhee to kiss her and outside her Quarters at that.

She dressed as quickly as she could and presented herself at the Wing Commander's office.

"Sir," she saluted, "you sent for me?"

Lexie had never seen his face look more serious.

"Take a seat," he said, linking his fingers in front of him and levelling his eyes with hers.

"There's no easy way of saying this," he said almost to himself. He drew in a deep breath as Lexie became more anxious at what he was about to say to her.

"I have to tell you," he said, "I have received a telephone call from a Mr John Anderson in Dundee..."

Lexie frowned, why would John Anderson be telephoning the airbase?

"There has been an unfortunate accident and your stepfather, Euan MacPherson, has been killed."

Johnny Johnson continued with more words about the unexploded bomb but Lexie heard no more. "Euan's dead!" she heard herself say, disbelief in the words.

Lexie's whole body began to shake uncontrollably as she tried to stand up, but instantly fell back down again into the chair.

Johnny Johnson rushed round the side of his desk and called for assistance.

An ACW responded immediately and ran into the Wing Commander's office. She could see immediately that something was far wrong.

"Take ACW Melville to the sick bay," he said, "she's just had some sad news and the shock has affected her quite badly."

The ACW helped Lexie to her feet, slowly making for the door.

"When you've recovered from the shock" he said quietly to Lexie, "arrangements will be made to get you back to Dundee as quickly as possible."

The same doctor who had treated Lexie after the ditched bomber rescue attempt, guided her to a bed and administered a strong sedative, putting her into a deep sleep. Tomorrow would be time enough to deal with the journey she would have to make back home, but now, her body needed to rest.

Next day, Bo McGhee waited outside the NAAFI for Lexie to appear, getting more agitated as the minutes ticked by. Two o'clock came and went and airfield personnel who went into the NAAFI, then came out later, still found him pacing up and down outside.

By 3 o'clock, Bo gave up. Lexie had obviously changed her mind and he cursed himself for kissing her on their first date. He was muttering to himself as he made his way to Johnny Johnson's office to see if he knew where his 'Liaison Officer' was, then changed his mind before he got there. He didn't want to be seen to be 'checking up' on Lexie. If she didn't want to meet him again, then he'd just have to 'get over it.' His feet took him to the Officers Mess where he hoped to find solace in the company of his fellow pilots and a round of drinks, but nothing worked.

He headed back to his Quarters and wrote Lexie a letter, explaining how he felt and asking her to at least speak to him and let him know if she could give him a second chance. He'd put the letter in the camp's internal mail tomorrow, then all he could do was wait.

Lexie woke from her drugged sleep early the next morning,

her head ached and her throat felt bone dry. For a minute, she couldn't think why she was in the sick bay, then it all came back to her in a rush. Euan was dead.

She threw back the bed covers and was trying to stand up when a nurse ran towards her. "Hey, hey," she said, sitting Lexie down on the edge of the bed, "take your time dearie, there's an hour before the Doctor's on call, so just get back into bed and I'll fetch you a cup of tea."

Lexie knew there was no point in arguing and lay back down again, her mind reaching out to her mother, who she knew would be taking Euan's death very badly. If John Anderson had telephoned the base, then Isobella would be with her mum, she reasoned, pushing back the covers again, but it was she who should be there. She had to get out of here and back to Dundee as quickly as she could.

The nurse returned bringing a cup of tea and a glass of water.

She handed Lexie the glass of water and gave her two small, white pills from a brown bottle in her skirt pocket.

"Take these, dearie," she said, "then drink your tea. I've told the Doctor you're awake and he'll be with you directly."

"You don't understand," Lexie began anxiously, but the nurse stopped her from saying any more.

"I do understand," she said, kindly, "and you'll be going home soon enough, just save your energy for the journey."

Wing Commander Johnson, followed by the Doctor, came into the small Ward. "How are you feeling?" the Doctor asked, taking her pulse as he spoke.

"I need to get home," Lexie said, "there's been a death in the family..."

Johnny Johnson stepped forward. He handed Lexie a travel warrant and a Leave Pass. "The train is at 13.30 hours from Inverness Station. My driver will take you there and your Leave Pass is for seven days."

Lexie took the documents.

"Is she fit to travel?" the Wing Commander asked the Doctor.

"She'll do," he said, smiling at his patient. "Get some more sleep on the train," he counselled Lexie "and if it gets too much for you, take two of these." He handed Lexie the small brown bottle the nurse had brought "and do the best you can for your family," he added, sagely, "especially your mother."

It wasn't till she was on the train from Inverness to Perth, that she remembered her date with Bo. She looked at her watch, 14.00 hours. He'd be waiting for her at the NAAFI, not knowing what had happened and thinking she didn't want to see him again, but nothing could be done now and her duty was to her mum. If he loved her, Bo would understand, if he was still at Lossiemouth when she returned. The training on the Wellingtons would be over in a few days and he could be posted anywhere!

Lexie closed her eyes and tried to sleep, but couldn't, her mind was too busy looping from one dilemma to the next, none of which had any answers, while the train crawled onward toward Perth.

——-—oOo——-—

Chapter 25

Nancy opened her door to her father, her hair tousled and her eyes bleary with sleep.

"Dad!" she exclaimed, "it's 7 o'clock in the morning, what..?

The look on her father's face stopped her from asking anything further.

She helped him over the doorstep and sat him at the kitchen table.

He looked lost and hopeless as he stared at his hands. Nancy quickly got the kettle on and lit some newspaper and sticks in the grate to get a fire started and bring some heat into the room.

Nancy poured the tea and pushed a cup across the table to her father.

His eyes met hers. She'd never seen him look so bleak and her heart quickened. Something was terribly wrong.

"Is Josie alright?" she asked softly, "and the girls?"

Billy nodded and returned his eyes to the teacup.

"It's Annie," he said, so quietly that Nancy wasn't sure she'd heard right.

"Auntie Annie?" she asked, fearful of what she was about to hear.

"He's dead."

Nancy leant across the table and pulled his hand towards her. "Who's dead?"

Billy's eyes filled with tears. "Annie's husband."

Nancy let go of his hand and jumped up, panic now beginning to well in her heart. "What are you talking about?" she said loudly, "are you telling me that Euan is dead?" But the look on her father's face was enough to confirm the news.

Her hand flew to her neck as a wave of nausea hit and she rushed to the kitchen sink and vomited.

Billy watched in silence, till his daughter recovered and returned to the table, her face milky white.

"She wishes it had been me and not him who'd died in the blast."

He father was rambling with the shock, Nancy told herself, she had to find out from Annie herself what had happened to Euan.

Leaving her father sitting at the table, she went into the back room and roused the bairns. "Get dressed quickly" she said, "we need to go and see Auntie Annie at once."

Mary Anne quickly picked up on her mother's anxiety and helped wee Billy get his clothes on before pulling on her jumper and skirt.

When the trio returned to the kitchen, her father was gone.

"C'mon" she said, pouring out a glass of milk for each of them, "drink this then we'll get going. Breakfast can wait."

Dundee was still asleep as Nancy and the bairns silently hurried along Victoria Street before turning into Albert Street and Annie's close.

Isabella Anderson opened the door, a grim look on her face.

"Come in Nancy," she said, "I suppose you father's told you what's happened?"

Isabella ushered the bairns into the kitchen and sat them down to a plate of porridge each.

"I had been making it for Annie and me, but neither of us have an appetite."

"Is it true?" Nancy whispered, "about Euan?"

Isabella nodded. "Come through to the parlour, we don't want the bairns to be frightened."

Nancy followed her into the dim parlour. "Where's Auntie Annie?" she mouthed.

"Asleep in her bed," Isabella told her, "she's had the most dreadful shock." She went on to tell Nancy the horror of the bomb which had suddenly exploded, killing Euan and two ARP Wardens instantly.

Now she understood why her father was in such a state.

Nancy was too stunned to speak. Kind and thoughtful Euan, who'd helped her through the darkness of her husband's infidelity and made Billy see sense about marrying her when she was pregnant with their first child.

"Does Lexie and Ian know?" she asked, her voice still sounding unreal in her ears.

"John's phoned the RAF at Lossiemouth and Lexie's on her way, but Ian's somewhere in France and they can't get in touch with him yet." Isabella wiped a tear from her eyes. "It's all so bad," she said, almost to herself. Her eyes drifted skyward, searching for comfort from her God but finding none.

"Will you tell her I've been and I'll call again on Monday after work."

Isabella nodded. "She'd like that," she said, "we need to be strong for her just now," she added, "Euan was her life, especially since Lexie joined the WAAF."

Nancy gathered her brood together and hugged Isobella. "Thank God you're here," she whispered "and hopefully Lexie will be home soon."

During the walk home, Nancy couldn't get the enormity of Euan's death out of her head. Her Auntie Annie would be a widow now, with all the fears that situation would bring. Both Lexie and Ian were at war and just when Annie needed the strength of Euan around her, he'd been cruelly taken away from her. No wonder her father had been so upset for her. Fleetingly, she wondered if she should pay him a visit, make sure he got home alright, but Josie and the girls would be there to comfort him and she needed to get her own children home and settled before work began again next day at Baxters.

By evening, Nancy had time to herself and pondered about her own future, bringing up two, soon to be three, children without a husband. She wouldn't be able to work at the looms after the birth and with only Billy's money being paid to her by the Army, she realised that things were going to get much worse. And what if she became ill, she asked herself, a frisson of panic finding a space in her stomach, she remembered how ill she'd been after the birth of wee Billy and how she'd been totally dependent on her husband for months.

She now knew for certain that Jim Murphy wasn't going to be in her life as anything more than a bit of fun behind Jean's back, but the idea of sharing her husband with a prostitute hardened her heart again.

Like Annie, she realised angrily, she too was without her man.

John Anderson met Lexie at the railway station, the train had been over an hour late, but with the war on and shortages, this wasn't unusual.

He waved to Lexie to attract her attention and quickly took her holdall as he lead her to his motorcar.

"How is she?" Lexie asked, as John steered the motor along Union Street and into the Nethergate. "Isabella's with her," he said, "but seeing you, will be the best medicine she could have to help her recover."

Lexie watched as the streets and people blurred around her. She thought she'd left Dundee far behind her and was becoming a strong woman in her own right, but now, fate had decided that she return to her past and the future and Bo McGhee had been moved aside.

The sight of her daughter coming into the bedroom brought a tinge of colour to Annie's cheeks. "Lexie," she called out, "thank God you're here. He's gone, Lexie," Annie wailed, "Euan's gone."

Lexie rushed to her side. "It's alright," she said, tearfully, taking her mother's hand, "I'm here now, everything will be alright."

Isabella watched from the bedroom doorway. Poor Lexie, she thought, the war had given her a taste of the world outside Dundee and now, she would be expected to give it all up to look after Annie.

"Why don't we let Lexie have a rest now," Isabella counselled, "she's had a long journey and she must be exhausted."

Annie clung to Lexie like a drowning sailor to a life raft. "I understand," she murmured, unable to believe what Isabella was saying, she'd only just got her daughter back and Isabella was telling her to let her go again!

"Lexie needs to freshen up Annie," Isabella said, extricating Lexie from her mother's grasp. "And, we need to get into the kitchen and prepare her a hot meal."

Annie nodded. Making food for her family was what she was good at and Lexie would have missed her home cooking.

She let Lexie go and Isabella ushered her out of the bedroom, closing the door behind her. She pulled a chair up to Annie's bedside.

"You know me Annie," she began kindly, "and you know I wouldn't say this if I thought you weren't strong enough to hear it."

Annie's hands pulled the coverlet up to her neck and her eyes began to widen with fear.

"You need to understand that Lexie will only be home for a little while," she said, gently but firmly, then she'll have to go back to RAF Lossiemouth where she belongs."

Annie couldn't believe her ears. "She belongs here," she said, her voice gaining the strength of her conviction.

Isabella sighed. "I was afraid you'd say that," she said, "your daughter has a new life now Annie, and whether we like it or not, we can't ask her to return to the life she had in Dundee. That would be cruel and I know you're not cruel."

Annie felt a wave of self-pity envelop her. "But Euan's gone," she blurted "and I've got no one left but Lexie."

Isabella handed her a handkerchief. "Now, now Annie," she continued, "you've got John and me and Ian will be here as soon as he can and only today Nancy and the bairns came over to see if you needed anything..."

"Nancy?" Annie asked, "how did she know about Euan?"

"She said her father told her," Isabella explained, "he must have gone to see her after he left here this morning."

Billy's distressed face filled her heart as she remembered calling him a coward and wishing him dead instead of Euan. But she had to remind herself that he was the father of her first born son, John Adams and it wasn't he who had killed Euan, it was a horrible German bomb.

Annie pushed the covers aside. "I need to get up now," she said, "make Lexie's tea."

Isabella nodded. "I'll leave you to get dressed then my dear," she said, "we've been through some hard times together and we'll get through this."

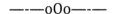

Chapter 26

The Courier had printed an Obituary on Euan's death and all who knew him had nothing but kind words to say about the policeman. He'd been part of their community for over thirty years and had helped many of them deal with the results of the drunkenness and domestic violence that beset their everyday lives, often offering a few well-chosen words of advice instead of marching the offender off to Bell Street Station.

The funeral had been arranged by John and Isabella and John himself would conduct the service in his role as Captain at the Salvation Army Hall.

As the days went by, Lexie began to realise that her mother wasn't going to insist on her returning to Dundee after all and she felt that Isabella had had a hand in the decision, as her mother kept referring to her sister-in-law needing her help with the war effort. Maybe her future could be returned to her after all and, along with it, Bo McGhee.

She looked at the telephone that had been installed by the Constabulary for contacting Euan in an emergency and thought of telephoning the camp. Maybe she could get word to Bo, tell him what had happened, but a knock at the door stopped her.

"Lexie!" Nancy exclaimed, "how are you?"

Nancy had come round straight from the mill and the smell of jute pervaded the lobby.

Memories of Baxters and her life back then, instantly filled Lexie's mind.

"Come in," she said smiling at her cousin, "mum's gone with Isabella for the messages, but they'll be back soon."

"How is she?" Nancy asked, draping her coat over a kitchen

chair and producing a packet of cigarettes and box of matches from her message bag. "Do you mind?" she asked, waving a cigarette in the air.

Lexie shrugged. It seemed that all women nowadays smoked, but it hadn't appealed to Lexie. "I'm sure mum won't mind," she said, filling the kettle, "I hope once the funeral is over, she'll begin to get back to some sort of normality."

Nancy blew smoke into the air. "What's normality," she said, meaningfully, wondering if Lexie knew about her pregnancy and also whether she would mention their encounter at the Palais, when she'd been clinging to Jim Murphy.

Lexie smiled and poured out their tea, producing the Biscuit Barrel with its Ginger Snaps.

"Did mum tell you I was pregnant?" she asked, dipping her biscuit in her tea.

Lexie's expression told Nancy the answer.

"I guess not," she said, "early days yet," she continued, "but I'm hoping it's born before the war ends and Billy's back home."

"Doesn't he know?" Lexie asked surprised at Nancy's words.

Nancy dipped another Ginger Snap into her tea. "They're about the only thing I can keep down," she said, popping the soggy biscuit into her mouth before answering Lexie's question.

"I suppose you've maybe guessed," she said, "having seen me at the Palais that time, that Billy and me aren't getting on, so, no, he doesn't know."

Surely, Nancy wasn't pregnant to another man!

"But it is his?" Lexie asked tactlessly.

Nancy frowned, "who else's would it be?" she asked feigning innocence.

Lexie felt her face redden. "No one else," she said hurriedly, "it's just that..." the words petered out.

"It's just that you saw me dancing with that bloke at the Palais and you put two and two together," she said, stubbing out her cigarette and picking up her coat to go.

Lexie felt terrible. "I'm so sorry Nancy," she said, her voice begging forgiveness, "I didn't mean..."

"It's my husband who's the adulterer," she added turning on

her heel, "ask anyone, him and Gladys Kelly are the talk of the Thrums Bar."

Nancy flounced out of the door, leaving Lexie shaken by the encounter. The last thing she had wanted was to hurt Nancy's feelings, she'd been counting on her to be of help to her mother once she returned to Lossiemouth. For her part, Nancy was pleased the way things had gone, now everyone would know that it was she who was the 'wronged party' and there would be no sympathy for Billy Donnelly, if and when he returned.

Lexie was still feeling guilty when her mother and Isabella returned with the messages. Euan's funeral was two days away and the wake was to be held at the Salvation Army Hall. Isabella had enlisted her fellow-salvationists to make tea and sandwiches for everyone who came back to the hall after the burial at the Eastern Cemetery. Lexie unloaded the shopping, such as it was, and decided now was not the time to broach the subject of Nancy and her pregnancy.

"Are you ready to go back to Lossiemouth?" Isabella asked, once Annie had left the kitchen to hang up her hat and coat and change her shoes. "I'm worried that you might feel it's your duty to stay," she added earnestly.

"I've thought about staying," Lexie said quietly, "but my life in the WAAF is what I want for the future, so, I will be going back to Lossiemouth."

"Good," said Isabella. "I know your mum, she's always been strong when faced with hard times and, with God's help, she'll cope again."

"And yours," Lexie said, smiling at her 'saviour', "without you here, I think I would have had to stay."

Annie came back into the kitchen. She was still looking shaken, but seemed to be taking Euan's death as 'God's will' and once the funeral was over, Lexie hoped her own departure would be bearable for them both.

The rain poured as the coffin was lowered into the grave. Six policemen from the Dundee Constabulary carried out the unhappy task and the rain masked many a tear from the crowd of Dundonians who had gathered to pay their last respects to the man who had been a friend to many and a loving husband and father. Lexie linked her mother's arm into her own as John Anderson conducted the burial service. She could feel her trembling with grief and, at that moment, wondered if she was doing the right thing in going back to Lossiemouth the next day. Her mother didn't feel as strong as Isabella had said.

The wake was attended by many, but the policemen had to return to their duties, as did the Air Raid Patrol men who had turned up to pay their respects. The Salvationists worked tirelessly serving tea and sandwiches and Annie stayed till everyone had gone home before her emotions took over and she wept in Lexie's ams.

Mother and daughter entered the empty house that held so many memories, both knowing that life would never be the same again.

Lexie saw her mother safely to bed, having given her the sedative the doctor at Lossiemouth had prescribed for her and tiptoed out of the bedroom, closing the door quietly behind her.

Tomorrow she would be leaving here and returning to Lossiemouth and Bo McGhee. The tears she had held back all day decided to flow as the loss of her lovely step-dad hit her. He wasn't her biological father, but he'd been her support and guide through the pain of Robbie Robertson and the breakup with Charlie Mathieson and had loved her as if she was his own.

Her head was telling her again to stay and look after her mum, but her heart was saying she needed to go back to Lossiemouth and hopefully, Bo McGhee, if he was still there and still wanting her.

The knock at the door brought her thoughts back to the present. Probably Isabella and John, checking if her mum was alright, she supposed. She brushed the tears away and blew her nose as she went to the front door.

The tall figure of an Army Officer stood before her. At first, she thought it was the Captain from the Bomb Squad, till she heard his voice.

"Hello, big sister," Ian MacPherson said, "can I come in?"

Lexie was stunned into silence. Ian had not been much more

than a boy when he'd left to enlist in the Army, but it was all too obvious, he had come back a man.

"IAN!" Lexie exclaimed. "You've made it." She threw herself into his arms, never so glad to see her 'little' brother in her life.

"Come in, come in," she whispered, signalling towards the kitchen door, "mum's sleeping."

Ian took off his peaked hat and undid his tunic, before heading for the cake tin.

Lexie almost laughed, no matter how much of a man Ian was now, he was still her little brother with the big appetite.

"Sit down," she said, "I'll get you some tea and, of course, a couple of mum's scones."

They sat across from one another at the table, each knowing what had happened and each worried about their mum.

"How is she?" Ian asked, leaving the tea and scones untouched.

"It was dad's funeral today," Lexie told him. "We tried to get in touch with you, but the Army said you were out of the country, but they'd try..."

Ian nodded, "I know, but I was in France and it was the French Resistance that got me to the coast and on a boat across to England."

Lexie realised how difficult it must have been for him to get here. She only had to get on a train from Inverness, but Ian had to risk his life to get back.

"How long have you got?" she asked.

"About another three more days," Ian said, "it took the first three days to get this far," he added, finally biting into his scone.

Mum will be so glad to see you," Lexie said, "especially as I have to leave tomorrow for Lossiemouth. I joined the WAAF a few months back and I'm stationed at RAF Lossiemouth, so was able to get here a bit faster."

"So, this is the only chance we've got to catch up?" he asked.

"I guess so," Lexie said, "I did consider leaving the WAAF and staying with mum, but Isabella talked me out of it." Why was she lying to her own brother, Isabella didn't need to talk her out of anything, she'd wanted to stay in the WAAF and enjoy her new life, especially now that Bo was in it. But Ian was no fool. He too had now experienced the world outside Dundee and had also found love in the shape of an English girl from Carlisle, who was a school teacher there. "And Isabella is right. The war has given us both a chance to see other places, meet new people and find another way of living." He leant across the table and grasped Lexie's hands in his. "I'll be here for a few more days and I'll look after mum, just like she looked after us and I'm sure Isabella and John will help her face the future without dad," Lexie relaxed, the guilt that she'd felt ebbing away."I know we don't say it often enough," she said, her eyes glistening with tenderness, "but I love you, my wee brother."I love you too, big sister," Ian replied, "and everything will be fine," he added, "just wait and see."

———oOo———

Chapter 27

Ian was as good as his word and made sure their mum was alright as they waved her off at the Railway Station, making Lexie's departure bearable. She settled herself into her seat for the return journey to Lossiemouth and promised herself she would write to her mother every week.

The train crawled through the landscape and it was dark before it pulled into Inverness. A small RAF truck was waiting for her to take her the rest of the journey and Lexie wanted nothing more than to get to her Quarters and her bed. Her heart dropped when she saw ACW Jenny McKenzie was the driver. She'd kept her very much at arm's length since finding out about her sexual 'preferences' but now they'd be side by side in the truck for the next three hours.

Jenny McKenzie saluted Lexie and opened the truck door for her to get in. Silently, Lexie returned the salute and settled herself into the passenger seat, folding her arms and closing her eyes. There would be no 'pally' conversation on the drive back to RAF Lossiemouth.

But Jenny had other ideas. She'd taken Lexie's rejection badly and was now going to get her revenge.

The camp had been abuzz with gossip about Bo McGhee keeping trying to find out where Lexie was, but with no luck, but Jenny had kept her ear to the ground and found out that the Canadian Pilots had been posted to RAF Montrose, to increase the bomber power there in the attack on Stavanger. And Captain McGhee was one of them.

Jenny smiled to herself, as she glanced at the closed eyes of Lexie. She coughed loudly and Lexie blinked her eyes open.

"Are you alright? Lexie asked, not really caring.

"Sorry," Jenny replied, "I was just thinking that a lot has changed since you went home."

Lexie bristled. "Hardly a holiday," she said crossly, "it was compassionate leave to attend a funeral." She closed her eyes again.

Now it was Jenny's turn to bristle as she dropped the bomb shell into the silence.

"Sorry," she said, "it's just that the Canadian Pilots have been posted elsewhere, now the training is over," she said smugly, so the WAAFs' are all a bit dejected and what with snow forecast, RAF Lossiemouth is not a happy base."

Lexie couldn't believe her ears. She'd only been gone a week and had longed to see Bo again, but to find out that he had been posted somewhere else was news she didn't want to hear."

"Posted where?" she asked tightly.

"Don't know," Jenny lied, relishing Lexie's discomfort. She'd have to yearn for her Canadian Pilot, just as Jenny had yearned for her.

Right on time, the snow started falling making the journey even slower, but Lexie managed to keep the tears from falling till she was safely back in her Quarters. Was she fated never to have love in her life again? Was love, for her, always going to have to end in tears? With these unhappy thoughts running around her mind, Lexie fell into an exhausted sleep.

Sgt Brady was as handsome as ever when she reported for duty next morning, but even the sight of him didn't bring a smile to her face. He noted Lexie's heavy eyes and put it down to the grief she was suffering from the loss of her step-father and in Sgt Brady's experience, there was only one antidote for unhappiness and that was hard work.

"There's a stack of paperwork to be sorted before you take over your shift on the Teleprinter," he said firmly, "and while you're at it, check our Internal Mail, it's not been looked at for a week."

Lexie saluted, her training forcing her to react immediately to an order from a superior officer. "Yes, sir!" she said, picking up the wire basket full to over-flowing with the documentation necessary for the running of an efficient Comms Room.

Despite herself, Lexie began to feel more relaxed as the demands of the work took her mind away from her own problems and focussed it back on the tasks in front of her.

Even Jenny McKenzie, who had hoped she'd upset Lexie with the news about the Canadian Pilots departure, was huffed to see her just getting on with the job.

Lexie had forgotten all about the Internal Mail and it wasn't till the end of her shift that she eventually got round to going to the Mail Office. There were the usual leaflets and general information for the Comms Room, but when she checked her own pigeon hole, there were three letters for her, two with stamps on them and one that had been dropped off. She popped them in her handbag and headed for the NAAFI. Lexie hadn't eaten since a breakfast of tea and toast in the Mess but maybe something more appetising to eat would help settle her grumbling stomach.

Lucy Ashford was sitting alone, pushing some mashed potato round the plate with her fork. Since her promotion to Corporal, Lexie had had to step back a bit from her friendship with Lucy, but right now, they were both off-duty and like Lexie, Lucy looked like she needed a friend.

"Mind if I join you?" she asked.

"I'd like that," Lucy said flatly, "and don't get the sausages, they taste like sawdust," she added, putting down her fork and picking up her cup of tea. "I won't" Lexie replied, looping her bag and gas mask over the back of the chair. "Be back in a jiffy'" she said, heading for the food counter and wondering why Lucy's usual cheeriness had deserted her. She didn't have long to wait to find out.

"Men," Lucy said, her arms crossed in front of her and a faraway look in her eye. Lexie waited, biting into a forkful of Fish Pie.

"Why do they always have to leave you, just when you get to...well, like them?" she said, more to herself than Lexie.

"Who's left you?" Lexie asked, immediately likening Lucy's situation to her own.

Lucy sighed. "His name is Brad Hollis," she said, "Pilot Officer Brad Hollis to be exact, Royal Canadian Air Force."

Lexie almost dropped her fork. Lucy must know what had happened and maybe even where they'd been posted.

She held her breath. "Where has he gone then?"

Lucy looked at her, suddenly remembering about Lexie's home leave. "Of course," she said, "you wouldn't know what's been happening you weren't in the Comms Room last week."

Lexie nodded, Bo McGhee once again foremost in her mind.

"Our favourite 'Lesbian' was on duty and word came through that the Canadians were needed at RAF Montrose, now their training was finished and just the day before the NAAFI dance when Brad Hollis and me were going to meet up." Lucy sighed again.

So, that was where Bo was, MONTROSE. Still in Scotland but he might as well have been on the moon, Lexie vexed and he'd still believe that she'd stood him up.

Lexie could empathise with Lucy, they'd both found and then lost the chance of finding love. "Fancy a beer?" Lexie asked, "drown your sorrows?"

Lucy grimaced. "There's not enough beer in the world," she said pushing back her chair and gathering her things together, "so, thanks, but no thanks."

Lexie was looking around her, hoping to find a reason to stay and avoid going back to her quarters, when she remembered the letters in her handbag and pulled them out.

She started with the unstamped envelope. Probably another camp leaflet about the joys of the forthcoming NAAFI activities, but Lexie could hardly believe her eyes when she read the letter. It was from Bo!

Dear Lexie

I don't know why you chose not to meet me, but it was perhaps that I kissed you on our first date and you didn't want to repeat the experience. I can't say how sorry I am that I've offended you, but if you can find it in your heart to give me a second chance, I promise I will be the perfect gentleman.

I await your response with hope and forgiveness.

Lexie read the letter again, tears of relief forming in her eyes.

"He does care" she whispered out loud and was now more determined than ever to find a way to reach him.

Sgt Brady smiled at the change in Lexie the next day when she reported for duty, confirming his 'work-theory' had been responsible.

"Feeling better?" he asked in a rare breach of the formality that was his usual approach.

Lexie saluted. "Yes, sir," she said briskly, "reporting for duty."

Sgt Brady saluted in return and immediately got back to business.

"Sit down," he said, pushing a sheet of paper towards her marked TOP SECRET in red ink.

'There is to be increased coastal sweeps off the Norwegian Coast targeting shipping in the North Sea carrying supplies to the German Army via ports in Norway. Due to heavy losses experienced by Bomber Command, especially Blenheims, all personnel and bomber aircraft at RAF Lossiemouth, not required to meet immediate needs, are to be posted to RAF Montrose.'

Sgt Brady took back the order. "This was received the day you left the base and during your absence, two squadrons and twelve Wellington Bombers, along with the newly-trained Canadians have been sent to Montrose."

Lexie nodded, so that's what happened, she thought, fear building in her system at the thought of the danger Bo and the other pilots would have to face over the North Sea.

"The weather here is only going to get worse, but RAF Montrose has more chance of getting our bombers off the ground. The long-range forecast for the next four weeks for Lossiemouth is snow, snow and more snow, so it looks like we'll all be grounded for a while."

Sgt Brady handed Lexie another sheet of paper. "I want you to be in charge of monitoring activities at Montrose and keep me up to date with how our personnel are faring, number of sorties, any loss of aircraft etc."

"Are these the codes for Montrose?" Lexie asked, recognising the sequence of numbers required to be entered into the

Teleprinter before sending a transmission.

"They are," replied Sgt Brady and I don't want anyone else in the Comms Room getting access to them. There's been some leaks of information lately and I don't want there to be anymore," he said, firmly.

"Your contact at Montrose is ACW Winifred Adams. Make sure she's on duty before you begin your transmissions."

Lexie could hardly believe her ears. WINNIE, her friend from

RAF Wilmslow was now based at RAF Montrose! The last she'd heard, Winnie had been sent to Swindon to be trained to drive trucks?

"Sir," Lexie stood and saluted, "I'll get on to it right away," she said, "and I'll make sure there are no leaks coming from the Comms Room."

Jenny McKenzie would be watched very closely.

———oOo———-

Chapter 28

Nancy's morning sickness had begun to ease, along with her mind, now that Lexie knew that Billy was indeed the father of her baby and an adulterer to boot. She decided to visit her Auntie Annie again soon and make sure she had her support in the months to come, so it would come as no surprise when she rejected Billy's 'fatherly' rights to the bairn and with that, his conjugal ones.

Time was a great healer and Nancy was sure she was getting over her infatuation with Jim Murphy en, late one evening, there was a knock at her door.

"What do you want at this time of night?" she demanded to know, from a forlorn-looking Jim Murphy.

"It's Jean," he said, shuffling his feet and averting Nancy's eyes, she's thrown me out!"

Nancy almost laughed. A few weeks ago she would have welcomed him into her house with open arms, but now, things had changed.

She placed her hands on her hips. "Hard luck," she said, "try some other door, this one's closed." His eyes searched hers for understanding.

"I know I don't deserve help," he said, pleadingly, "but I've nowhere else to go and you did love me...once."

"More fool me," Nancy retorted, but wondered at the same time, if she should dismiss Jim Murphy so readily. She did love him once, but that's when he was with Jean, but now...the balance of power had changed.

"One night," she said decisively, "you can stay for one night only, but then you're out."

"Thanks Nancy, "Jim said, as he stepped over the threshold, cap in hand. Jean had made no bones about where her husband now stood.

As long as the neighbours were unaware of his shenanigans, she could believe he was faithful, but when a whore like Gladys Kelly had whispered in her ear that Nancy Donnelly had been 'entertaining' her man while Billy was away at war, that was the final straw.

Nancy didn't offer Jim her usual hospitality to visitors and the kettle remained cold on the stove.

"Well," she said, "what happened?"

"Someone told Jean that I'd been calling...on you."

"Someone?"

Jim shrugged. "I don't know who told her," he said, "maybe one of your neighbours saw me leaving and put two and two together..."

This wasn't good. If Jean knew, Nancy could be sure that the rest of Baxters would know before the week was out. The ace card that she was holding over Billy being an adulterer suddenly vanished. She would be seen as bad as her husband and could expect no sympathy from the other women in her world. She needed to think this new development through and any ideas of Jim Murphy sharing her bed, 'for old-time's sake' were gone.

"You can sleep on the floor," Nancy said tight-lipped "and don't be here in the morning."

She swept from the room. Tonight she would share a bed with Mary Anne in the back room and try to figure out her next move.

Jim had gone when she woke next morning and once she'd made a pot of porridge for the bairns, she set off for work, maybe Di would know what to do.

Nancy felt as if all eyes were looking at her as she walked into the weaving flat. She signalled to Di that they needed to speak later and as soon as the 'bummer' sounded for the 12 o'clock break, she hurried over to Di's looms.

"You look worried," Di said, biting into her cheese roll and waiting for the latest news on Nancy's love-life.

"Jean's thrown him out," she started, "but that's not the worst of it."

Nancy took a deep breath. "Someone's told her that me and Jim were having it off."

Di stopped eating. "Who?"

"If I knew that, I'd know what to do to put a stop to the gossip, but we were careful, so I can't think who it can be who saw him at the house."

"Well, it wasn't me," Di said forcefully, "if that's what you think."

Nancy pursed her lips. "I know it wasn't you," she said, "I think someone maybe saw us at the Palais and made up the rest..." but even as she said it, she remembered, Lexie Melville saw her and Jim together.

Nancy's blood ran cold. If she'd told Auntie Annie about what she saw, then she might have told others and...It didn't take a stretch of the imagination for Nancy to fear that one of Annie's Salvation Army friends would find out it was Jim Murphy and feel it their duty to let Jean know what her husband was up to.

She had to see her Auntie Annie and fast. Saturday couldn't come quickly enough and with two freshly-scrubbed bairns in tow, Nancy made her way to Annie's door.

As soon as Annie opened the door, Nancy could see that she was still far from her usual self, her pale skin and red eyes indicating that sleep hadn't come easily last night.

"How are things?" Nancy asked, quietly, parking Mary Anne and wee Billy on two of the kitchen chairs and feeling guilty about intruding on her Aunt's grief. She'd have to tread carefully.

"Oh, you know," Annie said, "getting by."

She filled the kettle and put some bread under the grill to toast for the bairns. "There are no sweeties, I'm afraid," she said to them, "Auntie Annie hasn't gone for the messages yet."

"Mary Anne can run the messages for you," Nancy said quickly, "she's a proper little shopper and wee Billy can help her carry things." The two children smiled encouragingly, Mary Anne being especially anxious to show off her prowess at going the messages.

Annie glanced at Nancy. She wasn't in the mood to face the shops and took down the message list from behind the kitchen clock.

"Are you sure?" she asked Mary Anne, who nodded vigorously.

Annie handed her the shopping basket and a purse with enough money to cover the cost of the groceries.

"Careful crossing the road now," Annie said, "and there'll be sixpence for each of you when you get back."

Nancy turned the bread under the grill and poured the boiling water into the teapot.

"Sit down Auntie Annie," she said, pulling out a chair and we'll have some tea and toast. That always makes things better."

Annie managed a weak smile, breakfast with Euan had always been the best way to start her day. Just seeing him sitting there with his newspaper and cup of tea, had always made Annie feel secure, but now, he was gone. She felt her eyes moisten and blinked it away.

"That'd be lovely, Nancy," she said, "and thanks for letting Mary Anne go for the messages, although I'm sure Isabella would have helped when she got here."

"Isabella?" Nancy asked, worriedly, "is she coming over today?"

Nancy had wanted to find out if Annie knew about Jim Murphy before having to confront the Salvationist. "Not till this afternoon," Annie continued, "so it's nice to have company twice in the same day."

Nancy breathed a sigh of relief and spread some margarine on her toast.

"How's Lexie?" she asked, bringing Annie's daughter into the conversation.

Annie's voice softened to a whisper, "oh, she's had to go back to Lossiemouth, to the WAAF you know, she's been put forward to get an Empire Medal for bravery," Annie continued, her voice becoming stronger as her pride in Lexie surfaced.

"Oh yes!" Nancy exclaimed, "the rescue attempt, we read about it in the Courier. You must be very proud."

Annie smiled and managed to swallow some toast.

The pair ate their breakfast in silence till Nancy broached the subject of Lexie again.

"Is Lexie still friends with Sarah Dawson?" she asked.

"I think so," Annie replied, "but there wasn't much time to catch up with friends this time, what with the funeral..."

Nancy tried again.

"I'm sure I saw the both of them one evening when she was home on leave before...this last time..." Nancy said cautiously, "I think she was just coming to the end of her WAAF training."

Annie tried to remember the time scale before Euan died, but it was all a bit of a blur.

"You'd have to ask Sarah to make sure," Annie said, "I can't remember exactly when she was here before."

Nancy relaxed. Lexie couldn't have said anything to her mother about seeing her with Jim in the Palais that Saturday, but this was replaced with a new worry. If it wasn't Lexie who told Jean Murphy, then who was it?

"How's your pregnancy going?" Annie asked, refocusing her mind away from Euan and Lexie.

"The morning sickness has stopped," Nancy said, "so that's a blessing, but I suppose as things go on, it'll get harder to keep at the looms."

Annie nodded, she remembered the problems Nancy had after the birth of wee Billy. "Will Billy be able to come home when the bairn's born?" she asked, "he's probably a bit worried about you coping with it all."

Nancy took her chance and dropped her own bombshell.

"He doesn't know," she said, "we parted badly when he went back to his regiment last time and I don't know if the marriage can be mended."

Annie sat back in shock. "Doesn't know!" she exclaimed, "but surely he has to know that he's going to be a father again?"

Nancy hung her head. "It's not that simple," she said "after wee Billy was born, I found out he'd been visiting a prostitute called Gladys Kelly. I was too ill to be a 'proper' wife he said, so what did I expect," she lied, making Billy sound as bad as she could.

"Nancy," Annie said, the word heavy with compassion for her niece, "you should have told your dad, he would have sorted Billy out."

Nancy shrugged, ignoring the comment.

"We've been trying to make it work for years now, but since the war started, things have got worse and that night you and Euan babysat for us to have a night out at the Palais and I came back alone..."

"I remember," Annie said.

"He'd gone to say 'goodbye' to HER, rather than spend his last night with me."

"Oh! Nancy." Annie felt her heart break for Mary's daughter, how like her mother she was, always needing the attention of a man to make her feel good about herself.

Annie felt helpless to do anything for her niece and she feared for the future of them all.

The murmur of small voices interrupted the gravity of the news, as Mary Anne and wee Billy came bustling into the kitchen, the basket laden with the shopping and wee Billy carrying a brown paper bag full of potatoes.

Both Nancy and Annie forced a smile to their lips.

"Well," Annie began, "what a clever girl you are Mary Anne and wee Billy, how strong you've got, carrying all those heavy potatoes."

The bairns beamed as Annie took back the purse with the change in it, extracting two sixpences, one for each of them.

Nancy stood up and placed an arm round each child.

"We'd better be going Auntie Annie," Nancy said, "I've my own messages to get and you're expecting Isabella later, so you'll need time to get things ready."

Annie escorted the little family to the door. "Now remember, if you need my help," she whispered, "you just have to let me know."

Nancy nodded. "Thanks, Auntie Annie, I'll remember."

Annie closed the door behind them with a sigh. Billy Donnelly should know what he's done, she surmised, but someone closer to home needed to know as well, Nancy's father, Billy Dawson.

Chapter 29

Lexie keyed in the special codes for Winnie's teleprinter at RAF Montrose, given to her by Sgt Brady. If Winnie was on duty she'd return the call confirming it.

The teleprinter clattered into life.

RAF MONTROSE

READY TO RECEIVE TRANSMISSION FROM RAF LOSSIEMOUTH.

ACW ADAMS

Lexie grinned. Winnie was in for a surprise.

RAF LOSSIEMOUTH

UPDATED INFORMATION ON LOSSIEMOUTH PERSONNEL AND WELLINGTON BOMBER SORTEES REQUIRED ASAP. AWAIT REPLY.

CORPORAL MELVILLE

Lexie didn't have long to wait. Winnie came through with the information almost immediately.

RAF MONTROSE

FOUR SORTEES IN PAST SEVEN DAYS.

NO CASUALTIES.

ALL RAF LOSSIEMOUTH PESONNEL PRESENT AND CORRECT.

ACW ADAMS

So, all was well at Montrose, Bo was safe and now Lexie would find out if anything happened to him in the future. She now had two more letters to write tonight, one to Winnie and one, very special one, to Bo.

Once her shift had finished, Lexie headed for her Quarters, she'd first write to her mother and ask her if Nancy had been in touch and depending on her mother's reply, she'd know if Nancy had told her about the pregnancy and her intention to have the baby without its father knowing.

Lexie had never cared much for Nancy, especially when she'd fallen pregnant with Mary Anne out of wedlock. Lexie had been horrified at Nancy being a 'fallen woman,' but Billy Donnelly had eventually done the decent thing. Everyone always seemed so concerned for Nancy, Lexie remembered, especially her own mother and it looked like history was repeating itself, a pregnant Nancy without a husband again.

The letter home to her mother was most difficult, Lexie had left so soon after the funeral that she wasn't sure how much to say about Euan's death, so decided instead to keep things simple. 'She'd returned to base safe and well and hoped that Ian, along with Isabella and Nancy had helped her to cope. The weather was terrible, snowing heavily but hopefully, things would ease by Christmas.' Lexie signed with love and put the letter in an envelope ready for posting.

She did not to seal the envelope, as although it was benign, she knew
the contents would be checked for any information that may give a clue to the enemy about aircraft numbers or personnel movements.

The letter to Winnie was, therefore, also difficult. Their teleprinter communications were top secret, so any reference to them would cause both of them trouble. Lexie kept the letter short.

Dear Winnie

Hope things are well now you are home and hope we can get together soon. Sadly, Euan died two weeks ago but mum is coping well.

Let me know how you are, if you can and look forward to hearing from you by return post.

Lexie

This letter too was put into an unsealed envelope before Lexie turned her full attention to writing to Bo.

Dear Bo

Thank you for your letter, just received. Apology accepted, but no need, as not the reason for my disappearance. My step-father died suddenly and I went home to be with my mother. Back now.

Till we meet again,

Lexie

Lexie read the letter over and hoped Bo would be able to read between the lines and know that she was as disappointed as he was that their meeting didn't happen.

Lexie handed her letters into the Mail Room and hoped that they would be delivered uncensored, especially the one to Bo and that there would be a window in the weather to allow an aircraft to take off and fly the mail out.

But, the weather was relentless and all aircraft were grounded, so Lexie had to depend on information from Winnie at Montrose to know what was happening with the sortees over the North Sea and subsequently with Bo.

Work in the Comms Room continued unabated despite everyone having to take on snow clearing duties to keep the path to the door clear and Lexie was surprised to be summoned to Wing Commander Johnny Johnson's office at once. She ditched her shovel and headed to the camp offices, tidying herself as best she could before presenting herself to the Wing Commander.

"Corporal Melville," the Wing Commander said, acknowledging Lexie's salute, "sit down Corporal, I have news for you."

Lexie held her breath. "I've received a letter from the War Office in London, confirming that you are to receive the Empire Medal for bravery and you are to present yourself at Holyrood Palace in Edinburgh on the 17th December to receive the honour." Johnny Johnson looked up and smiled at her.

The Empire Medal! Lexie had almost forgotten about it, but now, they wanted her to go to Edinburgh to be presented with it.

"I don't know what to say," she said, stunned at the thought of being awarded the medal and also going to Edinburgh, a place she'd never been before.

"No need to say anything," Johnny Johnson said, "just know that the WAAF and the RAF are very proud of you." He handed Lexie a travel warrant and the letter. "You've got a few days to get ready for the journey and I'm told the weather is set to improve, so there shouldn't be any problem on the railway," he told her, standing up and extending his hand. "Safe journey," he said, "and well done Corporal Melville."

Lexie went back to the Comms Room in a daze. She'd have something to write home about now.

"You look pleased with yourself," Sgt Brady said as Lexie reported back to him, "all this snow clearing must suit you."

"I'm going to Edinburgh," she said, almost in a whisper, "to collect my Empire Medal at Holyrood Palace."

She held the travel documents up in front of the sergeant, "on the 17th of this month."

Sgt Brady nodded. "Well done," he said, cordially, "nice work if you can get it."

Lexie grinned and shook her head. "If I'm dreaming," she said, "don't wake me up."

But Lexie wasn't dreaming and on the 16th of December, she set off on the journey of a lifetime. As before, an RAF truck took her to Inverness Station where she boarded the train South to Perth. There she would transfer to the train bound for Waverley Station and Edinburgh.

How life had changed for her, Lexie thought, as the miles rolled by, her confidence in herself as a desirable woman that had been knocked by Robbie Robertson, had returned since meeting Bo and the knowledge that she was doing her bit for King and country, filled her with pride. Growing up in Dundee had bred in her a strong sense of how to deal with adversity, which had stood her in good stead, but nothing had prepared her for being a medal winner and the attention that would bring. She hoped she wouldn't make a fool of herself in Scotland's capital and especially not at Holyrood Palace.

The first thing that assailed Lexie's ears was the noise and bustle of Edinburgh, as she emerged from Waverley Station. Despite being used to the roar of the aircraft taking off at Lossiemouth, the noise of the city was difficult to pinpoint. It seemed to be everywhere, with uniformed men and women mixing with civilians as they hurried about their business. The small hotel that had been booked for Lexie was in a street off Princes Street and, to her surprise, she found it easily.

With relief, she dumped her travel bag on a chair and flopped down on the single bed. The room was small but there was a tiny sink where she could wash and, although the windows rattled when the wind blew, nothing would stop her sleeping tonight, the train journey had seen to that.

She checked her watch. 19.00 hours, no wonder her stomach was rumbling. A quick sandwich somewhere and then back to bed was the order of the day. Lexie headed out into the bustle of Rose Street.

She stopped a couple in the passing to ask where she could find somewhere to eat. "Everywhere," said the woman, looking up and down the long street, before they moved on.

Lexie shrugged and went through the door of the nearest eating place. There was a bar down one side and a few tables set out for eating down the other. She approached the barman. "Can I get something to eat here?" she asked, raising her voice to be heard over the noise of the drinkers at the bar.

"There's soup and a cheese roll," he said, looking around him, "if you want to take a seat somewhere, I bring them over to you when I get the chance."

Lexie nodded and scanned the tables for a seat in the busy eatery, finally spying one at a corner table at the back of the room.

There was a man sitting with his back to her at the table, eating a roll with his pint of beer.

Lexie tapped him on the shoulder. "Do you mind if I sit here?" she said, sitting down before he could refuse her and unbuttoning her RAF coat.

For a second, Lexie could only stare in disbelief as Captain Rainbow McGhee stared back at her.

"BO!" she exclaimed, her voice trembling with joy, "is it really you?"

"Lexie," Bo whispered, standing up and pulling her to her feet before wrapping his arms around her. "Don't say a word, just let me hold you."

Lexie closed her eyes and clung onto Bo, terrified that if she opened them he'd disappear.

A discreet cough from the bartender told them that Lexie's meal was waiting to be served.

"One soup, one cheese roll," he said, depositing the food on the table, but Bo and Lexie were oblivious of everything and only had eyes for one another. The barman shook his head, smiling to himself, "young love," he said, "you canna beat it."

When Bo finally released Lexie back to her seat, the meal was forgotten as they both silently thanked fate for bringing them together again.

"Did you get my letter?" Bo asked anxiously, as his heart raced in his body. Lexie nodded, "but by the time I'd got it you'd already gone, so I couldn't let you know what had happened."

"What happened?" Bo asked, "you just disappeared and no one seemed to know where you were."

Lexie leaned forward. "My step-dad died," she whispered, an unexploded bomb in the park near where we live." She leaned back, "Wing Commander Johnson gave me compassionate leave and I got the first train out of Inverness..."

Bo took her hands in his. "You poor darling," he said, "but why are you here, in Edinburgh?"

Lexie felt herself blush. "I'm here to be presented with my Empire Medal" she giggled, "at Holyrood Palace, tomorrow."

"Bo gasped in surprise. "Well," he said, "you clever little thing."

"Thank you kind sir," Lexie said coquettishly.

"Can I come and watch?" Bo asked, "I'm on R & R till Monday."

So that was why Bo was in Edinburgh, Lexie realised, he must have been flying quite a few of the sorties over the North Sea, to be given some Rest & Recuperation so soon.

"You're not hurt are you?" she asked, suddenly worried that he'd been in a scrap with the Lufwaffe.

"Nothing you can't mend," he murmured, looking round the crowded room. "Let's take a walk," he said, "find somewhere we can be alone."

Bo didn't have to ask twice. "I know just the place," Lexie said, "and it's not far from here."

They crept up the stairs of the small hotel leading to Lexie's room.

"It's not very big," she said, indicating the size, "but at least we can be alone."

Lexie kicked off her shoes and draped her WAAF coat over a chair before turning to face Bo. "I don't want to lose you ever again," she said softly "and I think I owe you a kiss."

All Lexie's fear of intimacy was gone, replaced by an overpowering desire to make love to Rainbow McGhee.

"I think you may be right," Bo whispered into her hair as his lips found hers. Nothing else in the world mattered any more, there was just the two of them and their love for one another.

"When this war is over Lexie, will you come to Canada...with me?"

Lexie snuggled down beside him in the little bed, all inhibitions lying on the floor along with their clothes. "I'll go anywhere in the world with you Bo, as long as we're together, that's all that matters."

"I was hoping you'd say that," he whispered, "because I'm never going to let you go. I love you Lexie Melville."

Lexie could feel tears blurring her vision. "And I love you too Rainbow McGhee," she said, safe at last in his strong arms.

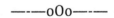

——-—oOo——-—

Chapter 30

Billy was busy in Baxters General Office when he got the message. As Works Manager, he was responsible for making sure the mill was kept running at full capacity.

"What is it?" he said sharply to the Lodge Keeper, "you know I don't like interruptions on Friday."

The Lodge Keeper took a step back and tipped the edge of his bonnet.

"Sorry Mr Dawson, but the lady says it's important that she sees you."

"Lady?" Billy queried, impatiently, "what lady?"

"She says her name's Mrs Melville and she needs to speak with you."

Annie was here and wanted to speak with him?

Billy rolled down his shirt sleeves and reached for his jacket.

"Show her into my office in five minutes," he told the Lodge Keeper, his voice losing its edge "and ask Joanie to fetch us some tea."

"Rigt-e-o Sir," the man said, sourly, "I'll do that right away."

Billy hurried to his office, a mixture of panic and longing to see Annie, filling his soul.

He forced himself to stand up from his seat behind the desk, on legs that seemed unable to support him as he waited. He could see the blurred shape of Annie through the frosted glass panel in the door and he felt his jaw muscles tighten as she knocked.

"Come in Annie," he called hoarsely, "the door's open."

The brass knob turned, the door swung open and the sight of her almost brought tears to his eyes. The grief since Euan's death had left its mark, dark shadows were evident under her eyes and deep lines had formed around her lips. But her blue eyes still drew him in, as she attempted a small smile.

"May I sit down?" Annie asked, quietly, "I tire easily these days."

Billie hurried round the side of the desk and eased her into the facing chair. He opened his office door and called to Joanie, the Office Administrator who was trying to fill Lexie's shoes since she'd gone to join the WAAF's, but with little success.

"Is that tea nearly ready?"

"Just coming Mr Dawson," Joanie called back, walking slowly towards him with the tray of tea things.

"Here" Billy said as she got to the office door, "give that to me and make sure I'm not disturbed...for anything."

He placed the tray on his desk, pushing aside papers and his diary.

"Is it still milk and one sugar?" he asked, pouring out the hot liquid.

Annie nodded and accepted the cup gratefully.

She'd come to him for help, Billy was sure of that, but perhaps, just perhaps, she needed him too. Billy lit a cigarette and waited, watching as the hot tea brought some colour to Annie's cheeks.

"What is it Annie?" he finally asked, unable to bear the suspense any longer, "you know I'll do anything I can to help you."

Annie put down her cup and took a deep breath. "I've had a visit from your daughter," she said, "Nancy."

Billy flinched. "She's alright isn't she?"

"I hope so," Annie replied before telling him of the reason for her visit.

"Did you know she was pregnant?" she said, hoping that he did.

By Billy's reaction, it was obvious he didn't.

The last time he'd spoken with Euan was to be told that he'd followed Nancy and a man back to Victoria Road at the end of an evening's dancing at the Palais and the pair had gone together up the stairs to Nancy's house.

Billy looked up to the ceiling. Surely, Nancy wasn't that stupid to get pregnant with another man while Billy Donnelly was away at war.

"And Billy doesn't know he's going to be a father again," she added.

Billy Dawson was putting two and two together. Of course Nancy wouldn't want her husband to know. She'd been bedded by another man and all Hell would break loose when Billy came back. All the rumours and whispered gossip was coming home to roost and now he knew why Jean Murphy had thrown her husband out. But there was more to come.

"Do you know someone called Gladys Kelly?" Annie asked, evenly.

Billy felt his blood run cold. "Why do you ask?"

"Nancy says, Billy's been visiting her every chance he gets and she's a...prostitute."

Billy felt anger rising in his chest. So, Billy Donnelly hadn't taken heed of either Euan or himself and still went to the whore.

He ran his fingers through his hair. "What a mess," he muttered, "each is as bad as the other."

"So, what Nancy said is true?" Annie asked, "Billy was going to a prostitute instead of loving his wife?"

Billy realised that only the truth would find a way forward for them all. He poured Annie more tea and told her everything, from Billy's first encounter with Gladys Kelly to the warnings from Euan and Billy over the years, but it looked like he'd strayed back to the woman again and again. And now, Nancy was pregnant.

"Did she mention anyone else?" Billy asked, lighting another cigarette, "there's been rumours for months around the mill that Nancy's been out dancing at the weekend with one of the other weavers called Di Auchterlonie."

"Who else would she mention?" Annie asked, now sure that Billy had more to say about his daughter.

Billy's lips tightened. "Did she mention anyone called Jim Murphy?"

"No," Annie said, "why do you ask?"

Billy braced himself to say the words. "He may be the father."

Annie almost spilled the tea as her hand began to shake.

"I'm sorry," said Billy, taking the teacup and saucer from her, "I thought Euan must have told you. "Euan!" Annie exclaimed, unable to understand why Billy had brought her dead husband into the conversation.

Billy sighed. The last thing he wanted to do was make Annie's grief any worse by speaking of Euan, but there was no way back. As gently as he could, he told Annie of the night Euan followed Nancy and a man back to Nancy's house.

"And, the man didn't come out again, so you can guess the rest," he said through clenched teeth. That man is Jim Murphy."

Annie felt embarrassment and hurt flooding her mind. How could Nancy be so heartless, she thought, shaking her head in disbelief. Billy Donnelly spending his time and money on a prostitute was bad enough but her niece behaving like one behind her husband's back, was just as horrifying.

It was plain to Billy that Euan hadn't spoken to Annie about that night and he could see why. She seemed beyond hurt as her tearful eyes met his.

"Will you speak to Nancy?" Annie asked, "please?"

Billy wanted more than anything to take Annie in his arms and make her world alright again, but he remained seated.

"Leave everything to me," he said grimly, "and I'll be speaking to Mr Murphy as well," he added, "we need to get to the bottom of this."

Billy felt a wave of love sweep over him as he watched Annie leave his office. There was no more to be said or done that day, but in the days to come, Billy was determined to find a way to put Annie's mind at rest.

The confrontation with Jim Murphy was almost immediate. Billy was waiting for him in the Buckie when Jim finished his shift the next day.

"Mr Dawson?" Jim said, feeling a knot of panic forming in his gut at the sight of the Works Manager obviously waiting for him.

"What can I do for you?"

"I have a question for you?" Billy said, evenly, "and depending on your answer, I'll know if any further action is needed."

Jim frowned in confusion. "I don't understand, Mr Dawson," he squeaked, "the yardage is being produced by the weavers and..."

Billy stopped him in his tracks. "It's not about the yardage," Billy said, moving towards the Buckie door and leaning against it, blocking Jim's exit.

"It's about my daughter, Nancy," he said, a spark of anger glinting in his eyes, "and you and your visits to her house."

Jim felt the panic increase as his legs turned to lead and his face drain of all colour. Now he knew why Billy Dawson was here and there was no escape.

He hung his head, fearful of what was to come. It was bad enough that Jean had thrown him out, but getting Billy Dawson on his back spelled disaster.

Billy watched the man cringe and knew the truth of it.

"Are you the father? Billy now demanded to know, "and if I find out you're lying about any of this, I'll kill you myself."

Jim's eyes were wide with fear as he raised his head, only the truth would do.

"Nancy and me did...go to bed together," he murmured, "but she says the bairn's Billy Donnelly's." Billy clenched his fists.

"How sure are you of this?"

"Totally certain, Mr Dawson," Jim Murphy replied, his mouth so dry he could hardly speak. "We only did it the once," he added fearfully, "and I was careful...what with being married myself and all."

"Pick up your cards at the office first thing tomorrow," Billy spat, "you're not fit to be a Chargehand."

Jim almost began crying. "But, Mr Dawson," he whined, "I've nowhere to live and with no money..."

Billy turned ice-cold eyes on the man. "You should have thought of that before you began prowling around my daughter like a mongrel dog. And incase you didn't get the message. You're sacked."

Billy's visit to Nancy had to wait till the weekend when, once again, he knocked on her door early on Sunday morning, but this time she knew the reason for his visit.

"I've been expecting you," Nancy said, letting him into the kitchen.

Billy removed his bonnet and pulled up a chair.

"That's not all your expecting, I believe," he said, waiting for his daughter to confirm what Annie had told him.

"I take it you've been speaking to Auntie Annie," Nancy said, wondering just how much she'd told her father.

"I have," said Billy "and she's got enough to cope with without you bringing more trouble to her door."

Nancy swung round to face him, "I'll not be any trouble to Auntie Annie," Nancy retorted "she understands about me and Billy and that whore from Dens Brae."

My God, thought Billy, she's pretending she's the one who's been wronged.

"And does she also understand about Jim Murphy?"

"Who?" Nancy asked shakily.   If her father knew about Jim Murphy, it could only have come from Lexie.

"Don't pretend you don't know who I'm talking about," Billy snapped, "the Jim Murphy who brought you home from the dancing and stayed the night."

Nancy felt faint. "And who told you that lie?" she asked, forcing herself to calm down.

"The man's dead now that told me, but you can be sure, he was no liar."

Nancy's mind was racing. She'd not only been seen by Lexie, she realised, but it looked liked Euan MacPherson had also seen her and Jim Murphy that night..

Nancy knew there was no way out and burst into tears. Billy watched her as she wept. He'd seen the drama before and knew that it was how Nancy got attention and help, but not this time. He'd been fooled by Mary's tears when she'd turned up on his doorstep all these years ago, pregnant with Nancy and had married her, forgoing forever any chance of being with his true love, Annie.

"Who's the father?" Billy asked coldly as Nancy quietened her wailing.

"It's NOT Jim Murphy, if that's what you're thinking," she sniffed.

"Are there any others you want to name?" Billy asked, knowing this would hurt his daughter, but the question had to be asked.

"NO," Nancy replied, her voice hoarse with shock at her father's question. "How could ask such a thing?" she whispered, but Billy wasn't finished.

"So, your husband is the father then?"

Nancy nodded, before trying again for Billy's sympathy. "But you can't ask me to stay with him, not after what he's done!"

"I'm not asking you Nancy," Billy said, pulling his bonnet on and standing up, "I'm telling you, so listen hard and do what you're told for once in your life."

Nancy's eyes widened, in genuine fear.

"You'll write to Billy tonight and tell him about the pregnancy and when he comes home you'll welcome him back as a wife should."

Nancy cringed and tears began, once more, to fall. "You're the mother of two children," Billy continued, "soon to be three and they need a mother AND a father and that father is Billy Donnelly."

"But...what about Gladys Kelly," Nancy gulped, "how can you ask me to love a man who goes to a prossie every chance he gets?"

Billy's lips tightened in anger. "Leave Billy Donnelly and Gladys Kelly to me," he said, "and by the way, Jim Murphy has been sacked from his job at Baxters." He watched as this news hit home. "No one wins when this game is played," he said, "but I won't see my grandchildren suffer through your lust or Billy Donnelly's."

The door banged shut as her father left and all Nancy's plans for happiness went with him.

Two sleepy voices called through from the back room.

"What's all the noise?" yelled wee Billy.

"Sssshhhh," hushed Mary Anne. "Go back to sleep," she said, too wise for her years, "mum's busy." But Mary Anne had heard everything and although she didn't understand it all, she knew something was very wrong. She closed her eyes and silently prayed. 'Please God, bring dad home soon, mum needs him.'

Chapter 31

Bo watched as Lexie's medal was pinned on her uniform. He couldn't stop smiling, his Lexie, he thought, a heroine. She'd told him the story of the ditched Wellington Bomber, saying anyone would have done the same, but Bo knew different. He'd been piloting bombers while crewmen had been vomiting with fear and who would have ran a mile away from the action if they could.

Once the ceremony was over, the couple walked hand in hand to Waverley Station. Bo had another couple of days R & R before he had to return to Montrose, but Lexie was expected back on the earliest train out of Edinburgh.

She told Bo about the link between Lossiemouth and Montrose.

"So, I'll know if you're safe," she said, "and God willing you will be."

Bo's arms tightened around her. He knew that the odds of surviving the war, especially as a pilot, shortened after each successful sortie.

He tilted her face up so he could see her eyes, glowing with love.

"Nothing will stop me coming back to you," he said, hoarsely, "just remember that I love you and once this war is over, we'll be together for the rest of our lives."

The guard's whistle and the slamming of the carriage doors signalled that it was time to part. Bo kissed Lexie soundly and helped her board the train. "I love you," Lexie mouthed, her voice drowned out by the steam engine rushing into life. Bo reached for her hand and placed a tiny package into it, folding her fingers around it. "Never forget I love you," he shouted above the noise, before stepping back from the train.

Lexie waved from the carriage door window till the platform and Bo were out of sight, her chin quivering with emotion and already missing him.

She gathered up her things and found a seat on the crowded train, the little package still held tightly in her hand. Her heart beating rapidly, she gently unfolded the tissue paper, inside was a small blue silk bag and in the bag was a beautifully carved ring. Lexie looked at it closely, it was made of what looked like ebony and intricately carved with tiny leaves and flowers. It was the most beautiful thing Lexie had ever seen and she slipped it on the ring finger of her left hand. It fitted perfectly.

Lexie closed her eyes and summoned up the picture of Bo blowing her kisses as the train pulled out and now, there was his ring. Her heart calmed down and a sense of 'knowing the future absolutely', swept over her as she turned the ring round and round on her finger.

Nothing and no one, not even Hitler was going to keep her and Bo apart and one day, when they were married and living in Moose Jaw, she'd tell their children about how they'd met. Then, she remembered her mother, now a widow with no one but Lexie and Ian to turn to. Almost imperceptibly, the picture of the future wobbled. Going to Canada with Bo would mean leaving her mother forever. Lexie wished she hadn't let the thought enter her head, but it was too late, it had already sown the seed of doubt.

The rest of the journey dragged by and again, it was late before the steam train from Perth puffed into Inverness Station. The RAF truck was waiting with Jennifer McKenzie at the wheel.

"The snow's eased," she said, briskly, opening the door of the vehicle for Lexie, "so we should make good time back to camp."

Lexie nodded. The last thing she wanted was another conversation with Jenny. "If you don't mind," Lexie said, "I've got a terrible headache, so wake me up when we get there ACW McKenzie," and with that, Lexie feigned sleep for the rest of the journey.

The snow had stopped the day Lexie had left for Edinburgh and although it wasn't melting, it didn't require any further shovelling. Lexie breathed in the cold air as she made her way to the Comms Room to report for duty the next day. She'd taken off Bo's ring and returned it, carefully, to its silk resting place vowing that the next time she wore it would be on her wedding day.

"Reporting for duty Sergeant," Lexie said, saluting Sgt Brady.

"Where is it then?" Sgt Brady asked, smiling broadly.

Lexie blushed. How did he know about Bo's ring? she asked herself, before realising it was the Empire Medal he wanted to see.

"Oh, the medal!" she said, "it's not something I'm going to be wearing every day, but I'll bring it with me tomorrow if you like."

Sgt Brady nodded and they got back to the business of the day.

"Just to update you," he said, "the first flight went out from the base late yesterday, so if the snow stays off, we'll be fully operational again by the end of the week."

Lexie's heart quickened. "Does that mean that the crews who transferred to Montrose will be coming back?"

"Not yet," the sergeant said, "the Norwegian Coast is closer to Montrose than we are and easier to target from there, so you'll need to continue liaising with them to keep tabs on what's happening to our boys."

Lexie's mood deflated, but at least she would still have contact with Winnie and find out what was happening to Bo and with the first flight out yesterday, there was a good chance he would get her belated letter.

That night, she wrote again to her mum saying she was well but making no mention of the medal or of Bo. Again, she asked how Nancy was and if she was visiting, hoping there would be more news about the pregnancy and if Nancy had told her husband yet. Christmas was only a month away and Lexie suggested her mum should spend it with Isabella and John Anderson. She knew she wouldn't be home for Christmas, nor would Ian. It was going to be hard for her mum to cope with her first Christmas alone, but with the war on, there was nothing Lexie could do.

Despite shortages, RAF Lossiemouth made every effort to sprinkle some Christmas happiness around the camp and by the time Christmas Eve came around, everyone was getting into the Christmas Spirit.

"The NAAFI looks great," Lexie said to Lucy, as they queued up for a quick lunch before going back on duty.

"Have you heard from Brad Hollis," Lexie asked, knowing that Lucy had been desolate when the Canadian pilot left for Montrose. Lucy shrugged. "Not a cheep," she said, sighing, "but there's the Christmas Dance tonight, so I'm just going to forget about him and enjoy myself."

Lexie squeezed her arm, knowing that it was bravado that spoke so casually about Brad and that Lucy was missing him badly.

Lexie hadn't heard from Bo either, but at least she knew he was safe thanks to Winnie and her updates.

"I'm sure he'll get in touch soon," she said, unable to tell Lucy much more, "try not to worry."

Lunch over, Lexie returned to the Comms Room and contacted Winnie for the last update of the day.

She keyed in the code for Montrose and waited. A few minutes later, the teleprinter sprung into life.

Lexie felt her blood run cold as she read the report.

THREE LOSSIEMOUTH WELLINGTON BOMBERS LOST. ONE DITCHED INTO NORTH SEA. ALL CREW MISSING. ONE SHOT DOWN BY ANTI-AIRCRAFT FIRE FROM GERMAN GUNBOAT. NO SURVIVORS. ONE AIRCRAFT MISSING, SUSPECTED LOST OVER NORWEIGIAN SOIL. NO FURTHER INFORMATION ON CREW AT THIS TIME.

Lexie responded with shaking hands.

REQUIRE ASAP BOMBER DETAILS AND CREW MEMBERS IDENTIFICATION.

Lexie waited, barely able to breathe as the list of names came through along with the aircraft details. Brad Hollis was amongst the names and, to her horror, so was Rainbow McGhee.

Lexie felt faint and leaned over to force the blood back to her brain.

Sgt Brady noticed and quickly came over to her.

"What's wrong?" he asked, placing his arm around Lexie's shoulder as he read the teleprinter report. He tore it off and helped Lexie to her feet.

"Go to the sick bay," he said, "I'll take this to Wing Commander Johnson."

Ten crew were dead and five missing, Lexie counted in her head as she stumbled to the sick bay, the shock igniting a rush of adrenaline through her limbs. One look was enough for the duty doctor to know the WAAF was in total shock.

He called for a nurse and led Lexie to the same bed she'd found herself in when she'd heard the news of Euan's death. She had felt bad then, but this was one hundred times worse. This time, the news was about Bo.

Lexie felt the jab of a needle in her arm, then darkness. "That should calm things down for a while," he said to the nurse, "let me know when she comes round."

Wing Commander Johnson read the printout from the Comms Room.

"Do we know the names of the crew who got to Norway?" he asked solemnly, looking to Sgt Wilson for the answer.

"Not yet," the sergeant said, "but I'll get on to it right away."

"Let me know as soon as possible," Johnny Johnson said, "the Norwegian Underground network is pretty strong and if any of our men have survived, they'll know about it."

Sgt Brady saluted. "And by the way, Sergeant," the Wing Commander added, bleakly, "Christmas is cancelled."

Despite being top secret, news of the doomed bombers and their crews somehow filtered through the 'grapevine' at RAF

Lossiemouth leaving no one in the mood to celebrate Christmas anymore.

Lexie was discharged from the sick bay on Christmas morning, to be sent for by Sgt Brady. All she wanted to do was bury herself under the blankets and wake up to find it was all a dream. She hurried to her Quarters and freshened up as best she could, trying to regain the sense of duty that had deserted her. She closed her eyes and prayed. "Bring him back to me," she whispered to God, "I can't live without him."

In the silence that followed, Lexie reached for the blue silk bag and took out Bo's ring. She didn't care who knew about her love for him now as she slipped the ring on her finger again. "I'm wearing your ring Bo," she said aloud into the emptiness, "and I'll never take it off, no matter what."

Sgt Brady was waiting for her in the deserted Comms Room and motioned her to sit down.

He handed Lexie a sheet of paper. "This is the names of the crew who got to Norway," he said, "but we don't know if they're alive or dead." Lexie read the names and hope sprung up in her heart, Bo and Brad Hollis, as pilot and co-pilot had been on the plane that had managed to get to Norway. A wave of relief washed over her, she felt for the ring through her glove. As long as she wore Bo's ring, she told herself, he'd return to her. She only had to wait.

But there was still no news of their whereabouts as 1942 began.

The weather had worsened again and everything was grounded, including Lexie. She continued writing letters to her mother in the hope that, one day, she'd receive them and it was the same with letters coming from home, varying from infrequent to never.

One flight, however, did get through and Lexie had two letters to open.

One was from Bo and one from home. She ran to her Quarters, clutching the precious envelopes and immediately opened the one from Bo.

The letter was dated the day after their meeting in Edinburgh and brought back the wonderful memory of their love for one another. Sadly, since then, Lexie had to cope with the news that Bo was missing somewhere in Norway, hopefully alive, and she held the letter to her lips and kissed his name, as tears blurred her eyes.

She drank some tea and tried to calm her heart down, before opening her mother's letter. It was with some relief that Lexie read that

Her mum had got through Christmas, with the help of Isabella and John Anderson, but the letter went on to tell Lexie all about Nancy, her pregnancy and Annie's visit to Billy Dawson. Lexie read on.

'Nancy's not wanting anything more to do with her husband and it looks like there's another man in her life, so I'm hoping that her father can make her see sense about everything. I'll let you know what happens.'

The rest of the letter was about missing Lexie and hoping to see her soon, but Lexie was transfixed with the news about Nancy. So, she was with the man from the Palais that night and Lexie came to the same conclusion that he was the father of her bairn, despite Nancy having denied the fact. She just hoped that her mother would stay out of things, but already it was obvious this wasn't going to happen. She'd gone to see Billy Dawson and was already involved.

—·—oOo—·—

Chapter 32

Billy Dawson had never wanted to set eyes on Gladys Kelly again, but if Billy wouldn't listen to sense, he was going to make sure that the prossie did.

The blackened door creaked open and Mrs Kelly's lined face and narrowed eyes looked round the side, but her eyes widened when she saw who was standing there.

"Mr Da'son," she murmured, knowing him of old and opening the door wider, "you'd better come in."

Billy stepped into the dark kitchen, the only light coming from the glow of the fire in the range.

"It's not you I've come to see," he began, "it's..." but before he could finish the sentence, a voice interrupted him.

"It's a'right ma," Gladys Kelly said coming into the kitchen from the back room, "Mr Da'son's here to see me."

The old crone made herself scarce, while Gladys lit the gas mantle above the range.

Billy watched her as she slowly lit a cigarette, pulled out one of the kitchen chairs and sat down, her eyes fixed on the smoking cigarette.

"If you're here to ask about Billy Donnelly," Gladys said flatly, "save your breath, he's long gone."

What in heaven's name drew Billy to this desperate woman, Billy thought, everything about her was pitiful and the thought of bedding her turned his stomach.

"I know where Billy Donnelly is," Billy said, tightly, "he's fighting somewhere in this God-forsaken war, instead of being home with his wife and bairns."

Gladys's eyes met his. "How many bairns is it now then?" she asked, a sneer in her voice, "twa is it, or mibee, THREE?"

Billy flinched. So the prostitute knew about Nancy's pregnancy, but her emphasis on the word 'three' made him wonder if she also knew about Jim Murphy.

"BILLY will be the father of Nancy's THREE bairns when the third one comes into the world," he said, menacingly, "unless you know otherwise?"

Gladys lips tightened. The word in the Thrums was that Jim Murphy and Nancy were 'at it' and his wife had thrown him out, so it was possible he could have got her rival pregnant, but no one knew for sure.

Billy waited, but she said no more. He felt his muscles relax, now it was time to play his Ace card.

"I want you gone from here long before the birth happens," he said, his voice brooking no objection.

It was Gladys's turn to flinch. "Gone!" she exclaimed, "gone where?"

"I'm thinking Lochee will be far enough," Billy said "but if you want to go further than that..?"

Gladys stood up, her eyes full of fear. Billy Dawson was well-known in Dundee, with powerful friends who could make life difficult for her.

"And if I stay where I am?" she said, her voice beginning to shake. She was no match for Billy Dawson and she knew it.

"That's not an option Gladys," Billy said evenly, taking out his wallet and extracting four £5 notes. He placed them on the table in front of her.

"This should be enough to set you up in Lochee," he said, before producing a small iron key with a brown label attached to it by a length of string. "The address is written on it," he said, tossing the key on the table and turning towards the door "and I'll be back in two days," he added, "make sure you're not here."

Billy had used one of his Masonic friends to procure the single-end in Lochee, no questions asked and once the prossie was gone from Dens Brae, Billy reasoned, it would be nigh impossible for Billy Donnelly to find her.

What he didn't know, however, was that Gladys knew how to

get in touch with Billy and she would be letting him know all about Billy Dawson's visit and Nancy's pregnancy, not forgetting to mention Jim Murphy. She looked at the address on the label, she'd make sure it was clearly written at the top of the letter. Billy Donnelly could still be hers.

Satisfied that both Jim Murphy and Gladys Kelly had been dealt with, Billy felt he would be able to tell Annie that she could stop worrying about Nancy and once Billy came home his daughter would also do as she was told and welcome him back with open arms.

He even caught himself whistling as he climbed the stairs to home, but his good mood was quick to evaporate when he saw the look on his wife's face.

Josie had become more and more withdrawn and anxious since the death of Annie's husband, Euan MacPherson and Billy was constantly being bombarded with questions about where he was going when he left the house and where he had been when he got back. Tonight would be no exception.

"At the Lodge," Billy said, trying to keep his voice neutral in answer to Josie's question.

"Again?" Josie snapped, knitting furiously. "That's the third time this week you've been 'at the lodge'," she muttered, "you'll be moving your bed in there next."

The clicking of the knitting needles quickened further.

Billy sighed. He was getting mighty sick of Josie's jealousy of Annie Melville and her constant questioning was only driving him further away.

Josie had always known that Annie had been Billy's first love and despite their marriage and three daughters, she still obsessed about the past. And now, with Euan's death, Annie had become more of a threat than ever. She was a woman alone and still attractive and Billy, she was sure, would want her again. It was difficult for Billy to disagree with her as he'd never stopped loving Annie and would leave Josie and his daughters at the drop of a hat if she asked him to.

"I've also been to see Nancy," Billy said, "if that's alright with you, she's going to have another bairn and with Billy away in

France somewhere, she's finding it difficult to manage. So, if I'm not here or at the Lodge," he added patiently, "that's where I'll be."

The knitting stopped. "Pregnant!" Josie exclaimed, "with a war on?"

Billy lit a cigarette and inhaled deeply. "Yes Josie," he said, "even with a war on, these things happen you know."

Josie hadn't expected that particular piece of news. She'd never had much to do with Billy's daughter since wee Billy was born, but now she'd make sure she went to visit her, just to check if it was true.

"Well," she huffed, "more fool her."

"If there's nothing else you want to ask me" Billy said sarcastically, "then I'll take myself off to bed. Goodnight," he said into the silence, but there was no answer.

He hadn't meant to use Nancy as an alibi, but now that the seed was sown, he reasoned, he'd be more able to visit Annie in the future.

There was good news to tell her and Billy knocked at her door the following day when he finished work at Baxters.

She was looking a bit more relaxed, Billy thought and seemed less hesitant in inviting him in.

He following her into the kitchen, where the table was set for one and he could smell the Smokie warming in the oven.

"I didn't mean to interrupt you at teatime," he said, removing his bonnet and tentatively sitting down, but I thought you'd want to know how things are with Nancy."

Annie leant forward at the table, hoping to hear good news about her niece. "Is she alright?" she asked.

"She's fine," he said, before telling Annie about his confrontation with Jim Murphy, and his ultimatum to Gladys Kelly "and Nancy will be writing to Billy to tell him he's going to be a father again," he added.

Annie sat back, the tightness in her shoulders easing as she realised how much trouble Billy had taken to resolve things and keep her from worrying.

"So, when Billy comes home, I'll be there to make sure Nancy does as she said she would and he forgets all about *that woman* and behaves like a husband and father again." Billy looked anxiously at Annie for a sign that she, at least, appreciated his help.

For the first time in a long time, Annie felt herself smiling at Billy Dawson.

"I'm sure Nancy and Billy will work things out, now that you have paved the way for them," she said "and you have my thanks for the way you've come to her rescue...and to mine."

Billy felt his heart leap in his chest. Annie didn't hate him anymore, he told himself, emphatically, he could see it in her eyes, hear it in her voice. It would be a long time, maybe never, before she began to like him again, but for now, her thanks were enough. He stood up to leave.

"Keep in touch," Annie said as he reached the kitchen door, "especially when Billy comes home."

Billy had to force himself not to turn back and take Annie in her arms, his heart was racing, *she wanted to see him again*, he told himself, the years between suddenly dropping away and he was a young man again and Annie the young, innocent Irish lass, who'd given herself to him in love, now sat just yards away from him. Calm down, he cautioned his heart, let her trust you again and then..."I will," Billy said, "but if you should need me for anything else, just say the word" and with that, he left the kitchen and Annie Pepper alone.

After Billy left, Annie busied herself with making her tea and ate the Smokie slowly, with a slice of bread and margarine. Her thoughts began to roam in the silence. How things had changed since the start of this war, her two children no longer with her and Euan, her security for so long now dead and buried. She felt the tears of loss begin to fall, but she brushed them away and began to gather up the tea things and start the washing up. Again, the loneliness weighed down on her, Euan had always helped with the dishes, drying the plates while she washed them.

But now, it was just her and would be *just her* till the day she died.

She went into the parlour and added more coal to the fire, before picking up her knitting and trying to force her thoughts onto other things. She would go and see Nancy soon and help if she could, but the memory of Billy Dawson's visit returned before she could decide when next to visit her niece.

She saw his concern etched on his still handsome face and his willingness to help her. Over the years, she'd had to ask him for help with Lexie and with Joe Cassiday and again now with Nancy and Billy Donnelly and every time, he'd sorted things out for her. Even Euan had reason to thank Billy for his help and Annie found herself smiling again. Despite everything that had gone on in the past, she had to admit that Billy Dawson had always been there when he was needed and in her loneliness Annie realised she needed his strength more than ever.

Billy Donnelly was back on English soil having spent the last five months in France defending a French bridge and roads leading to the Capital, by scuppering German troupe movements. Billeted at a temporary camp in Dover, the mail eventually caught up with him and he immediately recognised Nancy's writing. He lit a cigarette and stared at his name on the envelope, remembering how they'd parted and expecting a 'Dear John' letter. Anger building, he tore open the envelope but instead read Nancy's news. "PREGNANT" he said aloud. Three pairs of war-weary eyes turned his way. Billy coughed and apologised, waving the letter at them, by way of explanation, before turning back to re-read it.

The birth of wee Billy flooded his brain and the doctor's words returned to him. "Another pregnancy could kill your wife, so it's either your catholic religion or your wife Mr Donnelly, make your choice" he'd said and that was how his lust for Gladys Kelly had begun and his love-making with Nancy had stopped.

He'd forgotten his drunken night of forced sex with her before he'd been sent to France and his mind put two and two together, if it wasn't him who'd made her pregnant, then Gladys had been right, Jim Murphy was the father and on reading his other letter from Gladys Kelly his worst fears were confirmed. " The whore," he cursed under his breath, she'd pay for this and so would Jim Murphy.

Chapter 33

In 1942, the Americans had joined in the war and brought much needed troops into the conflict as well as equipment and other essential supplies, shipped over the Atlantic by fleets of Merchant Navy vessels, which ran the gauntlet of German submarines with every crossing.

The cargo ship, MV Northern Way, captained by Robbie Robertson had been torpedoed twice, the second time forcing Robbie to abandon his ship. Fortunately, one of the Destroyers in the convoy had picked up the crew and brought everyone safely back to Glasgow.

Robbie returned home to Dundee on leave, till his next ship was made ready and spent his time looking up old friends in the Thrums bar and catching up on the news. The pavements were still slushy with melting snow and the lack of street lighting made for many slips and broken bones, but he was home and to his surprise, far from wanting to escape from Dundee and get back to sea, Robbie realised how much he'd missed the old place, the smell of the jute, Harry Duncan, his boyhood employer and Lexie Melville, especially Lexie Melville..

Since reading about her and her Empire Medal in the Courier on his last leave home, she'd crept back into his consciousness more and more. She had been his first love and he had been hers, but his hot-blooded advances had made her reject him and Sergeant MacPherson had made sure he kept away from her.

But most of all, he'd regretted taking revenge on Lexie years later, by rejecting *her* love, even though he knew how much it hurt her. He'd 'played the field' ever since and became a typical sailor with 'a girl in every port,' but the horrors of the war had changed him, making him realise what was important in life and finding Lexie again bacame the most important thing of all. He took out his wallet and ran a finger over her photograph torn from the Courier and nestling alongside it was the silver ring he'd given her as a token of his love and his promise of marriage. He smiled grimly to himself, recalling Sergeant MacPherson handing it back to him. The hurt he had felt had been almost unbearable, but the love he had felt for Lexie had never left him.

Harry Duncan was working in his butcher's shop, trying to make sausages from minced scraps of everything he could bone out when Robbie came in.

"Robbie," he cried, immediately recognising his butcher boy who he'd seen change from an awkward youngster into a fine man, thanks to the Merchant Navy. And now, he was the Captain of his own ship and braving the North Atlantic to keep supplies coming in from America.

"When did you get home?" Harry asked, excitedly, beckoning him into the back shop and making him a mug of tea.

"You're looking grand" he fussed, settling down to hear of Robbie's adventures, the shop ignored for the moment "and still sailing the seven seas?"

"Still sailing the seven seas," Robbie confirmed, taking a drink of dark brown tea from the mug. He told the old butcher about his last trip and the rescue by the Destroyer as Harry sat agog. "Whew!" he exclaimed, "how lucky was that!"

Robbie smiled to himself, "maybe it was luck, maybe not," he said, "but here I am and wanting to know all the news about what's been happening here."

Harry's brow furrowed, "I'm afraid there's not much to shout about in Dundee just now, what with the freezing weather and food shortages." Sadly, he waved his hand around him, "we're even short on liver and lights," he said, "and as for pork and beef, well..."

"But that famous Dundee spirit is still alive, I'm sure," Robbie said, encouragingly, "not everyone's away fighting."

Harry looked at Robbie wondering if he knew about Sergeant MacPherson's death. He remembered the policeman speaking with Robbie outside the back shop, just before he joined the Merchant Navy and, although Robbie had said nothing at the time, the rumour was that it was something to do with young Lexie Melville.

"We had an unexploded bomb in Baxters Park," Harry began, watching for Robbie's reaction, but there wasn't one. "Well," he continued carefully, "when I say unexploded, it did go off before the bomb squad could defuse it and three people from the ARP were killed."

Robbie put down his mug. "No one we know I hope?" Robbie asked.

"Aye," Harry said, slowly, "Sergeant MacPherson and two of his men were guarding it till the Army got there, but..."

Robbie felt the air rush from his lungs, making it hard to speak.

"Are you sure?" he managed to stammer, "the policeman?"

Harry nodded. "No doubt about it," the butcher confirmed, "there wasn't much of him left," he added, solemnly, "but the folks nearby at the time witnessed what happened."

Robbie thought he was going to vomit. "I need some air," he mumbled, heading for the door, "I'll see you later."

He lowered himself onto the dyke outside the back shop in Todburn Lane and breathed deeply till the nausea passed. Euan MacPherson was dead and he could have been too if the Destroyer hadn't rescued him from the Atlantic Ocean. The Hand of Fate took no prisoners he realised and what of Lexie, where was she now, maybe dead too for all he knew.

Fear now forming in his mind, he made his way up Princes Street to Albert Street and Lexie's home. Whether he was welcome or not, he had to find out if Lexie was alive and the only one who could tell him that was her mother, Annie MacPherson.

He tapped gently on the door, not knowing what to expect. Annie opened it and furrowed her brows in confusion. "I think you must have the wrong door," she said, beginning to close it. Robbie placed his foot over the doorstep. "It's Robbie Robertson," he said as softly as he could, "I've come to offer my condolences."

Annie opened the door again. For the first time, she came face to face with the man who had hurt Lexie so much. "I'm not sure you're welcome here," she said, "but thank you for your kind thoughts." Annie began to shut the door again, but again Robbie stopped her.

"Please, Mrs MacPherson," he said, "I just want a few minutes of your time, to say I'm sorry...for everything...and if I could put the clock back, I would."

Annie looked at the handsome man at her door, now full-grown, dark and bearded with eyes that seemed to beg her understanding. He'd just been a boy when Euan had to speak to him about Lexie, so how could she still be angry at a boy.

She stepped back and allowed Robbie to enter.

He looked around the comfortable parlour as Annie went into the kitchen to get them both some tea. He'd never been in Lexie's home before and he tried to picture her living in this very room.

Annie brought the tray through, offering Robbie his tea in a china cup and saucer and a teaplate with two pancakes on it. "I'm sorry it's margarine," she said, indicating the yellow spread, "but I've already used up my butter ration."

Robbie felt his fingers were all thumbs as he tried to balance the cup and saucer in one hand and find a way to eat the pancakes with the other.

Annie smiled to herself, Robbie Robertson was still a lad at heart despite looking every inch a man. She could see why Lexie had been besotted with him and tried to understand why he had broken her heart the way he did.

"Harry Duncan told me about your husband Mrs MacPherson," Robbie said, once he'd managed to eat the pancakes and drink the tea. "I know I behaved badly when I was young," he continued, "but Sergeant MacPherson made me see the error of my ways and, well, I'm now the Captain of a Merchant Ship." Robbie studied his clasped hands "and I hope you'll forgive the way I behaved towards Lexie like I did. I know now that two wrongs don't make it right, so the next time you see her, maybe you could tell her how sorry I am."

Annie acknowledged Robbie's sincerity, it had all been a long time ago and Lexie was happy now in the WAAF, despite there being a war on.

"I'll let her know you've visited," Annie said kindly, "next time I write to her."

Robbie felt his whole being relax. "Write to her?" he asked, "is she in touch then?"

Annie nodded. "She's not allowed to say much," she added, "but she's fine. She came home for Euan's funeral, but couldn't stay long..."

Annie's voice trailed off into silence and Robbie sensed it was time to leave.

He stood up, towering over Annie as he did so. "I won't intrude further," he said, heading for the door, "I'm home for a couple of weeks," he added, "so if there's anything you need doing, fixing or mending, or such like, you only need to ask. Harry Duncan knows where to get me."

Annie saw him to the door and returned to the parlour to clear away the tea things. How the past kept coming back, she thought, rinsing out the teapot and the cups. first Billy Dawson and now Robbie Robertson. One had figured largely in Annie's life and the other in Lexie's life, but what did it all matter now, she shrugged, sometimes fate let you win and other times you lost and the only thing she was sure of was that life goes on regardless till it stops.

Robbie Robertson felt happy for the first time in a long time. Lexie was alive and her mother had forgiven him. It was a start and if the fates were kind, they'd meet again, but this time, it would be different. Lexie would keep his ring.

But Lexie was miles away in Lossiemouth and her thoughts were far from home and Robbie Robertson. Her thoughts were all of Bo.

It would soon be March and still no news, but she consoled herself that Lucy was going through the same waiting game as she was and they tried to keep one another's spirits up as the weeks wore on.

"You'd think someone knows something," Lucy said, exasperated by the lack of information, "doesn't anyone in the Comms Room know what's happening anymore?"

Lexie grimaced "it's not going to come through the usual channels," she said, "it'll be up to the Norwegian Underground to get them back home if they can, so we won't know anything till they're back on British soil...provided they're still alive that is..."

The girls fell silent, both trying to push the thought from their minds.

"C'mon," said Lexie, finishing her tea, "let's go for a walk, it's a nice day and it'll maybe help stop us worrying for a while."

They were just about out of the camp when Jenny McKenzie came running after them.

"Sgt Brady wants to see you at once," she told Lexie breathlessly "and he won't take no for an answer."

Lexie frowned, "Alright ACW McKenzie," she said formally, "tell the Sergeant I'll be there in a minute."

"Sorry Lucy," Lexie said, "duty calls."

Lucy shrugged, "I'll go on my own," she said, turning towards the gate.

"I'll go with you," Jenny said, hopefully, but Lucy ignored her and left the camp alone.

Lexie gave Jenny an annoyed look. Did this woman never give up! Couldn't she see Lucy wasn't interested in her?

Irritated, Lexie marched off with Jenny trailing in her wake.

Sgt Brady was at his desk as usual, despite it being Saturday and beckoned Lexie over. She had told him about Bo McGhee and explained the significance of the ring he had given her, but she wasn't prepared to hear what he was about to say.

The Sergeant leant forward, lowering his voice, conscious of Jenny McKenzie filing paperwork nearby.

"Don't react," he said to Lexie, "but I have news about the Canadians."

Lexie almost jumped out of her chair, drawing a look from ACW McKenzie, but the sergeant hushed her to sit down again and pretended to shuffle some documents on his desk. Jenny turned away.

Lexie's heart was racing but her mind was rigid with fear.

"They're safe," Sgt Brady said, "all of them," he added. Don't ask me how I know," he continued, "just believe me that it's true."

"Where are they?" Lexie asked shakily. "They've been snowed-in in Norway," the sergeant replied, "nothing's been able to be moved for two months, but now it's getting easier and the Norwegians have managed to get the guys to the north of France. They're with the French Resistance now and arrangements are being made to get them across the channel and home."

Lexie almost wept with relief. She wanted to hug Sgt Brady till her arms ached, but now wasn't the time or place. She stood up and saluted instead, "thank you Sir," she said loudly, before hurrying towards the door. She had to find Lucy and tell her the good news.

She found her sitting on a Capstan at the harbour, aimlessly watching the seagulls swooping and diving around the fishing boats.

"Lucy," she called, waving her arms to get her attention.

Lucy turned, standing up and watching Lexie draw closer.

"They're SAFE," Lexie breathed, before wrapping her arms around Lucy and hugging her tightly. Lucy fought to be released, her brows furrowed in confusion. "Who's safe?" she asked.

"BO AND BRAD," Lexie said, "ALL OF THE CREW ARE SAFE."

Lexie thought Lucy was going to faint as she dropped back down onto the iron Capstan. "Are you sure?" she asked, her voice quivering.

Lexie nodded vigorously and told her the good news without mentioning Sgt Brady. "It looks like the Comms Room got word from RAF Montrose this morning, but keep things to yourself," Lexie added, "it's not for public consumption yet."

The two friends made their way back to the camp, the wait was almost over and both Bo and Brad would be back with them soon.

—·—oOo—·—

Chapter 34

The winter in Dundee had been bitter and Nancy felt more and more tired as she trudged back and forth through the thawing slush of William Lane to Baxters Mill in King Street.

There was no denying she was pregnant now and her bump seemed to be getting bigger by the day. She'd written to Billy as her father had asked, but as yet, had heard nothing. Nancy knew that she wouldn't be able to carry on working at the looms for much longer and the money the Army sent to her would be all she had, once she had to stop the weaving.

All thoughts of leaving her husband and setting up home with Jim Murphy had been well and truly laid to rest by her father and Nancy knew now that her only chance of keeping her children fed was down to Billy Donnelly.

Her Auntie Annie had been her saviour, looking after Mary Anne and wee Billy while she got some rest and dropping by with a basket of home-made scones and biscuits, using her own ration of sugar and margarine to make sure the bairns got a weekly treat.

"Have you heard back from Billy?" Annie asked, one Saturday as she popped a blob of Apple Jelly onto a scone for each of the bairns.

Nancy sighed, "not yet," she said, "but even if he's happy to be a dad again, it won't rekindle the love we had, not with Gladys Kelly still around."

"But she's not around," Annie told her, surprised that Nancy didn't know, "your dad's sent her packing."

"Packing?"

Annie nodded. "He went to see her and told her to leave Dens

205

Brae and never come back," she smiled, "so I don't think you need worry about her any more, Nancy, just you make sure Billy finds a happy wife when he comes home from the war."

Nancy couldn't believe her ears. For a long time, Gladys Kelly had loomed large in Nancy's life and now...she was gone!

Nancy allowed herself to think about the future. With Gladys out of the way, maybe she and Billy could...after all, she reasoned, her father had given her no choice in the matter, maybe he'd give Billy no choice either. She looked at Mary Anne and wee Billy scoffing their scones, they were what mattered and when the new bairn came along, maybe, just maybe, it could be a new beginning for them all. But Nancy's hope for the future would soon be shattered, Billy Donnelly was on his way home. He'd been given Compassionate Leave due to the pregnancy, but it was the letter from Gladys Kelly with the news that Jim Murphy could be the father that was driving him wild, as the train puffed over the Tay Bridge into Dundee.

Billy had been battle-hardened by his time in France and he knew Jim Murphy would be no match for him, he could wait. But his visit to his wife could not. He looked at the Steeple clock, almost three, he'd be home before Nancy had finished her shift at the Mill and he'd be waiting.

He heard a key turn in the lock but it was Mary Anne and wee Billy who came into the kitchen. Their eyes lit up when they saw their dad and Mary Anne flung herself into his arms, followed by wee Billy.

"I knew you'd come," Mary Anne beamed, "I asked God to send you home to mum, she's going to have a bairn and me and wee Billy are gonna help look after it."

Billy felt tears of remorse fill his eyes as he looked at the eager faces of his bairns. Innocent, he thought, they don't deserve a whore for a mother and his resolve to make Nancy pay, strengthened again.

"I need to get the tea started," Mary Anne announced, donning her mantle of 'housewife' in her mother's absence, "and wee Billy will get the fire going." Billy watched as his daughter and son went about their chores. Nancy had taught them well and by the time her key turned in the lock, the table had been set, the fire was lit and three Bridies were heating in the oven. "You can share mine," she told wee Billy, "dad can have yours."

Before Nancy had a chance to put her foot in the door, she could hear squeals of excitement coming from her children.

"What's all the noise about?" she asked, bending down to unwrap them from her skirt.

"DAD'S HOME" Mary Anne shouted. Nancy looked up and felt her heart lurch in her chest. "Billy," she said, trying to keep calm, "welcome home."

"Mary Anne has made me welcome," Billy said, his voice controlled, "so I don't need a welcome from you and all."

"Not in front of the bairns," Nancy murmured, "they're innocents in all this."

She turned to the oven and brought out the hot food. "Me and wee Billy's sharing," Mary Anne piped up proudly, "so dad can have a whole Bridie."

Nancy forced a smile and cut the Bridie in two, putting a half on each plate. "Now," she said, "I want you both to take your tea outside on the stairs and when you're done, you can stay out to play for a bit."

She looked at Billy for support. "Daddy's tired and needs to get a sleep before his tea," he said, "but later on, I'll take you both to Johnny the Italian's ice cream shop for a wee cone."

The two didn't need telling twice. "Thanks dad," Mary said, suddenly solemn, "for coming home to mum."

Nancy took the other two Bridies and brought them on the table.

"Aren't you hungry?" she asked, cutting into the pastry. Billy stared at her as she ate and waited.

Nancy could feel her insides rebel as she forced the food down.

"I take it you got my letter," she said as calmly as she could, instinctively knowing this wasn't the time to cross swords with her husband.

"I believe his name is Jim Murphy," Billy said through gritted teeth.

Nancy slowly set down her knife and fork. Someone had somehow told Billy that Jim Murphy was the father of her unborn child and she could see he believed it.

"Then you believe wrong, Billy," she said, feeling as though she was walking through broken glass, "the bairn's yours."

Billy leapt to his feet. "You haven't let me near you for almost a year," he spat, "so it looks to me like it's either a miracle or you're LYING."

He brought his fist down onto the Bridie, fragmenting the pastry and spilling the mince onto the table.

Nancy pushed back her chair and backed away towards the door but Billy came after her, pinning her against the bunker, his face white with temper.

"I'll kill the both of you," Billy raged, "you AND your fancy man."

Nancy could feel the spit from his mouth pepper her face.

"Are you forgetting you RAPED ME Billy Donnelly?" Nancy shouted desperately, "after that night at the Palais."

Nancy held her breath as the fire in Billy's eyes was replaced with confusion. His grip loosened and he stepped away from her.

The memory of that night forced its way back into his brain, fuelled by drink and frustration, he grimly remembered pushing Nancy onto their bed and demanding his 'conjugal rights'.

Billy shook his head and sat down heavily as the rape, for he knew it was rape, filtered back into his mind and heart.

"So," Nancy said shakily, "you remember now?"

Billy felt all of his anger ebb away. How had it come to this, he asked himself, raping the mother of his bairns and fathering another poor innocent in the process. But before he could say anymore, the kitchen door flew open and one of the neighbours, her eyes wide with fear, burst in.

"It's Mary Anne," she cried, "she's fallen off the shelters and she's not moving!"

Billy and Nancy leapt to their feet as one and rushed down the stairwell onto the slope of the back green, where Mary Anne lay surrounded by the other bairns and two more of the neighbours.

"There's an ambulance on the way," one said breathlessly, "but she hit her head on one of the stones hidden in the grass and..."

Billy knelt down beside his daughter. "Mary Anne," he whispered, "dad's here now, everything will be alright." He could feel tears welling in his eyes, little Mary Anne, who gave up her Bridie for the love of him.

Two ambulance men with a stretcher hurried down the steep slope.

"We'll take over now," one of them said, briskly, "she'll be in good hands at the Infirmary," he reassured them, as they gently lifted Mary Anne onto the stretcher.

The sound of wee Billy crying and shaking reached Nancy. She hurried over to her son and held him tightly. "It's alright," she said, "Mary Anne will be alright, she's going to the Infirmary to get fixed."

"I didn't mean to ppppush her," he said trembling, "I was just pretending to be a German..." Nancy held him closer, "I know," she whispered, "it wasn't anyone's fault, Mary Anne just fell, that's all."

Billy came beside her as the ambulance men carried the stretchered child up the slope to the ambulance. "I'll go with Mary Anne in the ambulance," he said, "you stay here with wee Billy."

Nancy nodded silently. Billy's arm reached around her shoulders.

"I'll be back as soon as I can," he whispered, "look after wee Billy till then."

The shock of the past few hours hit Nancy as she waited for Billy's return. She had been so concerned about herself, she hadn't realised how much Mary Anne and wee Billy missed their dad, or how much Billy loved his bairns. Her father had been right, her place was with her family and that included her husband. Her hands were clenched into fists when she heard Billy's footsteps coming up the stairs. She jumped up, pulling wee Billy to her side, fear surging through her veins.

Billy's eyes were raw and the muscles in his face twitched.

"She's going to be alright," he said hoarsely, running his hands through his hair, "she came round in the ambulance, but the doctor's keeping her in for a wee while." Nancy felt her breathing ease, "are you sure she's fine?" she asked. Billy nodded "and she says to tell you she forgot to put on her parachute before she jumped," he said smiling at his son.

Wee Billy's eyes lit up. He wasn't to blame after all and hurried to the door. "Can I go and tell Georgie and Davie about Mary Anne?" he asked his mum, his childlike conscience now clear.

Nancy ruffled his hair. "Off you go," she said, "but NO PLAYING ON THE SHELTERS," she added sharply, "we don't want any more accidents."

"I think it's time we talked," Billy said, quietly, as Nancy handed him some hot, sweet tea. She nodded, sure that whatever Billy had to say, especially about Gladys Kelly, it was not going to break her. She was going to fight for her marriage and her bairns.

—·—oOo—·—

Chapter 35

It was April before Lexie heard that the Canadians were on English soil. Sgt Brady, who seemed to know everything, had told her that the Free French had ferried the men across the English Channel, under cover of darkness, in a small fishing boat.

"Does that mean, they'll be coming back to Lossiemouth?" Lexie asked, holding her breath.

But, Sgt Brady shook his head. "That I don't know," he said, "it will depend on how the men are and if they'll be fit and able to resume their duties."

Lexie's eyebrows formed into a worried frown.

"Bo's alright, isn't he?" she asked, conscious of overstepping the mark of seniority, but desperate to know more.

Sgt Brady met her worried gaze.

"You'll have to wait and see on that one," he said, "now they're back on British soil, I don't expect to hear any more news except through the usual channels."

There was nothing else for it but to wait, hope and pray. Lexie and Lucy shared a table in the NAAFI that evening, the war and everything about it weighing heavily on their shoulders.

"What if we never hear from any of them ever again?" Lucy asked dismally.

Lexie patted her arm. "We'll hear from them," she said, "one way or another, they'll get in touch."

Lucy brightened. "Maybe they already have," she said, "have you checked your pigeon hole lately?"

Lexie felt a surge of hope. "Let's check first thing in the

morning," she said, "if they're at an English airfield, there are bound to be ways of getting letters out."

Next morning, with hope renewed Lexie checked her pigeon hole. She could see there was mail there, but was there anything from Bo?

Her heart sank. There was a letter, but it was from her mother.

Absently, she opened it, there was the usual update on how things were at home but then, Lexie stopped dead. *I had a visit from Robbie Robertson today,* Lexie read *he's the captain of a Merchant Navy ship and home on leave. He seemed very concerned about Euan's death and wanted to say sorry for the problems he'd caused in the past, so I said I'd pass on his apology to you, Lexie. He did seem truly sorry, so I hope you accept it.*

Lexie stared at the words, her mind flashing back to the last time she'd seen Robbie Robertson and aware that her heart was racing and her stomach churning. She pushed the letter into her handbag and headed for the Comms Room, determined to push the memory of Robbie Robertson back down into the darkness where it belonged, but the more she tried to ignore her feelings, the more they surfaced.

How dare he visit her mother, she fumed and pretend that he cared, especially about her! She forced her thoughts back to Bo. Where was he, her heart demanded to know, and why isn't he here now that I need him more than ever? Questions without answers rumbled around her brain till her shift finished and she headed for the NAAFI to seek out Lucy and find out if she'd had better luck in hearing from Brad.

Lucy was pushing rice pudding around her plate with a spoon. Lexie grimaced, Lucy didn't look happy.

"Any letters?" she asked feigning brightness, "from Brad I mean."

Lucy shook her head, "nothing," she said, "how about you?"

"Nothing," Lexie said, "but I did get a letter from home." She handed the letter to Lucy to read.

"Who's Robbie Robertson?" Lucy asked, handing back the letter and wondering why Lexie had shown it to her.

Lexie sighed and told Lucy the whole sorry story about their childhood engagement, Robbie's cruel rejection and the real reason why she had joined the WAAF. "So, you see," Lexie concluded, "no matter what I do, the past seems to follow me wherever I go, even to Lossiemouth."

Lucy frowned. "But, you've got Bo now, haven't you, the love of your life...remember?"

"Have I!" Lexie exclaimed hotly, "I don't know where he is, or what he's thinking, or even if he still loves me," she finished, exasperation colouring the words.

Lucy took her hands, "of course he still loves you," she said emphatically "and when he comes back, AND HE WILL," she added positively, "this Robbie Robertson will be back where he belongs, IN THE PAST."

Lexie felt her shoulders relax and a weak smile formed on her lips.

"You think so?" she asked softly, "I do love Bo so much."

"I know so," Lucy replied, "and until then, we just have to wait."

The wait lasted another three weeks before Sgt Brady told Lexie the news.

"The Canadians are coming home," he said with a flourish. "They've been debriefed and their ETA is 16.00 hours TODAY."

Lexie almost fainted. "TODAY," she repeated in disbelief, her heart soaring. "Are you sure?"

"Of course I'm sure," Sgt Brady said, grinning, "so you'd better get ready to welcome Captain Rainbow McGhee back home."

"At last," Lexie breathed, before beginning to entertain a whole range of doubts. Would Bo still love her, would he even remember her, did he still think of Edinburgh. The list went on and on, but Lexie needn't have worried. The minute Bo disembarked from the aircraft, his eyes found Lexie, her arms wrapped around herself to keep out the cold.

He hurried towards her, not caring who saw him and swept her off her feet and into his arms. "Lexie," he murmured, "I've missed you so much."

Lexie's eyes filled with tears. Everything was going to be alright.

"Have you missed me too?" Bo asked, almost anxiously, because if you haven't then..."

But Bo didn't have a chance to finish the sentence.

"MISSED YOU!" Lexie echoed, "only more than life itself," she told him, tightening her grip on his arms.

Bo grinned from ear to ear. "And the ring?" he asked next, "have you still got it?"

Lexie took off her glove and wiggled her hand. "It's never left my finger since you went missing and now you're back safely, it never will."

One of the crew whistled to Bo and waved him over.

"I have to report to the Winco," he said, "but I'll pick you up at your Quarters around 20.00 hours and we'll celebrate."

Lexie nodded. "I'll be waiting," she whispered, "I love you, Bo."

Lexie watched as Bo blinked away a tear, or maybe it was just the Scottish wind making his eyes water. He held her hands tightly.

"I love you too, Lexie Melville," he said, "more than you'll ever know."

Lexie waved as Bo joined the rest of the crew, including Brad. Lucy would be in for a surprise tonight, Lexie smiled to herself, as she made her way back to the Comms Room, all thoughts of Robbie Robertson gone.

Robbie may have been replaced by Bo in Lexie's heart, but she was now firmly back into Robbie's. Since his first visit to Lexie's mother, Robbie had made several more visits to the flat in Albert Street, re-painting the kitchen and the front door as well as bringing Annie some extra meat rations from Harry Duncan's shop. By the time his leave was up and his new ship was ready to take on the North Atlantic runs again, he felt he had not only made up for the past, but had also made a friend of Annie Melville.

"I'll drop you a line, if I can," he said on his last visit, "if you don't mind that is?"

"I'd like that," Annie said, "and may God go with you, Robbie," she added, "wherever the fates may take you."

They shook hands before Robbie left and Annie returned to her lonely life without Euan. She was considering what to cook with the minced beef that Robbie had brought when there was another knock at her door.

She wasn't expecting Isabella nor was she expecting Billy Dawson, who she found standing on the door mat.

"Billy?" she asked, "nothing's wrong I hope?"

Billy shook his head, "no Annie, nothing's wrong, in fact I've come to tell you that Billy Donnelly is back."

Annie's hand flew to her neck and clutched the little silver heart Euan had given her for their last Wedding Anniversary.

"Come in, come in," she said, "have you spoken to him, is Nancy alright, have they sorted things out?"

Billy held up his hands in mock surrender. "One question at a time, Annie," he said, "and some tea wouldn't go amiss."

Annie's hand fluttered to her hair, pushing a stray whisp back under the Kirby grip.

"Tea," she repeated, "of course, come into the kitchen."

Billy removed his coat and bonnet and followed her through to the kitchen, his nose taking in the smell of paint. "Someone's been busy," he said, wondering who had been painting Annie's kitchen as well as her front door.

"Oh that!" Annie exclaimed, filling the kettle and lighting the gas ring.

"Robbie Robertson's been giving me a hand while he was on leave from the Merchant Navy," she told him, "he left just before you came to the door, it's a wonder you didn't see him in the close."

Billy shook his head, frowning, "isn't he the one who upset Lexie so badly?"

Annie set two cups down onto the table and spooned some tea into the teapot. She wasn't sure how much Billy knew about Lexie and Robbie, but whatever he knew, that was in the past and now, she needed to know about Billy Donnelly and Nancy.

"They had a misunderstanding, that's all," she told Billy, dismissively, "but that's in the past and Lexie's fine now, but tell me about Billy and Nancy, please."

215

"They've patched up their differences," Billy told her, "for the sake of the bairns. When he got Nancy's letter, Billy came home immediately, not believing that he'd fathered the bairn, but now he knows he did." Billy drank his tea and continued with the news. "It wasn't a pretty picture, I'm afraid, he was drunk and, well, wasn't careful that night before he went back to his unit, but it was Mary Anne's accident that brought them together again."

"ACCIDENT!" Annie squealed, leaping to her feet. Billy steadied her and sat her down again. "It's alright," he said, calmly, "Mary Anne's fine, but it gave them both a bit of a shock." Annie's breathing steadied.

"I think they realised what we've known all along, that the bairns are the most important thing and they need their mum AND their dad."

Annie nodded slowly, wondering if Billy was trying to tell her something. Two of her own children were now without a dad, but the father of her first born, John Adams, was still here and sitting at her table. Billy Dawson.

They hadn't spoken about their son since Annie had told Billy the truth and John's letters had made no mention of his father contacting him.

Billy spoke into the silence. "It's good news, Annie," he said quietly, "I thought you'd be pleased?"

Annie brought her thoughts back to the present. "I am pleased," she said, "I was just thinking..."

"About John," Billy said, "I can see it in your eyes, how much he means to you, just as he means everything to me."

Annie looked at her hands, Euan's ring still encircling her finger, "have you been in touch with him?" she asked.

"I have," Billy replied, "only by letter, but one day in the future, I will go to Ireland and tell him how much I love him."

Annie felt her chin quiver. How could one mistake, all those years ago, when Billy had married Mary instead of her, still have such a hold on her heart.

"I think it's time for you to leave," Annie said, shakily, "Josie will be wondering where you are."

"She won't be wondering where I am, Annie," Billy said, softly, standing up and moving towards the kitchen door, "she'll know." He pulled on his coat and bonnet. "She's always known."

——-oOo-—-

Chapter 36

At exactly 20.00 hours, Bo tapped on the door of Lexie's Quarters.

"May I come in Corporal Melville," he grinned, when she opened the door.

Lexie stepped back and swept a welcoming arm into the room. "You can, Captain McGhee," Lexie smiled, before throwing herself into his arms. Their time apart had only strengthened their longing for one another and nothing was going to stop Bo from showing Lexie how much he'd missed her. It was against all the camp rules, but at that moment nothing else mattered for Lexie, except being with Bo.

In the dimness of her Quarters, as Lexie lay contented in his arms, he quietly asked her to give him back his ring. In an instant, Lexie felt her blood run cold, as the past and Robbie Robertson's rejection filled her heart and now Bo was doing the same thing! She'd been fooled again.

With tears filling her eyes, she took off the strangely carved little ring and placed it on the locker beside her bed. Turning away, she pulled on her dressing gown tying it tightly around her. She had been so sure of Bo's love, but like Robbie he'd thrown it back at her.

"I think you should go," she murmured, her ears straining to hear the door of her Quarters closing, but instead she heard footsteps as Bo came behind her. He held her shoulders tightly as he whispered in her ear. "I only want the ring back," he said, "so I can give you this."

He turned Lexie round to face him and in his hand was a small box that he held in front of her.

"Will you marry me Lexie Melville?" Bo said, lovingly.

Lexie blinked in disbelief.

"Marry you?" she murmured.

Bo nodded. "Well?" he said, "will you?"

Tears of happiness flowed down Lexie's face. "YES," she said, "yes, a thousand times."

Bo opened the box and there was a gold ring with a solitaire diamond set in its claw. Lexie took it from its velvet box and let Bo slip it on her trembling finger. "That's until I replace it with a wedding ring," he said, guiding her back to her bed.

Lexie gazed at her engagement ring. "Do you like it?" Bo asked, donning his uniform again. "I love it," Lexie replied, "but where are you going?"

Bo sat back down beside her. "Now that we're official," he said, "I need to inform Wing Commander Johnson that once we're married, you'll be discharged from the WAAF and become Mrs McGhee from Moose Jaw, Saskatchewan."

Lexie was dumbstruck. "Don't we have to plan things?" she asked, "tell my mum and..."

"Hush now," Bo said, "it's wartime and there are ways of speeding things up, if you know the right people."

Lexie sat for a long time after Bo left, unable to take in the changes that were about to happen in her life. She got out her writing pad and pen. Her mother had to know, at once, what was happening and that she'd be in touch with more details as soon as she knew them.

It was with a mixture of excitement and confusion that Lexie addressed the envelope. Would her mum understand about Bo McGhee and his proposal and...how she was going to live in Canada when they were married!

Lexie slept little that night and the next day, Sgt Brady had another surprise for her. "Hope you had a chance to give that boyfriend of yours a kiss or two," he said, "their return to Lossiemouth was just a stop-over on their way back to Canada."

Lexie's eyes widened. "What do you mean, stop-over?" she asked, still reeling from Bo's proposal.

"It means that they fly out at midnight tonight," Sgt Brady

told her, "so your hello kiss will be turned into a goodbye kiss before the day is over."

Lexie muddled through her shift unable to concentrate on anything anymore and hurried to the NAAFI to find Bo. But he was nowhere to be seen, nor were any of the crew.

Fear began to pull at her insides. Where was he!

Lexie hurried to her Quarters, her head down and her thoughts scattered.

"Hey, what's the rush?" Bo said, stopping her in her tracks.

"BO!" Lexie exclaimed, "where have you been, what's happening?"

"Let's get inside," Bo said, "and I'll tell you everything."

Lexie's emotions were all over the place, so much was changing, but Bo seemed in complete control.

"I have to fly out tonight," he said, "back to Moose Jaw, "to train more Canadian flyers about operating the Wellingtons, so our wedding will have to wait a little longer." Lexie listened intently, a part of her glad things were slowing down a bit. "As soon as I'm home, I'll make arrangements for you to come over by ship to Halifax and instead of getting married in Scotland, we can get married in Canada." He searched Lexie's eyes for understanding.

Lexie nodded, it was all such a rush and not like she'd expected her wedding to be.

"So, the Wingco has agreed to give you the time off to make the journey and once we're married," he continued, "he'll officially discharge you from the WAAF."

Bo held her hand tightly as he spoke. "How does that sound?" he asked at last.

Lexie was lost for words as she tried to piece it all together.

"Will everything be alright?" she asked Bo, unable to think straight.

Bo pulled her towards him. "Everything will be fine," he said confidently, "just leave everything to me and once I've arranged your passage to Halifax, all you have to do is be on that ship. OK"

"OK," Lexie repeated, before Bo kissed her soundly.

"See you in Halifax," he said, checking his watch. "Remember

I love you."

Lexie managed a smile. "I love you too," she said. Then Bo was gone.

Annie heard the rattle of her letterbox and put down her breakfast cup of tea. She didn't get much mail these days, so it was always a pleasure to hear the postie at her door.

"Two letters," she murmured in surprise, checking the postmarks before opening them, one was postmarked Glasgow and the other Lossiemouth.

She spread some toast and opened the letter from Glasgow.

Just a quick word to say thank you for your hospitality when I was home on leave and your good wishes. I hope you are well and perhaps, when I'm next home, I can visit you again. It was signed Robbie.

Annie smiled at the thoughtful note and felt she'd really found a friend in the young man.

But it was the letter from Lexie that pushed all thoughts of Robbie away.

I have some wonderful news. I'm going to be married. He's a Canadian pilot called Bo McGhee and although we haven't known one another long, I know he's the only man for me. Please be happy for us and I'll let you know more very soon. Lexie

Annie stared at the words. Lexie getting married, Annie told herself in disbelief and to a Canadian! Only Lexie could be so headstrong Annie thought, first it was Robbie, then Charlie Mathieson and now...she looked at the name again...Bo McGhee! What kind of a name was that?

Annie felt as if her whole world was falling apart, first Euan dying and now Lexie marrying a 'foreigner'. She wasn't sure exactly where Canada was, but knew it was very far away. "Oh Lexie," she whispered into the emptiness, "not you as well." And where was Ian, she hadn't heard a word from him for weeks, not since he'd gone back to his Unit after Euan's funeral. She walked to the window and although it was June, the sky was cloudy and rain was drizzling down the panes of glass. Annie had never felt so alone. Her mind went back to the poorhouse where she'd spent her confinement, waiting for the labour pains to begin when she'd received the worst letter of her life. It told her that Billy and her sister were married and it was only the stirring of new life in her womb that had kept her from going insane with grief.

So long ago now, but still the birth of her illegitimate son reverberated through her world. But he was in Ireland, a doctor of medicine now and had his own life, but what had she to cling to, Annie pondered, with so much of her world now gone.

The noise of the door knocker brought her mind back to the present. She hesitated from opening the door, not wanting to see anyone, but the insistent knocking continued till Annie answered it.

Isabella bustled in. "You took your time answering the door," she said, "is everything alright?" she asked, taking off her hat and noticing Annie's face for the first time.

"Annie!" Isabella exclaimed, "you look dreadful. What's wrong?"

Annie showed Isabella the letter. "Getting married to a Canadian!" Isabel read, frowning, "she never mentioned anything about this when she was home for the funeral." Isabella slapped her hand over her mouth. "I'm sorry Annie," she said, "I didn't mean to bring it up..."

Annie waved a hand in dismissal and turned her sad eyes towards her sister-in-law. "I suppose it had to happen sooner or later," she murmured, "I just didn't expect it to happen so soon."

Isabella made the tea, her mind whirling as to how to deal with Annie's distress. She'd just been coming back from Euan's death and now this.

"I don't think you should stay here alone for a wee while," she said, "come and stay with John and me, there's plenty of room and just until you feel more like yourself again."

Annie nodded. There was no fight left in her and Isabella and her kindness came as a relief. She looked around the little kitchen where she'd spent so many happy times but now it was more like a prison than a home.

"Let's get you out of here," Isabella said, "you're not alone Annie," she said, decisively, "you'll always have me, I'm not going anywhere."

The two friends walked slowly to Isabella's house in Janefield Place.

"You need a bit of fattening-up," Isabella said, "some decent food and a warm bed will soon put you to rights. "That would be nice," Annie said, weakly, maybe she should have moved into Isabella's house immediately after Euan's funeral, instead of trying to soldier on by herself, but now with Lexie's news hitting her hard, she gratefully accepted Isabella's support.

Could you let Nancy know I'll be here for a while?" she asked Isabella.

I said I'd help her out during the pregnancy and I don't want her to find a closed door."

"Leave everything to me," Isabella said, "just get some rest and stop trying to solve all of the world's problems yourself."

Once Annie was settled in and fed some soup and bread, Isabella went to John's study and picked up the telephone. Billy Dawson answered it after three rings.

"It's Isabella Anderson here," she said. "I think we need to meet up...it's about Annie."

Billy felt his grip on the telephone receiver tighten. He turned away from Josie and lowered his voice. " I'll be at the Masonic Lodge in Princes Street in an hour, will that do?"

"I'll be waiting," Isabella said and hung up.

"Who was that?" Josie asked, realising Billy wasn't going to volunteer the information.

"There's a problem at the Lodge," Billy replied, pulling on his jacket and stubbing out his cigarette in the ashtray by the telephone. "I'll be back as soon as I can." He leant over and kissed her on the top of her head.

"But, what's the prob..." Josie started to ask, but the question went unfinished as Billy disappeared out the door.

She picked up the book she'd been reading and marked the page.

Life with Billy was becoming more and more silent. He spoke

only when he had to and left the house as often as he could find an excuse to do so and this felt like one of those times. She sighed and went into the kitchen to fill the kettle. Was this what her life with Billy was going to be till one of them died, she wondered, feeling his indifference weighing heavily on her heart. With the girls independent now and her teaching days over, Josie felt useless and unloved. As usual, when she felt blue, her thoughts turned to Annie Melville, a widow now and free as a bird, she surmised, able to go where she wanted and do anything she wanted, unlike her, trapped in her silent marriage. She straightened her back, when Billy came home, she was going to speak to him about their life together, she decided, he wasn't going to ignore her any longer. Things had to change and change for the better.

Chapter 37

Isabella was waiting when Billy arrived. "Will you walk with me," she said, to Baxters Park?"

Billy nodded, and the pair set off along Arbroath Road.

"How's your daughter, Nancy?" Isabella asked.

"She's fine now," Billy said, "her husband's home on leave and they've cleared up the misunderstanding about the new bairn."

"Good," Isabella said, "because, I don't want her bothering Annie just now."

Billy flinched. "What's wrong with Annie?" he asked, anxiously, "if she needs anything, she just has to ask, she knows that."

Isabella turned to face him. "You love her, don't you?" she stated bluntly.

Billy stared at the honest woman before him. "Is it that obvious?" Billy said.

"She's had a letter from Lexie saying that she's going to be married to a Canadian pilot and it looks like they'll be going to live in Canada."

Billy's eyes searched the darkening sky. "Not Lexie as well as Euan," he said more to himself than to Isabella.

"Exactly," she said, "she's living with me and John just now, till she's strong enough to go home, but I don't know if we're going to be enough.

Billy waited. She needs to be loved again," she said, evenly, "she needs you."

Billy stopped in his tracks. "Did she say that?" he asked disbelief in his voice.

"No, she didn't," Isabella replied, "but there's no one else, but

225

you, who can bring some light back into her life. Question is, can you do it?"

"May I call and see her when she's stronger?" Billy asked, immediately.

Isabella smiled for the first time. "I'll let you know when to visit."

She was taking a huge risk by speaking with Billy Dawson as she did, but Lexie didn't deserve to be laden with guilt just when she'd found love in her own life and if Billy was half the man she thought he was, he'd find a way to bring the colour back to Annie's cheeks.

Josie had been nursing her grievances, real and imagined, for two hours since her husband left and was ready for Billy when he returned.

"Well," she said sharply, "has your precious Lodge burned down then?"

Billy frowned. "Is that supposed to be a serious question?" he asked, draping his jacket over the back of a chair and foraging in the pocket for his cigarettes.

Josie put down her knitting. "No, Billy," she said, "but I have a serious question and I'd appreciate if you'd give me a serious answer." Billy sat down and lit his cigarette. His wife usually accepted the status quo regarding the Lodge, but now...

"Fire away," he said, his good mood dissipating into the tense atmosphere that surrounded Josie.

"Do you love me?" she asked, her eyes never leaving his face.

Billy hesitated too long.

"I thought as much," Josie muttered, darkly, "ever since Euan MacPherson died, you've been itching to get back with that Annie Melville woman ...haven't you!"

Billy knew that his only reply had to be the truth. "Yes."

Josie froze, this wasn't the answer she had been looking for at all, she'd wanted Billy to deny he had feelings for the woman, as he usually did, but instead, he'd said 'yes.'

Anger and fear flared in her eyes. "So, you admit it," she screamed, "I've been right all along about you and her...haven't I?"

There was no turning back now. "Yes," Billy said again, relief washing over him that, at last, his love for Annie was out in the open.

Josie slumped back in her chair, Billy had confirmed what she'd always known, he didn't love her, he loved Annie Melville.

Billy knew there was no going back now, even if Annie rejected him, his life with Josie was over.

"I'm sorry," he said, "I'll find somewhere to stay tonight and come back tomorrow for some things, if that's alright?"

Josie said nothing, her face set in stone. After all these years, Annie Melville had won and she had lost.

Billy closed the door quietly, he didn't know where he would go that night, but it didn't matter, the sense of freedom was euphoric. No more pretending, no more making excuses, whatever the future held, he would deal with it. Images of Josie filtered through to his brain, all she'd ever done was love him and this was the way he treated her. A shimmer of guilt grew into a wave and he determined he would make sure she didn't suffer financially and the girls would be told their mother wasn't at fault, especially Sarah, who'd always saw him as infallible.

He walked though the dark city, his shoes sounding louder in his ears the further he walked, till he found himself outside the church in the Nethergate, where he'd found solace all those years ago when he'd came back from the Great War, shell-shocked and broken.

A door was open and Billy stepped inside. Two tall candles burned in the gloom and as Billy's eyes adjusted he saw a figure kneeling at the altar. Billy cleared his throat as the figure stood up, turned and came towards him.

"Can I help?" the old clergyman said. "I think I need to talk," Billy said, "and maybe confess." The clergyman nodded. "The Lord is always listening," he said simply.

The two men sat side by side in one of the pews while Billy told his story. "So, I can't live a lie anymore," he finished, "but my decision has caused much hurt for my wife...and probably my daughters, but the other woman needs me now and I can't turn away from her."

"You've put yourself on a hard road," the clergyman said, "only the Lord knows what's in your heart and he'll guide you in truth and love if you let him."

Billy knew then, there would be no easy answers.

"I will pray for you all and may God go with you," he said, disappearing back down the aisle to the altar.

Billy spent the rest of the night on a bench at Magdelane Green, watching the river's relentless flow into the North Sea and by the time the first streaks of dawn had appeared, he felt calm and ready to face the future, whatever it held.

For the first time in weeks, Annie slept soundly, whether from exhaustion or feeling safe in Isabella's home, she didn't know, but when morning came, she felt some peace had returned to her heart.

Isabella was bustling about her kitchen when Annie came down.

"Annie," Isabella said, "you're looking better already, now come and sit down and have some scrambled eggs and toast, one of John's friends keeps a few hens and hands some eggs in every now and again.

Much better than those powdered things," she added, scooping a spoonful onto a plate. "They look wonderful," Annie said, her appetite awakening at the sight, "are you sure, I'm not using up your own rations?"

Isabella tutted as she popped two slices of toasted bread into the toast rack. "Silly girl," she said, smiling, "now eat up and when you're finished, we can take a nice walk in the fresh air, get some colour back in those cheeks."

Annie obliged and felt herself relax even more, thanking God for Isabella and her kindness.

The two women walked together up to the ponds at the top of Pitkerro Road and sat on a bench, watching a pair of swans gliding gracefully through the shallow water. Euan and Annie had been at this very spot many a time, but the memory of her husband this time, brought a smile instead of a tear.

"Have you had any further thoughts about Lexie," Isabella asked, wanting to gauge Annie's feelings about her daughter going to live in Canada.

"I've missed her since the day she joined the WAAF," Annie said, softly, "but she's a grown woman now and maybe it's time I realised she's got her own life to live and...that life may be in Canada."

Isabella took her hand and squeezed it. "I'm glad to hear you say that, Annie," she said, "I've never had children of my own, but I've seen the bond mothers have for their offspring, girls or boys."

Annie clasped her hands together. "I just hope Ian survives this horrible war," she said, at the mention of 'boys', "but I've never expected him to spend the rest of his life living with me, so why should I expect it of Lexie?"

"We've been through a lot together, "Isabella said, remembering her brother's suicide "but I think it's made us stronger." Annie nodded to herself. Isabella only knew about her life since she'd married Alex Melville, but long before that, there had been Billy Dawson and their illegitimate son, John. Only Billy and herself knew he was John's father and about his existence in Ireland, but he seemed to have tied them together for life.

"Penny for your thoughts, Annie," Isabella said. Annie considered telling Isabella about the past, but hesitated, it was all so long ago and she didn't feel up to delving into her heart again."

"I'm thinking that it's time I counted my blessings," Annie said, "and maybe I could start by helping you with the mums and their bairns who come to the Salvation Army for help, instead of feeling sorry for myself."

Isabella beamed. "Do you feel strong enough?" she asked, "the children are sometimes in great need?"

Annie stood up and took a deep breath. Maybe she couldn't look after her own children any more, but there were others who truly needed looking after and she felt compassion rise in her heart.

"I'd like to try," she said, "with your help."

Annie was going to be fine, Isabella decided, with or without Billy Dawson's love.

—·—oOo—·—

Chapter 38

It was six weeks later when the letter from Bo arrived.

Home safely, my darling, she read *and missing you like mad. Hope you're missing me too. I've arranged your passage to Canada, as we planned, on the MV City of Glasgow, a cargo ship also taking a few passengers, to Halifax. It sails from Glasgow on Saturday 2nd August and is due to dock in Halifax on the 23rd. So I'll see you very soon sweetheart and we can plan our wedding together. Check with the Wingco for your leave pass and embarkation papers.*

Love you so much, Lexie and can't wait to see you again. It was signed with love and kisses.

Lexie had only received one letter from her mother since breaking the news that she was to marry a Canadian and that response had been noncommittal to say the least. But now, with the arrival of Bo's letter, she had no option but to confirm she was going to Canada to live and be married to Bo.

Lexie tried to keep the words positive but she knew there was nothing positive about the content, Lexie would be living thousands of miles away from Scotland and home and there would be no way she would be able to see her mother again. Lexie felt a shiver run down her spine at the thought. She folded the letter and slipped it into its envelope for posting, the finality of what she was telling her mother, weighing heavily on her young shoulders.

Wing Commander Johnson welcomed her into his office. "ACW Melville," he said warmly, "I believe we're to be losing you soon, marriage and such like to Captain McGhee?"

Lexie saluted. "Yes sir," she said, "I've received a letter from

Bo, I mean Captain McGhee, telling me about the travel arrangements and my Leave Pass."

"Yes, yes, I have them here," the Winco said "and I believe your ship sails on the 2nd August, from Glasgow?"

"Yes sir," Lexie said, "so I'll need a couple of days to get to Glasgow and I'd like to stop off and see my mother before I sail, so may I request my leave starts from 27th July?"

Johnny Johnson sat back and folded his arms. "It's a long way to Canada," he said, "are you sure this is the right decision for you?"

Was she sure? She knew she loved Bo and that he loved her, but could she spend the rest of her life in a foreign land, never seeing her home or family ever again?"

"I'm sure," she said, decisively, "I made the right decision when I enlisted in the WAAF, even when everyone thought I was mad and I think I'm making the right decision now, to go to Canada."

The Wing Commander nodded sagely. "Only the young," he murmured to himself, "and the brave."

He stood and shook Lexie's hand. "Here are your documents," he said, "and once I see the Marriage Certificate, you'll be honourably discharged from the service."

Lexie saluted. "Thank you sir," she said, softly, taking the paperwork, "and thank you for all your help."

Back at her Quarters, Lexie looked at her Embarkation ticket as a mixture of excitement and trepidation flowed over her. She clutched them to her chest. There was no turning back now, she told herself, she was on her way to the New World and her future.

Two weeks of being looked after by Isabella saw Annie back on her feet, she was beginning to enjoy helping the poor women and their bairns who came to the Salvation Army Hall, making her own problems seem easier to bear.

"I think it's time I moved back home," she said to Isabella and John as they shared an evening meal, "I still have Ian and there's Nancy and her brood to look out for, so going back home feels right."

"I couldn't agree more," Isabella said, "you're certainly back to being your old self again, but if you need us, we're here."

The women smiled at one another, knowing what they both owed one another and acknowledging a friendship that went beyond the everyday.

"That's settled then," Annie said, "I'll move my things back tomorrow."

As it turned out the move back home was just in time and it was late in the evening when there was a loud pounding on her front door.

Annie glanced at the clock. It had gone nine and Annie felt a frisson of concern.

Cautiously, she opened the door. "Mary Anne!" she exclaimed, "what on earth..."

"Mum sent me," she said breathlessly, "you have to come, the bairn's wanting to be born."

Without a second thought Annie grabbed her coat. "Then there's no time to waste," she said, hurrying Mary Anne out of the door and into the darkness of the close.

Nancy was white with the pain when Annie arrived.

"Is the Doctor coming?" Annie asked quickly, judging that Nancy's labour was well advanced.

"Di Auchterlonie's gone to get him," she said, her teeth clenched.

Annie hustled Mary Anne and wee Billy into the back room. "Now, just get yourselves to bed and when you wake up tomorrow. you're new brother or sister will be here."

At the sound of their mother's screams, the two youngsters ran from the kitchen, covering their ears.

"Will mum be alright?" wee Billy asked anxiously.

Mary Anne shrugged. "Don't know," she said, the sound of her mother's pain almost freezing her to the spot, "but Auntie Annie's here now, she'll know what to do," she said trying to sound grown up. "I wish dad was here," wee Billy whispered. "So do I," Mary Anne said, as she knelt to pray to God for her father's return.

Di and the Doctor rushed in as Nancy moved into the

final stage of her labour. "PUSH" the Doctor urged, "the bairn's almost here."

With a strength that seemed to come from nowhere, Nancy bore down and with a squelch, her third child shot into the world.

The Doctor picked the newcomer up by its ankles and gave its bum a slap. The resulting yell was all he needed to know. The baby were fine.

"I think some tea would be in order," he told Annie, "it's thirsty work bringing bairns into the world." Annie nodded, as he turned his attention back to Nancy, but Di had already set about filling the kettle and spooning tea into the teapot.

"What is it?" she whispered to Annie. "It's a boy," she said, quietly "and he looks just like his dad." She watched as Di sighed with relief. It looked like Annie wasn't the only one who doubted Nancy's word.

She tiptoed into the back room where both children lay like soft bundles on their beds. "Mary Anne," Annie whispered, "are you awake?"

A small head with wide-awake eyes looked over the covers.

"You have a new brother," Annie said, "and everything's just fine."

Mary Anne threw her arms around Annie's neck and hugged her tightly. "Now all I need is for dad to come home and I'll know God answers prayers," she said, her eyes wide with wonder.

"Your dad will be home soon," Annie said, reassuringly, "now get some sleep, mum's going to need your help tomorrow."

"How are you Nancy?" Annie asked, once the Doctor had finished his work and had gone.

Nancy gazed from her new born son to Annie. "Everything will be alright," she said, "Billy's wanting this bairn as much as me."

"Good," Annie said, turning to Di. "Can you stay for a while?" Annie asked, just for tonight and I'll be back tomorrow."

Di nodded, "I've nothing to rush home for," she said, "I'll stay as long as Nancy wants me to."

Annie reached for her coat, only now realising how exhausted she felt, but it was a good exhaustion at a job well done. "I'll see myself out," she said warmly, "I'll telephone Bell Street and see if they can send a motor to take me home." Her husband's help was with her still, she realised, even though he was now dead, his memory had ensured that the whole of the Constabulary were at her disposal at any time of the day or night.

"Can you tell dad and Josie?" Nancy called to Annie's disappearing back. "They'll want to know they're grannie and grandad again."

"As soon as I can," Annie called back, "they'll no doubt be as pleased as I am."

As fast as Annie's world was contracting, Billy and Josie's world was expanding and the feeling of loss crept into her soul again. She pushed the feeling deep down inside her, there was no going back to feeling sorry for herself, she decided, as she walked to the Police Box in Wellington Street, her life was to be in the service of others and that was that.

Annie woke late the next morning and after breakfast and tidying herself and the house, she made her way to Billy and Josie's home to tell them the good news.

Josie answered the door and it was clear that something was very wrong. She stood with the door ajar and waited, not inviting Annie in or saying anything.

"Nancy sent me," Annie said, "to tell you and Billy that she's given birth to a son, last night and..."

"And you couldn't wait to tell your precious Billy the news."

Annie flinched. "I'm sorry Josie, if this is a bad time, but Nancy wanted you both to know..."

"Well, here's something YOU should know. "He's left me," she spat, "and all because of YOU." The door slammed in Annie's face with a resounding bang.

Annie knocked again, but there was no answer. What was Josie talking about, she fretted, Billy had left Josie because of HER?

She hurried down the stairs and out into the street. What was she talking about! But Annie knew there was only one other person who could tell her.

She almost ran down Albert Street to Baxters Mill and straight up the stairs to Billy's office, brushing aside the Lodge Keeper in her hurry.

Billy was speaking on the telephone when she rushed in.

"I'll speak with you later," he said into the receiver, "something's come up."

He put down the telephone and waited.

Before she could say a word, Annie broke down into tears.

"I've just seen Josie," she managed to stammer.

Billy's lips tightened, this wasn't the way he wanted Annie to know, but now it was out, there was no turning back.

"And she's told you I've left her," he said, "and it's all your fault," he added grimly.

Annie turned tearful eyes on Billy, searching for an explanation. She hadn't done anything to hurt anyone, especially not Josie.

"I don't understand," she said, wiping the tears with her gloved hand.

"I know," Billy said, "and you shall understand, "but this isn't the time or the place." He stood and came round the desk to her side, his eyes pleading for her patience.

"I'll explain everything tonight," he said, "if you'll let me come and see you. Please?"

Annie felt she had no choice. If she was going to hear what Billy had to say, she was going to have to agree.

She nodded and left the room without another word.

By the time Billy knocked at her door, Annie had calmed down.

She would listen to what he had to say and then he could go.

"Thanks for seeing me Annie," he said, removing his bonnet and waiting to be offered a seat.

Annie indicated a chair opposite from where she sat.

"Please, just hear me out, before you judge me," he said, sitting down and leaning forward to be nearer to her.

"I've lived a lie," he said, quietly "for most of my life, in fact. First of all with Mary and then, when you married Euan, I turned to Josie." Annie felt herself bristle, "I don't think we need bring Euan's memory into this," she said. Billy nodded. "I'm sorry," he said, "but I need you to understand how it felt to see the one you...love...happy with someone else."

Annie clasped her hands together. "I think I do, Billy," she said evenly, remembering Mary's letter "and I need YOU to know how it felt giving birth to your son in the Poorhouse while you married my sister."

Billy sat back in the chair. So there it was, the decision he had made all those years ago to marry Mary, pregnant and destitute and demanding he do right by her.

"I didn't know, Annie," he said, passionately, "why didn't you tell me?"

Annie looked at her hands, the memories flooding back through the years. "Because it was all too late for us," she said, "the damage was done and nothing could undo it."

"Until now," Billy said simply. He reiterated his conversation with Josie,

"she always knew I loved you" he said "and I won't be going back to her, no matter what."

He stood up to go. "So, now you know it all, Annie Pepper," he said, "from the beginning to the end and through it all, I love you as much now as I did then."

He pulled on his bonnet and withdrew an envelope from his pocket, placing it on the table beside Annie.

"Read it when I've gone," he said, "then the choice is yours."

She watched as he left the room and she heard the door close and his footsteps fade into nothingness.

She opened the envelope. A boat ticket from Glasgow to Belfast fell out.

She read the note.

I'm going to visit our son in Belfast Annie. This ticket is for you to come with me. If you don't use it, I'll understand and I won't bother you again, but please, please come. Our son deserves both of us.

A wet tear dropped onto the notepaper as she gazed at the words.

Would the past, with all its tears and human failings, be able to be forgiven by her heart? The memory of Billy Dawson making love to her by the river while the flax waited to be harvested, settled in her soul. She had loved him so much then, but what did she really feel now?

"What will I do, Euan?" Annie asked the stillness, but there was no answer. Euan had gone.

Chapter 39

Lexie arrived on Annie's doorstep the day after her letter had, giving neither of them time to prepare for what could be their last meeting.

"But, I posted it days ago," Lexie explained, looking around her home.

"It doesn't matter," Annie told her, "you're here now so let's make the most of our time together."

Once Lexie had taken her bag through to her old bedroom, she joined her mother in the kitchen, who was making tea as usual.

"Are you happy for me?" she asked "marrying and going to Canada, I mean?"

Annie looked at her daughter and compared her to Nancy, with her three children and her hard life keeping the children fed and a roof over their heads. Even with Billy Donnelly back by her side, their life was going to be one of a struggle to survive. If Lexie stayed in Dundee, that could be her life too?

Lexie had made the right choice to join the WAAF and it had been selfish of Annie to try to stop her and now, she was making the right choice again.

"Does this Bo make you happy?" Annie asked simply.

Lexie nodded. "Very."

"Then your choice is simple. Go to Canada and marry the man."

"But, what about you," Lexie asked anxiously, "will you be alright?"

Annie hugged her daughter. "I'll be fine," she said, "and before you go, remind me to tell you something."

Lexie frowned. "Can't you tell me now?"

"No," Annie replied, "like I said, before you go will be soon enough and, anyway, I think tomorrow we need to go and see Nancy's new bairn.

They're calling him Kevin," Annie said, changing the subject, "his dad says there was once a King Kevin in Ireland and that's what he's going to be when he's grown."

Lexie giggled. "King Kevin," she said, "I like it."

Nancy was a little unsure of Lexie at first, but soon realised that she had her own life to think about and couldn't care less about the past.

"Isn't King Kevin beautiful," Lexie whispered, at the sight of the new-born. One day, she and Bo would have their own little King, Lexie mused and she couldn't wait.

"So, off to Canada," Nancy said, trying to keep the envy out of her voice, as she cradled Kevin. "You always did do more than the rest of us," she added, aware that her life had become a repeat of her mother's.

"Just different," said Lexie "and look at you with your lovely family."

Nancy grimaced. "I'll be glad when their dad's back from this war," she said, "bairns need their dad as well as their mum."

Changed days thought Annie, glad that Nancy had seen sense, thanks to her father.

Annie tucked two half-crowns under Kevin's pillow in his Moses basket and left the usual treats for Mary Anne and wee Billy on the table.

"Time we were off," she said briskly, "Lexie wants to say goodbye to her friends and then on Friday, she's off to Glasgow to join her ship to Halifax."

"It all sounds so exciting," Nancy said, almost adding 'I wish it was me.'

"I just hope I'm not seasick," Lexie told her, "we'll be at sea for quite a long time."

"You'll be fine," said Annie, "now let's get going before the shops close."

Mother and daughter made the most of their time together,

but on Lexie's return from visiting Sarah the next day to say goodbye, her good mood had evaporated.

"Sarah's dad's left home," she said, stunned at the development "and her mum says it's YOUR FAULT."

"Sarah's mum's wrong," Annie said clearly. "Remember, I wanted to tell you something before you sailed for Canada?" Lexie nodded. "Well, it looks like you need to know now what that something is."

Annie told her daughter her story from start to finish, while Lexie's eyes grew wider with the telling. "So, you and Billy Dawson have a SON!"

she exclaimed in disbelief. Annie went to her handbag and took out the ticket and letter. "Read this," she said, "then tell me if any of it was my fault."

Lexie had never felt so confused. John Adams was her mother's illegitimate son! Now she knew why it was essential that Sarah had been kept away from him, they both had the same father!

"Did Euan know?" she asked.

"Yes and no," Annie replied, "he knew about my son, but not that Billy was the father.

Now Lexie knew why Billy Dawson had always been so helpful to her, getting her the job in Baxters and always looking out for her. He loved her MOTHER!

"So you see, Lexie," Annie said gently, "life isn't always plain sailing and doesn't always do what we want it to, but whatever the fates throw at us, we have to learn to deal with it."

"We never really know anyone, do we?" Lexie said faintly.

"That's why it's important that you go to Canada and be with the man you love and don't let anything or anyone stop you," Annie said firmly. Billy Dawson made that mistake all these years ago and...so did I."

After Lexie had gone to bed, Annie wondered if she had been wise telling her about the past, but somehow it had seemed right to tell her the truth, no matter the consequences.

The next day, Annie went with lexie to the train station. As usual it was bustling with servicemen and women, moving to where they were needed and Annie was glad that, at least, Lexie would be safe in Canada away from any of the fighting.

Mother and daughter stood facing one another, then without warning, Lexie flung her arms around Annie. "I love you mum, no matter what happened in the past and I want you to be as happy as me, whatever you decide."

Annie hugged her back as the train steamed to a halt and the doors were flung open.

"I love you too, my daughter," she said, "safe journey to Canada and to Bo."

Lexie's eyes were blurred with tears as she boarded the train.

"Write soon," Annie called through the noise.

"I will," said Lexie, imprinting the image of her mother on her brain.

Annie blew her a kiss as the train pulled out. "God keep her safe," she said into the noise, as she waved till the train picked up speed on its journey into Lexie's future, without her.

The train journey went almost unnoticed by Lexie as she tried to take in all that her mother had told her and fit together the events she had experienced, but never really understood till now. Euan's worries about her mother's behaviour, especially being seen kissing a young man, who Lexie now knew was her SON. Then there was Billy Dawson shouldering the expense for Mary Anne's christening and Nancy and Billy Donnelly's wedding and making sure he'd married the pregnant Nancy, instead of leaving her to be a burden on her mother. She recalled how Billy Dawson had made sure she became an office worker at Baxters and not a Weaver as she'd wanted, of course, at the behest again of her mother. In fact, Lexie realised that whenever her mother had a problem, it was always Billy Dawson that she went to, in order to find a solution. He must love her mother very much, she realised, but did she still love him?

The brooding brickwork of Glasgow hove into view as the train pulled into the huge station. Lexie was familiar with Edinburgh, but Glasgow was completely new to her. She asked a porter the way to the docks.

"Just follow your nose to the River Clyde," he said, tapping the side of his nose, there's plenty docks there, lassie. He saw Lexie's perplexed look. "Is it any dock in particular you're looking for?"

"I'm due to sail on the City of Glasgow to Canada, she said, feeling very modern, "so wherever it's berthed..?"

He whistled over to another porter and shouted Lexie's query above the echoing noise of the station. He came back nodding his head, "Jimmy's brother drives a wee van," he said, "he says he'll take you there for one and sixpence if you'd care to wait five minutes."

Lexie quickly agreed. The quicker she got on board the City of Glasgow and settled in, the better. She didn't like Glasgow with its smoke and dark streets and didn't want to spend any more time there than was necessary.

The van was more used for transporting fish than people and Lexie held her breath as much as she could as it rumbled along the cobbles towards the river.

Dockers were loading cargo onto the ship when they arrived. "This is it then, lassie," the man said, "there's a gangway over there," he added, pointing to the wooden, roped structure, "it's the only way on board, but it'll be slippy, so watch your step as you go." Lexied eyed its steep slope and was glad she was in uniform and wearing sturdy shoes. "I'll be careful," she said, rummaging in her bag for her purse. She handed the man two shillings.

"Keep the change," she said, "and thanks for your help.

The man tipped his bonnet. "Right you are missus," he said, "and I hope you get where you're going safely."

Lexie had never been so close to a large ship before and hoped there would be others coming aboard, like her, who were also going to Halifax. and who could give her moral support at least.

A seaman was waiting at the top of the gangway and helped her step aboard. She showed him her travel documents and followed him down steep iron steps to a corridor running the length of the ship. He stopped at one of the doors and opened it with a key, indicating Lexie should enter. He nodded as he gave her the key and handed her a note.

All passengers will be expected to join the Captain for dinner that evening in his Quarters. Passengers will be escorted at all times and access to the deck was not permitted without authorisation. Lexie read.

She went to thank him, but he held up his hand and indicated that he was deaf and dumb, before closing the door and leaving Lexie alone in the small cabin. The note also said that the ship would be sailing at midnight on the next high tide and there would be a safety drill at 09.00 hours the following morning.

Lexie look around the confined space. A small bunk, a tiny table and chair and an alcove strung with a rope which she assumed was to act as a wardrobe. A small cabinet beside the bunk completed the furniture with no sign of washing or toilet facilities except for a metal po on the floor of the alcove. This was going to be a long, long journey, Lexie realised and she was glad that, at least, she had brought a couple of books to read and her writing pad and fountain pen. Apart from her uniform, she had very little in the way of civilian clothing, so decided to wear her uniform as much as possible and only resort to the rest of her meagre collection when necessary.

She was looking through the small porthole at the dockers winching the cargo on board when there was a knock at the cabin door.

The deaf seaman was back. He handed her another note, but before she read it she beckoned him to come in. She didn't want to spend the next three weeks or so not even knowing his name, so she got out her writing pad and pen.

What is your name?

The man took the pen.

Danny Doyle.

Lexie nodded and wrote that her name was *Miss Melville.*

Will you be my escort?

Danny nodded.

Can you show me round the ship?

He nodded again and indicated that she should follow him.

Lexie kept hold of the paper and penl incase she wanted to

ask him anything else and fell in behind him back along the corridor to the stern.

Lexie saw the stark washing and toilet arrangements and hoped she'd get used to them, giving Danny a weak smile as she followed him to the Galley. The cook welcomed her aboard and told her to come and see him if she needed anything to eat or drink, but not without an escort, he added. "But, Danny can't hear me," Lexie said shrugging slightly.

The cook pointed to a bell above the counter. "There's a bell pull in your cabin," he said, "give it a tug, it'll ring here and I'll send Danny along right away." He smiled at Danny. "He can lip read a bit," the cook said, "he was too near an exploding torpedo that hit our last ship and it rendered him deaf and dumb from that moment."

Lexie frowned in concern. "I'm sorry," she said.

"Don't be," the cook smiled, "he's the Captain's favourite and his lucky charm, if it hadn't been for Danny, he would have drowned when this German fighter plane flew over the ship all guns blazing and the Captain was knocked overboard. Without thinking of his own safety, Danny jumped in and held on to him till we got them back on board."

Lexie remembered how she had waded into the sea at Lossiemouth to try to save the crew of the crashed Wellington, but that was nothing compared to diving into an ocean.

She turned to Danny and beamed. "You are very brave," she said slowly, forming the words carefully with her lips. The seaman's face reddened with embarrassment, but he was smiling too.

"Danny will come and fetch you for dinner with the Captain at six o'clock," the cook said, "there are four other passengers, so you'll get to meet everyone else then."

Lexie thanked him. "I'll look forward to that," she said, and meant it.

Once back in her cabin, Lexie located the bell pull and picked up the note Danny had brought for her.

Looking forward to meeting you again at dinner, it said. No signature.

Looking forward to meeting me again?" she pondered. She'd only met Danny and the cook. Must be one of the other passengers, she thought, maybe one of Bo's friends was also travelling home.

She smiled at the thought of Bo and being able to speak to someone

who knew him. Lexie was feeling better and better about the trip and decided she'd change out of her uniform and into her one and only dress for dinner.

At a quarter to six, Danny knocked on her cabin door. His eyes lit up when he saw her in the floral print frock and he nodded appreciatively.

Lexie grinned and shook her head in mock modesty as she followed him past the galley and along another corridor to a door marked CAPTAIN.

The rest of the passengers were already seated at the round polished wooden table and all eyes turned to her when she entered the room. "Welcome aboard," said a deep voice, triggering a shimmer of shock through Lexie's whole body.

Captain Robbie Robertson smiled. "Nice to see you again, Miss Melville," he said, "come and join us."

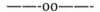

———-oo———-

Chapter 40

After her talk with Lexie about the past, Annie felt a lightness fill her whole body. Her daughter had heard the worst about her past and she still loved her. There would be no more secrets, no more pretending and no more worrying what anyone thought about her. She felt free to live any life she chose, but as with any choice there would be consequences. Annie had to get it right this time, her future happiness depended on it.

She needed to talk things over with someone who would understand and Isabella was the obvious choice. Hopefully, she'll be able to find a way through the dilemma, Annie thought, as she approached the Salvation Army Hall.

It was business as usual at the Hall, with Isabella in the thick of things handing out clothing for the bairns and sausage rolls to their mums, gifted to the Army by a local baker.

"Annie," she called, as she saw her sister-in-law come in, "the water should be boiling and we girls could do with a cuppa." She smiled at three of the mums, their faces and bodies showing the extent of their poverty.

Annie bent to the task and soon the tea was made and drunk by the women.

Isabella wiped the sweat from her brow as she closed the Hall door. "There," she said, heading for a chair, "that'll keep 'the wolf from their doors' for another day."

Annie poured out two cups of tea and brought them over to where Isabella sat, getting her breath back.

"Sorry I'm a bit late this morning," Annie began, "but I was seeing Lexie off at the train station."

Isabella sipped her tea thoughtfully. "She's gone to Canada

then?" she asked. Annie nodded, "It's for the best," Annie said, firmly, "she has a chance of a better life with the man she loves and, well, I couldn't hold her back, even if I'd wanted to."

"I'm glad to hear that," Isabella said, relieved that Lexie was able to go, free from guilt about her mother.

"We had a talk before she went," Annie began, before hesitating.

"And?" Isabella said.

Would Isabella, with her Salvation Army background understand about her past, she wondered.

"And..." she continued, "when I was a young girl in Ireland, I met a man who I fell in love with and I became pregnant with his child." Annie took a deep breath.

"I gave birth to a son, in the Poorhouse in Belfast." Isabella's eyes radiated concern. "He was taken by the nuns for adoption and with nowhere to go and no one to help me, when Mary asked me to join her and her husband and new baby girl in Scotland," Annie shrugged, "I came."

Isabella nodded in sympathy. "You poor thing," she said, kindly.

"Did the father know of all this?" she asked, quietly.

"Not at the time," Annie said, "but he does now."

Isabella looked confused. "How so?"

"My son's father...is Billy Dawson."

Isabella almost dropped her cup. So that was what Billy's feelings for Annie were all about! "But wasn't he married to Mary at that time?"

Annie nodded and looked at Isabella for understanding. "Billy only found out about his son a year ago, when Euan was still alive and he's been trying to make up for his mistake ever since."

Isabella sat back in her chair. Annie had somehow managed to keep her secret for thirty years, even from her brother, the obsessive Alex Melville and her late husband Euan MacPherson. No one deserved to live like that, she frowned, especially not Annie.

"Billy has left Josie and the girls," she murmured, "he came to tell me himself and he gave me this." Annie took the envelope with the letter and ticket in it and handed it to Isabella.

"I don't know what to do," she said, a tremble in her voice.

More and more details emerged as Annie unburdened herself while Isabella listened, without interrupting.

How could one moment of love reverberate through two lives for all those years, Isabella thought, neither of them able to break away from society's conventions that had kept them locked into their personal prisons.

But now, Annie and Billy were free!

"Do you love him, Annie?" Isabella asked, gently.

"I don't think I ever stopped," Annie admitted, for the first time, "but so much water has flowed under the bridge, I don't know if it's all too late."

Isabella handed the letter back to Annie.

"I've seen you at your best, Annie and I've seen you at your lowest, but I've never seen you as a coward," Isabella counselled, "so don't be a coward now." She grasped Annie's hands. "Follow that heart of yours," she said, "just like you told Lexie to do and if it all goes wrong, then I'll still be here for you, like always."

Tears of gratitude and friendship spilled onto both Annie and Isabella's cheeks.

"Thank you for not judging me," Annie whispered.

"Only the Lord judges the heart," Isabella replied, "and if he finds yours wanting, then he's no God of mine."

And with these words, Annie decided.

Lexie forced her legs to unfreeze and walked to the last remaining seat at the table, directly facing Robbie. A babble of conversation started up around her, but she heard none of it and wished the ground would open up and swallow her. How could this be happening? Focusing her eyes on anything except Robbie, she forced some food down herself, but the nerves in her stomach, coupled with the comfusion in her mind, threatened to throw it right back up.

She dabbed her lips with a napkin. "Excuse me," she stammered, pushing back her chair and making for the door, "seasick." The fact that the ship was still in dock didn't matter,

Lexie just had to get away from Robbie Robertson and any excuse would do.

The rest of the company exchanged querying glances and shrugs, but no one said anything as they returned to the business of eating.

"We'll be sailing at midnight," Robbie said, at the end of the meal, "so could you all make sure you're in your cabins by then." Everyone acknowledged the Captain's instruction. Robbie stood up, "your escorts will see you back to your cabins," he advised them, "sleep well."

Left alone with his thoughts, Robbie lit a cigarette and poured himself a measure of Rum. He didn't understand how fate had managed to deliver Lexie to his door, he only knew that he had three weeks to convince her of his love for her and make her his again.

Captain Rainbow McGhee didn't know it yet, but he had a fight on his hands and Robbie intended to win.

Danny Doyle had almost jumped out of his skin when Lexie ran past him.

He caught up with her as she tried to unlock her cabin, his eyes questioning her haste. But Lexie just shook her head and slammed the cabin door behind her, before breaking down in tears.

The next morning when Danny knocked at her door, she handed him a note.

Please bring all of my meals to the cabin, he read. *Thank you. Miss Melville.*

She looked out of the porthole window at the sea rushing past and thought of Bo. How she wished he was with her, but he was five thousand miles away in Canada. Lexie was going to have to face Robbie Robertson alone and make sure he knew how much she hated him and the sooner the better.

By the third day at sea, Lexie felt calm again and ready to face the man who'd broken her heart. But the weather took a turn for the worse and everyone was confined to their cabins, as the ocean boiled around them. This time, Lexie really did feel seasick and after suffering the nausea and vomiting for hours, she finally asked Danny to escort her to the ship's sick bay.

"You'll soon get used to it, lassie," said the medic, giving her a shot of something in her arm "and once the storm clears, I suggest you spend some time on deck, that'll bring the colour back to your cheeks."

Lexie nodded weakly, as another wave of nausea hit her. If she was going to have to suffer seasickness for three weeks, she questioned whether she would survive the journey.

The storm lasted into the evening before blowing itself out and it was with relief that Lexie finally managed to get some rest and by morning she returned unsteadily to her cabin, helped by Danny as usual.

She managed her breakfast and began to feel stronger and when Danny knocked at the door to remove her breakfast tray, she asked if he could escort her on deck.

She donned a pair of slacks and polo-neck jumper as well as the waterproof jacket Danny had given her. She looked at her image in the small mirror in her handbag. A white face with dark circles gazed back at her. She looked dreadful.

Danny led her up the iron stairs onto the deck and took her to the stern of the ship where he'd set up a chair and a blanket. It was the most sheltered spot on the ship, protected from the wind by the bulk of the Bridge and hidden from the crew going about their duties.

Lexie closed her eyes and breathed in the salt air. The drumming of the engines driving the ship nearer to Canada comforted her and she smiled at the thought of Bo waiting to meet her in Halifax.

"Penny for your thoughts?" Robbie Robertson's dark brown voice hit her again. Lexie's eyes flew open and her knuckles gripped the blanket tighter. Robbie stood with arms folded and a smile playing round his lips.

"What do you want?" Lexie asked, her voice clipped and reedy-sounding in her ears.

"Just seeing if you're alright," Robbie said. Lexie said nothing.

"And, are you?" he repeated.

"I'm going to Canada to be married," she blurted out "and my

Fiancée will be waiting for me in Halifax, so just leave me alone."

Robbie grinned. "Can't do that," he said, "it's the Captain's duty to make sure the passengers have a safe trip, German subs and seasickness permitting."

Lexie's lips tightened further. "Well, I'm fine thank you and Danny is looking after me, so you can strike me off your duty list."

Robbie gave her a mock salute. "I'll never strike you off my duty list," he said, "and until we arrive at Halifax, your welfare will be my priority, just like the rest of the passengers," he added with a wink.

Lexie bristled. He winked at her, she fumed, how dare Robbie Robertson wink at her. She pushed the blanket off of her knees and strode to the ship's rail, her composure ruffled. She watched the trail of white frothing water stretching away from her before disappearing into the waves of the grey Atlantic. Then from nowhere, came the sound of a giggle. She swung round, but there was no one there, the giggle had come from her.

Lexie decided not to let herself spend time alone on deck again, but get to know the other passengers instead. Two of the four male passengers were Swedish and didn't speak English, another one looked Jewish and didn't answer when Lexie wished him good morning, on meeting him in the Galley. The only remaining passenger was an old man who turned out to be Welsh and preferred his own company and a book.

Lexie sighed. Whether she liked it or not, she had no option but to spend the rest of the journey alone. One week at sea and two more to go, she counted, wishing there had been at least one other woman aboard.

At the start of the second week, everyone was called on deck.

Robbie Robertson stood on the Bridge looking down at the passengers while the crew gathered behind them.

"U boats have been sighted in the area," he began, "so you will be expected to carry out the lifeboat drill morning and evening for the next few days." He looked towards his second mate. "Organise it," he said shortly.

He turned back to the passengers. "Do not on any account

wander onto the decks till your escorts tell you it is safe to do so and, if you hear the siren for Actions Stations, get into your lifejackets and wait in your cabins for further instructions."

The reality of their situation focused Lexie's mind and with it her dependence on Robbie and his crew for their safety. She didn't know how many trips he had made into these dangerous waters, but Danny Doyle's story about the German plane attacking their ship and catapulting Robbie into the water made her feel ashamed of the way she had responded to his presence.

Twice over the next two days the call to Action Stations sounded. Lexie sat in her cabin, life jacket on, listening to the hurrying feet of the crew as they manned their posts and tried not to think of what might happen if they were hit by a torpedo. She'd heard about the dangers to shipping the subs posed and now she was in the thick of it, her heart raced at the bravery of the men running the gauntlet to bring much needed cargos of food and munitions home.

At last, the signal to 'stand down' sounded and Lexie removed her lifejacket with a sigh of relief. "Come in," she called out in answer to the knock at the cabin door, before remembering that Danny couldn't hear her, but when she opened the door, it wasn't Danny, it was Robbie who stood before her.

"Can I come in?" he asked, weariness showing in the darkness of his eyes. Lexie felt a surge of gratitude towards Robbie that they were safe and stood aside.

"I just wanted to make sure you were alright," he said, "these things can be frightening if you're not used to them."

"I'm fine," Lexie said, sitting on the edge of her bunk, "thanks."

Robbie sat on the small chair.

"I've sent a signal to one of our Destroyers and it should be here before nightfall. That should be enough to give us protection till we reach Halifax, so you can sleep easy tonight."

As Lexie looked at his strong features, she began to wonder why she hated the man so much. His only crime had been to not love her when she'd wanted him so much, but looking at him now...the Captain of the City of Glasgow, responsible for all their lives, she realised how much she had misjudged him.

"I've something to show you," Robbie said, taking his wallet out from his coat pocket. He handed Lexie the clipping from the Courier with her photograph and the story of her Empire Medal.

"I read about it when I was home on leave," he told her.

Lexie felt herself colour under his gaze. "Anyone would have done it," she said, "I just happened to be in the right place at the right time."

Robbie smiled. "Only you would have been so brave Lexie," he said, "always rushing in where angels fear to tread."

Lexie felt the involuntary giggle rise up again.

"Will you have dinner with me later?" he asked quietly, standing to go, "for old times sake?"

Lexie tried to think of a reason to say no, but couldn't think of one. The word that came out was 'yes'.

Robbie felt a rush of desire to hold her again, but instead nodded in acknowledgement. "Danny will bring you to my Quarters at six," he said "and wear that floral dress again," he added, "it really suited you."

Lexie felt herself blush again, but said nothing as Robbie left the cabin.

Chapter 41

After her talk with Isabella, Annie didn't want to go home so decided to visit Nancy and the bairns.

Billy was still somewhere in Europe, fighting the war and unable to be of help, so she felt Nancy would appreciate some company. King Kevin, as he had become known, was making good progress and Mary Anne was always pestering her mother to let her hold him.

"She's spoiling him," Nancy told Annie as they both sat down for a cup of tea. Annie had brought a packet of Rich Tea biscuits, indulging Nancy's habit of dipping them in her tea before eating them. A habit she'd got from her own mother when she was alive.

"Dad was here a couple of weeks back," Nancy divulged, "he's left Josie and the girls and he's living with one of his Masonic pals in a house on Pitkerro Road."

Nancy dipped another biscuit. "Aren't you concerned?" Annie asked, glad that Billy had spoken to his daughter about the separation.

Nancy shrugged her shoulders. "I never liked her anyway," she said, in a matter of fact voice, "and the girls are grown now, so..." she shrugged again.

"Do you want to know something else?" Annie ventured. If confession was good for the soul, she decided that her soul must be jumping with joy.

"Did your dad mention me?" she asked.

Nancy's eyebrows raised. "No," she said, "why should he?"

In for a penny in for a pound, Annie decided. "I'm the reason he left Josie."

There was a moment of confusion before Nancy began to laugh.

"Why would dad leave Josie for you?" she said, smiling broadly, "you're my Auntie Annie, prim, proper and practical," she said, shaking her head and picking up King Kevin from his Moses basket.

She settled him in her arms. "He's due a feed soon," she said, "before Mary Anne gets in from school and starts fussing around him again."

"I wasn't always prim, proper and practical," Annie told her, "when I was younger than you are now, I gave birth to a bairn in Ireland."

Nancy paid attention. "Apart from Lexie and Ian you mean?"

Annie nodded. There was no stopping now, "he was illegitimate and adopted at birth."

Nancy's mouth dropped open. "I don't believe it," she said, shocked, "do you know where he is now?"

"He's in Belfast, in Ireland," Annie said, "and me and his dad are going to visit him soon."

Nancy returned Kevin to his basket and gave Annie her full attention.

"His DAD," she echoed. "You know who the father is?"

"I do," Annie said, "and now you know why he left Josie."

Nancy sat back down in the chair with a thump, lost for words.

"So you see, Nancy," Annie continued, "I've decided that with Euan gone and Lexie on her way to Canada, it's time I put my own needs first and I need to be with the man I've always loved, your father, Billy Dawson."

Nancy still said nothing.

"And now that I've told everyone that matters, I'm going to see him now and tell him my decision," Annie said, gathering her coat and bag, her longing to be with Billy strengthening with every word she spoke."

She felt sorry for her niece, but in Annie's new found freedom there was no room for secrets.

"Be happy," she said, gently, "and once that husband of yours comes home, don't ever let him go."

Billy was finishing the paperwork needed to close the Yardage Book for the day, when Annie came into the mill.

"Do you have a minute, Mr Dawson?" she asked, softly.

Billy's heart leapt at the sound of Annie's voice, but he couldn't bring himself to face her.

"I have all the time in the world for you Annie Pepper," he said, shakily, "but do you have any time for me?"

Annie stepped closer to him and brushed some jute fibres from the shoulder of his jacket. With eyes burning with love for her, Billy turned and faced her.

"I think it's time we visited our son," she said, tears welling in her eyes.

Billy wrapped his arms around her so tightly Annie thought she would stop breathing.

"Are you sure," he said, hoarsely, "really sure, Annie?"

The years rolled away in an instant, and once again, Annie was in the arms of the man she loved, the man she had never stopped loving.

"I'm sure," she said simply, linking her arm through his.

"I think we've a boat to catch."

—-—oOo—-—

Chapter 42

Robbie was waiting when Lexie was brought to his Quarters by Danny.

He wore his Captain's coat and had spent time on his appearance, trimming his beard and brushing his dark hair. Lexie wore the floral frock.

"Please," Robbie said, standing up, "come in."

He came around the table and pulled out the chair next to him.

Lexie sat down, suddenly feeling vulnerable as the door closed behind Danny.

"You look...lovely," Robbie said, "but you always were lovely."

Lexie smiled, pleased at the compliment.

Robbie picked up the decanter of wine nearby. "A gift from a grateful customer," he said, proceeding to fill a glass with the deep red liquid before offering it to Lexie and pouring one for himself.

He raised his glass encouraging Lexie to do the same. "For old-times sake," he said, clinking their glasses together. Lexie sipped the wine. "It's delicious," she said. "It's French," Robbie told her, "not that I know much about wines," he added, "but I'm told it's a fine Claret. The cook's made a special effort too," Robbie said, lifting the lid from a silver salver, "I hope you like beef stew."

The smell of the cooked meat wafted under Lexie's nose and she realised how hungry she was.

"It's my favourite dish," she said and meant it.

Lexie almost mentioned Harry Duncan's Butcher Shop but decided against it. Raking over the past was only going to spoil the evening and whether it was the wine or the company, she found herself warming to Robbie's tales of life at sea.

"If you were a Captain's wife," he ventured, "you could sail all over the world, visit countries like Portugal and Maderia, China and even Australia." He watched as Lexie's eyes grew wider, "but, of course, you'll be living in Canada with your new husband."

Lexie came down to earth with a bump. She'd made her decision to marry Bo and the dream that Robbie was spinning around her was just that, she told herself, a silly dream.

"I think it's time I turned in," she said abruptly, standing a bit unsteadily as the wine rushed to her head.

"Here," Robbie said, "let me help you."

He took Lexie's arm in his and escorted her to the door. "Danny will see you back safely to your cabin," he said, opening the door and signalling to the seaman. "Sleep tight Lexie," he whispered, "and sweet dreams."

Lexie lay on the small bed in her cabin, listening to the engines drone and trying to make sense of how she was feeling. She searched her handbag for the box holding Bo's engagement ring, removed it and slipped it on her finger.

This was what she wanted, she chided herself, to be with Bo for the rest of her life and live in Moose Jaw in Canada and never to see her mother again, or her home in Dundee. A feeling of unease and loneliness crept over her, as she turned the ring round and round, trying to conjure up an image of Bo. Lexie did dream that night, but it wasn't of Bo, it was of Robbie Robertson.

Overnight, the weather had worsened again and Lexie's seasickness returned.

It wasn't as bad as the last time, but bad enough to keep her confined to her cabin and with nothing to distract her, she kept reliving her dinner with Robbie. Had he meant what he'd said about being a Captain's wife and travelling the world, she wondered and where was his wife, if indeed he had one. Suddenly, it was important for Lexie to find out.

When the storm had passed and she had got back her

'sealegs' she asked Danny if Captain Robertson would allow her to go on deck again.

Danny went off to find out and returned five minutes later with a note for her.

Weather too changeable to risk the deck, but dinner is at six again if you'd like to join me.

Lexie couldn't control a shimmer of excitement at reading the note.

She showed it to Danny, who grinned from ear to ear and pointed to his heart.

Lexie blushed. "Don't be daft," she mouthed, feeling like a silly schoolgirl, "come back at six."

Just like the last time, the cook had conjured up another of his dishes. A fish of some sort, that Lexie had never heard off, but was totally mouth-watering.

"I thought you sailors survived on ships biscuits and rum," she joked.

Robbie felt his heart jump at seeing Lexie laugh, at ease in his company. There was only a week to go now before they docked in Halifax and Bo would be there to whisk her away from him. He felt his muscles tense. He couldn't let that happen.

They sat long into the night talking about home and Robbie's meeting with Lexie's mum. "Did she mention me in her letters?" Robbie asked, "she did," Lexie said, unsure whether to say anything more.

"I saw her just before I came to Glasgow to board the ship," Lexie said, remembering how her mother had spoken so well of him. Could he really have changed, she asked herself?

"She said she hoped you'd keep in touch," Lexie said, "but of course, that won't be easy, especially if you have a wife to write too."

Robbie eyed her through narrowed lids. "Who said I had a wife?"

Lexie took the plunge. "No one," she said, "but do you?"

Robbie leant towards her, refilling her wine glass as he did so.

"What does it matter to you if I do have a wife," he said, "you're about to marry a Canadian, Bo McGhee isn't it?"

Lexie felt as though a bucket of sea water had been poured over her.

Robbie was right, why did it matter to her if he had a wife. She felt a wave of jealousy wipe out the effect of the wine.

"I doesn't matter," she retorted, her heart and mind wanting to run as far and as fast as she could away from the truth.

She jumped up from the table, almost knocking the chair over in her haste to be out of the room, but Robbie's strong arms pulled her towards him and kissed her again and again till she stopped struggling and gave into her desire for him.

"Don't marry him," Robbie whispered, "marry me."

For a moment it felt like the world stood still and Lexie knew there was only one answer she could give.

She had loved Bo, she knew she had, but the depth of love she felt for Robbie, as he held her in his arms in the cabin of the City of Glasgow, could not be denied.

"Yes, Robbie," she said, "I will marry you."

Robbie felt in his pocket for his wallet and produced the silver ring he had given Lexie when she was fifteen years old and now, fourteen years later, he gave it to her again.

"I've never stopped loving you," he said, "and once we're married, we'll see the world together."

"Together," she echoed, "forever."

Within one day's sailing to the dock at Halifax, the Captain of the accompanying Destroyer was winched aboard. "As a Captain in the Royal Navy," Robbie told Lexie, "he has the authority to conduct our wedding ceremony, if you'll still have me, that is?"

Lexie had never felt so happy and certain about her future. This was the man she loved and who she'd spend the rest of her life with. She looked deep into his brown eyes. "I'll have you," she said, her blue eyes shining.

They would go to meet Bo together and Lexie hoped he'd understand her change of heart, as she placed his two rings into her handbag to give back to him. He'd make some woman very happy, Lexie smiled at the thought, but that woman wasn't her.

Lexie wore her floral frock and Robbie had on his Captain's

coat as they stood before Captain Morton in his full Royal Navy finery.

First, Lexie took her vows and then Robbie took his, placing the silver ring on the third finger of her left hand, to the cheers of the crew and the handful of fellow-passengers. Robbie kissed his bride, his heart so full of joy he felt it would burst.

"Captain and Mrs Robbie Robertson," Lexie whispered in Robbie's ear, "together, forever."

Lightning Source UK Ltd.
Milton Keynes UK
UKOW05f1154111016

284994UK00001BA/10/P